CRAWLEY HOUSE

THE HAUNTINGS OF KINGSTON

By

Michelle Dorey

DEDICATION

Justin and Elyse, this one's for you.

ACKNOWLEDGEMENTS

I need to thank those who made this book possible. Although my name is on the cover, it's a labor that had been touched by many hands, eyes, brains and hearts. Without your help, this would be a much lesser effort: Brenda Murphy, Rick Gagnon, dearest Corliss, and of course my favorite narrowback Irishman, Jim have been invaluable in improving this book. I will be forever grateful.

CONTENTS

Part I

Kingston, Ontario
1928

CHAPTER ONE

Melanie Crawley perched on the edge of the chair waiting. Her fingers gripped tightly to stop the trembling. It was a struggle to maintain the cool composure a lady must always exercise and she was losing the battle.

She wanted to scream.

The door to the office opened and Doctor Evans entered. He held a file folder in one hand and a smoldering cigarette in the other. There was a grim smile on his ruddy face when he took a seat behind his desk.

Melanie leaned closer to peek at the file folder he opened. But she didn't need to see it to know what the missed monthly's meant. Her breath caught in her chest. The bubble of joy at the prospect of carrying Kevin's son was about to be burst by the man sitting across from her.

Doctor Evans tapped the ash from his cigarette and turned back to scan her patient record. "My wife instructed you on the use of those feminine napkins, Mrs. Crawley?"

"Yes she did, Doctor."

"And you know the signs to look out for?"

"Spotting in the morning larger than a shilling, and I'm to telephone you straight away."

He lifted his hand and made a small circle with his thumb and forefinger. "I said a quarter."

She nodded. "And I'm more familiar with the size of a shilling, Doctor." With a weak smile she held her fingers in the same position.

He snorted. "Melanie, you've been here in Canada for almost five years—don't you think you should start being more familiar with our currency?"

"My husband handles the finances in our home, I don't have much opportunity."

"Very well, as long as we're in agreement on that part anyway. And for the second part?" His chin lowered and gray eyes peered at her above the spectacles.

"But Doctor, I have two children at home! How can I care for them from my bedroom?" Her hands knotted as she tried to calculate the additional expense of a live-in maid. Kevin had said that having Mrs. Dowd and Bridget part time was stretching the household finances as it was!

Doctor Evans leaned across his desk. "Mrs. Crawley... Melanie... I've known your husband since The Great War. It's a wise man who keeps his cards close to his chest with respect to his finances. But take my word for it—your husband has no vices other than a cigar and brandy every now and then. What a Major earns as salary isn't a pauper's wage. I'm confident that you will be able to afford the extra help."

"How can you be so sure, Doctor?" She and Kevin *never* discussed the household's financial affairs. He insisted it wouldn't be 'Lady Like'. As if an Irish lad from Canada had the slightest idea of how things were done in such a home.

Her mother, Baroness Darcy, knew where every ha'penny in the estate came in from. She also knew what it went out for. Melanie had to admit, it was a relief not having to be concerned about such matters in her own household. Until now.

"Melanie dear, every other Major stationed here in Kingston has at least *twice* the number of household staff as you." He tapped his desktop with his index finger. "Full time help, I might add."

She cringed inwardly at the doctor's familiar use of the word 'dear'. Keeping her expression neutral, she replied, "I sincerely hope you're correct, Doctor." *And the correct term, Doctor is 'servants' not 'staff'. Generals have 'staff', ladies have 'servants'.*

"Bed rest it is, then. Doctor's orders. No more than four hours a day on your feet." When she sighed in response, his tone grew sharp. "Mrs. Crawley. This is serious business. When you delivered your daughters, I told you that additional pregnancies would be a trial for you."

She stamped a foot on the floor in frustration. "My Kevin *deserves* a son!"

The doctor sat back in his chair, the squeak of the springs underscoring his annoyance. "Damn it, woman; he has no title to pass on! This isn't England!"

She sat forward. "But he has a *name* to pass on Doctor! When Agnes and Alice marry, they'll take their husband's name. Should Kevin's name go into the ground with him when he's gone?"

"That will not be for a long, long time, Melanie. Kevin's barely thirty years old." Doctor Evans smiled as he said it.

"He's the most remarkable man I've ever known, Doctor. He's—"

Doctor Evans cut her off with a wave. "I'm quite familiar with your husband's heroism, Melanie. I was over there during most of his exploits." He sighed. "He's the most remarkable man *I've* ever met as well." Shaking his head slowly, he continued. "No other soldier ever went from a raw private to his station and rank before." He looked up at her with a twinkle in his eye. "And for an Irishman like him to win the heart of a Baron's daughter... What a tale."

"He had his pick of the London Season I assure you, Doctor. *I'm* the fortunate one." Five years after their wedding, and two children at home, and she meant every word. Good Lord she loved that man so! She could and *would* give him a son!

"I assume he knows you're expecting?"

"I wanted to wait until I was further along to say anything. I'll tell him tonight." She wouldn't have even then, except for the bed rest order.

Stubbing his cigarette out in the ashtray, Doctor Evans concluded the consultation. "If he has any questions or concerns Melanie, I'm at his disposal."

***

As the taxicab drove away, Melanie paused in the walkway to examine her dormant rosebushes. They survived the winter easily this year because of dear Kevin's work at triple wrapping them in burlap last fall. Growing up in England, she loved her mother's rose gardens, and had planted bushes as soon as the house was built. But here in Canada, a great deal more work was required to ensure survival from season to season. These bushes were her second attempt.

Hitching up her skirts, she climbed the steps to the veranda and opened the broad front door. It wasn't a double door as in her parents' home, but it was a sturdy, solid door nevertheless. Also unlike her parents' home there was no front door servant to greet her. Her mouth was set firm. Kevin Crawley was not now, nor ever would be a Lord with a manor, but that was just fine.

Were they back home in England, no Irishman would ever, ever stand a chance of entering her social circle. But Kevin had been a member of the *Canadian* Expeditionary Force; despite his brogue, he wasn't technically an 'Irishman'. His majesty King George V *himself* had hung the Victoria Cross on him, and *then shook his hand!* Even the Times published an etching of the ceremony, captioning the picture 'Majestic Heroism'. That single gesture opened the door to every home and salon for Major Kevin Crawley in the *Empire*, let alone London!

And he chose *her*. From the first instant of their meeting, neither of them could tear their gaze from one another. She had taken the rule book of proper decorum for a young lady and absolutely shredded it! That memory of six years ago caused her to grin like a schoolgirl. And he, the charming and debonair 'Warrior of Ypres', 'Conqueror of The Somme', 'The Victor of Vimy Ridge' and 'Lion of Passchendale' to quote the tabloids, was a stuttering schoolboy in her presence.

To this day, they both laughed at how shy they were with each other when they were introduced.

"I survived bomb blasts and explosions, Melanie," he had said later that same evening. "But none of them prepared me for the thunderbolt that is you."

To his surprise, and her astonishment, she kissed him right then. The wedding took place six months later. Her mother insisted they wait an acceptable time. It was the most difficult six months of her nineteen years.

And the last five years have been the most joyful anyone could ever imagine.

Her lips broke into a smile so large it hurt her cheeks.

By God, she'd follow Dr. Evans' orders to the 'T' and give her Kevin the son he deserved!

From the foyer she could hear the twins chattering at Mrs. Dowd in the kitchen. Agnes must have done something quite saucy, because Alice's laughter tinkled over Mrs. Dowd's scolding, which transformed into a chuckle. She quickly strode to the rear of the house.

Entering the room, she saw Alice standing on a chair in the kitchen, an apron covering her dress like a smock to her feet and Agnes beside Mrs. Dowd, both of them with flour on their faces, laughing.

"Mummy!" They yelled in unison and ran to her, one on each side, burrowing their faces in her skirt.

"Mrs. Dowd's making baked apples and she's letting us help!" squealed Agnes.

"And Agnes wiped flour on her nose!" Alice giggled. "She's baaad and Mrs. Dowd is going to bake her with the apples and bake the saucy right out of her!"

Melanie couldn't help but laugh. She looked to Mrs. Dowd who was trying to look stern, but couldn't quite seem to manage it. She smelled the apples baking in the oven. Like the sweet and cinnamon scent, joy and laughter permeated the kitchen.

"A cuppa tea, ma'am?" the woman asked. Her words carried a brogue similar to Kevin's, but heavier. She prepared the pot and put the kettle on.

"Thank you, Mrs. Dowd. That would be wonderful." She bent over and gave the twins each a hug. Letting them go, she shoo'ed them out of the kitchen for a while to the back yard so she and Mrs. Dowd could speak privately.

"May we play on the swing, Mummy?" asked Agnes.

"Yes, but don't push your sister too high, dear."

They raced out the door squealing and laughing.

The two women looked at each other in silence for a moment.

Mrs. Dowd sighed and folded her arms. "Well?"

Melanie sat in one of the kitchen chairs and stared at the tabletop. "No more than four hours on my feet a day." She looked up at the older woman. "That's a bad sign, isn't it?"

"No, darlin' 'tis not. A bad sign is bed rest *all* day. The worst sign is they admit you to the hospital. I've seen both happen." The kettle began to whistle and she filled the teapot. "Four hours on your feet means you must take care, yes."

"But I'll have the baby?"

"Most likely," she added a nod. "I've had five of me own without any problems, aye." She creaked her back. "Lord a'mighty, and my youngest now eighteen!" She crossed over and rested a thick hand on Melanie's shoulder. "My sister Moira has four children, and had to spend six months in the bed *all day* for each of them." She gave Melanie's shoulder a pat. "So yes, most likely indeed, ma'am."

Melanie felt her chin tremble. "Are you telling me truly, Mrs. Dowd?"

7

"I am, ma'am." The woman nodded as Melanie's eyes filled.

She dropped her head composing herself while Mrs. Dowd prepared the tea and placed a cup before her. "Thank you, Mrs. Dowd."

"Ye'll be needing all day help now, ma'am. I can't do it, not all day with the wee ones ye have."

She nodded. "Any suggestions?"

"Aye. Bridey's here one day a week to do the household laundry. She's familiar with the home, and the girls like her."

"She hates that name, Mrs. Dowd. She prefers Bridget."

"She's Bridey to me, ma'am. And to Mister Crawley. We're all off the boat, and she'd be best to know her place." She huffed. "Although ye wouldn't know it to hear her speak, how she's worked at trying to get rid of her accent."

"Kevin has as well," Melanie smiled. "I think it's a charming way of speaking, frankly, unlike the plum in my mouth that was drilled into me." She giggled. "Three drams of Jameson's though, and he's an auld sod once more!" She tilted her head side to side like a schoolgirl. "Quite dashing if you ask me!"

"An English Lady calling an Irishman dashing!" Mrs. Dowd shook her head with mock grief. "What is this world coming to?"

"But you think Bridey can work out?"

"Aye. I'll keep an eye on her. I'm here every afternoon to do the cooking anyways. If she's here all the time, perhaps you can cut back on my hours. I can easily find other homes to fill in the gap."

"She can cook?"

"I'm sure! The eldest daughter in a family of seven? I'm positive! If ye pay her a fair wage, why she'll jump at the chance." She turned her head gazing around the kitchen. "A fine house as this, with her own room and central heating? She'll jump through hoops for the position."

Melanie clapped her hands. "That's wonderful, Mrs. Dowd! I'll offer her the position when she comes tomorrow! Oh, what a worry off my mind!"

She would barely live long enough to regret those words.

CHAPTER TWO

Bridget Walsh was a block away from the Crawley home. She should have been there by now, but she'd overslept that morning. Her head was still a little fuzzy, despite dipping her face into the cold water in the basin before dressing. Her stomach was still rolling too; all she could get down was a single cuppa.

Blast that Martin Meara! He *knew* she had work this mornin' when he bought her those *two* jiggers of Jameson's! She smiled to herself though. He had his scheme for her of course. Every man that purchased a lady a drink in the Ladies' Public Room at the Royal Oak had a plan.

Her plans certainly did not include snogging with a 'prentice blacksmith on a Thursday night in a dark corner of a Public House! So she drained both glasses quickly and immediately took her leave. Thank God she did; the whiskey hit her hard as soon as she got home. If she had stayed ten more minutes, who knows what would have happened?

The look of shock on his moon face when she said "Thank ye fer the drink, lad; and I'll be takin' meself home now" was priceless. He could have been in one of Charlie Chaplin's moving pictures, he looked so funny!

Settling down with the likes of Martin Meara was not in her plans at all; and she would put her plan in motion within a year. She had to. She was already twenty-one and had to get out to Hollywood before she was too old. She had been told too many times that she was as lovely, as pretty as any of those famous Hollywood actresses on the covers of her *Photoplay* magazines. Even Ma had said she had a face that would break hearts. She'd been practicing in her bedroom mirror when she had the privacy, rare as that was in a house of seven children and Ma and Da. She could pout like a waif, smile like a princess and laugh like a flapper girl.

She'd make a name for herself, she would; as sure as her name was Bridget Walsh.

But now she was payin' the price. And a week's worth of wash facing her. It wasn't yet eight a.m. and her arms already felt worn out. Bless the Lord 'twas Friday though. She'd not go out tonight, and had no other homes to look after 'till Monday.

Still, the Crawley family was her easiest washing. Only two bairns in the house. All of her other clients had at least four children, and many had a grandparent or two as well, livin' with them. His money was good for the work—a dollar *and* a dime for the day.

Aye, her easiest day, for sure. Even so, 'twas backbreaking work. The hauling of sheets and pillowcases, britches and shirts, tea towels, dish towels, table napkins by the score! Soaking and scrubbing the underwear stains, collar stains, and armpit stains in every article of clothing was but the beginning.

11

Even though they had one of those new fangled, Thor Automatic Washing Machines, 'twas a beast in its own right. She had to fill and empty its water with buckets. The only thing it did was churn the stinking mess for fifteen minutes. Getting that blasted beast running (and electric motors terrified her) while she wrung out the previous load was a burden. Each and every cycle-wash then two rinses-meant more filling and draining bucket after bucket!

Not to mention the delicate work to be done on the precious twins' dresses! And the dresses and blouses and underskirts and chemises of the 'English Crumpet', *Melanie Crawley*!

And after everything was washed and every stain removed, her work would be but half done! Then the hauling the wrung out slop to the lines and hanging everything to dry while the next damn load was being done. And all that work was mere preparation for the blasted ironing!

She was already exhausted when she turned up the drive to the side entrance.

She gritted her teeth and corrected herself. *The Major* called it the side entrance. The 'English Crumpet' called it *the servants'* entrance! Only the blessed and high born were permitted to use the front door of her little palace! All shanty Irish to the side door.

She had been in the employ of the Crawley's since the Major had the home built. God bless Mrs. Dowd for securing her the position, even if the old bat was strict. They paid her well, and when she had been with them for three months, the offers and pleas from other fine homes came pouring in and she had her pick. Everyone who was anyone in Kingston wanted their underwear washed to proper British standards!

Working for a woman who was an actual Baroness or whatever she was, had its advantages.

Even if the work was chafing her hands raw.

She pulled open the side door (*yes, the SIDE door, damn it!*) entered the mudroom, took off her boots, and hung up her coat and hat. She took a pair of shoes from the carpetbag along with her apron and cap. Properly turned out as the household laundress (*her mother could call herself a washerwoman, but not her!*) she stood at the bottom of the three steps that led to the kitchen door.

Through the door she could hear the twins yammering in the kitchen, arguing over their game of jacks above the sound of the bouncing ball. Silly girls—almost five years old and trying to play a game meant for older children. Agnes' grating voice let out a shrill laugh, and through the door she could hear that battleaxe of a housekeeper Mrs. Dowd, gently admonish the child. Better she gave her a clitther on her gob, but alas, that was not for the princess daughters of the 'English Crumpet'!

Oh sweet Jaysus a cuppa would be a grand thing to take before setting to work! But from the day she started in her position it had been made very clear she was to only enter the household proper when summoned. She'd take her afternoon meal down in the cellar; any tea she would have would have to come from her own lunch bucket.

She knocked on the door and called out in her sweetest voice, "I'm here, Mrs. Dowd, and I'll be getting to work now!"

"Bridey!" the twins cried in unison. She heard them scramble to their feet, flinging the door open a second later.

Agnes held the door in one hand, in her other she had a fistful of steel jacks. "We're playing jacks, Bridey, and I'm winning!"

Bridget held her tongue and stared at the child who returned her gaze with an air of defiance.

"Mummy told us to address her by her proper name, Agnes," her sister said quietly. "That's not nice." Alice turned to face her. "Good morning, Bridget, how are you today?" she said as kindly as she could.

Flitting her eyes from one child to the other, the thought crossed her head for what had to be the millionth time, how two small girls, mirrors of one another, could be so different? One as gentle as a spring morning and the other as loathsome as any demon.

"I am very well, Alice, and how are ye?" she said.

"It's 'you', not 'ye' Bridey!" Agnes' voice chirped, ending in a small laugh.

Mrs. Dowd had finally lumbered to the doorway. "Off with ye girls, Bridey has work to be doing." She glanced down, "A wee bit behind your time today, lass?" Her gaze was steady.

"Yes, Mrs. Dowd. Me own Ma needed help with one of the children," she lowered her eyes as demurely as she could.

"Don't be making a habit of it. Off with ye now," and she closed the door.

Bridget turned and opened the door leading down to the cellar.

She sighed. Put in her place by a four year old, and Mrs. Dowd let her get away with it.

***

14

With her stomach rumbling for her supper, she glanced up from the ironing when Mrs. Dowd appeared in the laundry room. She was wearing her coat and hat, purse in hand. She folded her arms and looked Bridget up and down.

She glanced up from the shirt and back down to it. It was one of the Major's uniform shirts; and like every stitch of clothing that man wore, she was attentive that every crease and seam be perfect. "Is something the matter, Mrs. Dowd?"

"How much longer 'till you're finished, girl?"

"Not too much." She lifted the iron and pointed it at one of the baskets in from the line. "One more shirt after this, and my day is over, thank God." She bent down to her work. "Why so curious, Mrs. Dowd?"

"I'm leaving for the day, Bridey. The Missus will be seeing you in the parlor when you're done down here."

She looked up sharply. "What's the matter? What's wrong? She *never* sees me unless it's my birthday or Christmastime." Her pay was always left by her boots at the end of the day.

"Just make sure you're as presentable as ye can be, lass. You're a sweaty wreck right now, and I thought fair warning's a fair thing."

"Mrs. Dowd, what is it? Am I sacked?"

"No, child," she shook her head from side to side slowly. "Just be as proper as ye can when ye go on upstairs, alright?" With a nod, she turned to leave.

"Mrs. Dowd!"

"Tisn't me tale to tell," she said over her shoulder and left.

Burning with curiosity and apprehension, Bridget bustled through the remaining clothing. Oh dear, summoned by the Missus with no warning! What on earth was the matter? Raising one arm, she sniffed her armpit and wrinkled her nose.

Oh dear!

She nicked one of the washcloths and hand towels from the basket and went to the laundry sink. She slipped out of her apron and blouse. She rubbed soap into the drenched cloth and wiped herself down, patting herself dry with the hand towel.

She would keep her apron and cap on, that way she wouldn't have to worry about her hair.

When she came through the door to the kitchen, she saw the twins playing on the swing outside. When she called out a 'halooo', she was summoned to the front of the house.

Melanie was seated on the chesterfield and waved her into the room. There was a tea service on the table before Mrs. Crawley. But only a single cup.

"Please, take a seat, Bridget," she said, gesturing to a thickly padded grey chair beside the sofa.

Bridget sat and perched on the front of the cushion just like she saw the fine ladies do in the moving pictures. She tilted her head at Mrs. Crawley. "Ma'am?"

"I have some news I'd like to share with you, and a proposition."

"Ma'am?" She made sure to keep her aching back straight and rested her hands on her lap.

Melanie's heart shaped face blossomed into a smile. "I'm having another baby, Bridget!"

Bridget let her face show a smile. Oh for the love of God! That was her big news? Jayzus, there wasn't a day gone by in Lowertown where one woman or another didn't have a bun in the oven! *"How wonderful, Ma'am! I'm so happy for you!"*

***

An hour later, Bridget entered her childhood home closing the door behind her. She sniffed the air. The smell of old cooking aromas, unwashed bodies and shitty diapers filled her nostrils. It would not be hard to say goodbye to this place. She immediately went upstairs to her bedroom, carrying the two bushel baskets she had managed to wheedle out of the vegetable monger down the street. The chiseler charged her a penny a piece for baskets he would be throwing into the trash!

Oorna, her twelve year old sister was lying in her own bed reading one of Bridget's older editions of *Photoplay*. Her dark eyes widened in curiosity when she saw Bridget go to her pasteboard dresser and begin loading clothing into the baskets.

"What are ye doin' sis?"

"Moving on to bigger and better 'ting's Oorna." She kept her eyes on her work at hand.

Oorna hopped out of bed in a flash. "Ye're leaving home? Are ye goin' to California?"

Bridget gave a small laugh. "Nooo... just over to the better part of town! I've got a live-in position with the Crawley family!"

Oorna's eyes opened wide. "The war hero Major? The family ye've been doin' the wash for?"

"Aye." She finished filling the first basket and went to the wardrobe where her coat and two dresses were hanging. "The Missus is having another bairn, an' wants me to look after her two girls and the house."

Tipping her nose into the air, she strutted across the room in her best La-Di-Da fashion . "It would seem that her delicate and ladylike constitution is not conducive to the act of child bearing." She turned and faced Oorna, fists on her waist. "So the weakling English Crumpet needs me help and is paying me a good penny *and* room and board!" She clapped her hands. "I'll be able to save almost all of me pay!"

"But…"

She spoke in a torrent of words to hold back the water flooding her sister's eyes. "And then I'll be able to afford to go to California after the babe's born! I'll become a big star in the moving pictures and send for ye, and we'll live by a swimming pool in the winter time! Isn't it grand, Oorna?"

"But ye'll be leavin' us, Bridey? Ye'll be goin' away?" Oorna burst into tears and was swept up in her sister's arms.

"Shhh…. Shhh… craitha'… I'll be only a short ways away…" She placed her hands on Oorna's shoulders and looked in her eyes. "Tis only over on Harvest Street!"

Oorna's eyes brightened, but just for a moment, looking down to the floor she said, "And then it's off to California…"

"Not for some time, darlin'!"

Hugging Bridget, Oorna's said in a soft voice, "Maybe 'ting's will change for the better and ye'll never leave."

CHAPTER THREE

Kevin Crawley closed the textbook on his lectern. He closed his eyes and took a breath. Opening them he looked out over the thirty uniformed cadets in the lecture hall. He despised this part of his guest lectures. "And now, I'll take any questions." Thirty hands flew up. With a sigh he pointed to a student in the front row.

The boy snapped out of his seat at full attention. "Major Sir! This Cadet is grateful for your instruction today and hopes that you can share with us some of your personal experiences in battle. While the textbook is a worthy source of information as to troop dispersals, objectives and resources applied, it lacks any sense of the human experience in such circumstances."

With a slow nod, Kevin bade the student to be seated. Another request for war stories. These boys were so eager to hear of the glory and fighting. They've gotten their tales from story books as far as he was concerned. No report, not any account, neither his nor any other man's could ever prepare one for the roiling hell of battle when the first shot is fired and the trench commander blows his whistle.

He took a deep breath. "Gentlemen, it is my fervent prayer that not one of you ever has need to rise from a trench to attack the enemy." He folded his arms. "But should that be your duty, show no mercy, grant no quarter until told to do so by a superior."

"Keep killing until told to stop, like you did in the trenches, Sir?"

Kevin nodded. "Killing a man face to face with a mounted bayonet is different than shooting at him from a hundred feet away, Cadet."

"You would know that, Sir. They called you Terror of The Trenches, didn't they?" The rest of the class sucked in their breath.

"Where did you hear that term, Cadet?"

"It was in the newspaper Sir, after the battle of The Somme." The lad shook his head slowly. "I never forgot the story."

Kevin's voice became low as he looked past the class to the rear wall of the classroom. His memory's gaze continued across the Atlantic to the fields of France on that bloody, vicious day. "There is no time to think, nor reload your rifle. And the more of the enemy you kill, the fewer of your own lads would die…" he refocused his gaze on his class. "And the sooner peace will come." He sighed. "At the end of that day, the mud in the trenches had thickened from all the spilled blood."

"But not yours, Sir."

He shook his head. "By the grace of God not mine, no." He wondered when God would call in that debt.

***

The best part of giving the guest lecture that day was he was able to go home early. He left the lecture hall and walked to the field where automobiles were parked. The chilly March winds whipped across his clean shaven face as he crossed the field. He rubbed his chin ruefully. He had tried to grow a beard after he returned home to Canada, but sad to say, it came in thin and scraggly. Perhaps in eight years when he turned forty, he would try again.

When he got to his automobile, Colonel George Larsen was waiting for him, leaning against the passenger side door, one foot up on the running board, and a cigarette between his fingers.

He snapped off a sharp salute to the man when he got within arm's length.

The Colonel lazily returned the salute. "Enough of the decorum, Kevin—let's get a move on, I'm dying of thirst!"

"Parched, eh, George? It's only March and you're acting like it's the dog days of August." He got behind the steering wheel and started the car as George got in the other seat.

"It's a Friday afternoon, and we're done till Monday. That's good enough for me. Onward Major! The Prince George Hotel forthwith, before they run out of beer!"

"Yes, Sir!" Kevin put the car in gear and began navigating towards the highway that would take them across the bridge and to the Colonel's favorite watering hole on Ontario Street. It had been their Friday afternoon tradition. Kevin would drive his friend to the bar dropping him off there and continue home to Melanie.

George twirled his mustache as he looked over to his friend and protégé. "Heard some interesting scuttlebutt at lunchtime mess today, Kevin."

"Oh? You're going to take a wife?"

"Perish the thought!" He arched an eyebrow. "Even so, my scuttlebutt may improve *your* bride's disposition."

"Oh really? My Melanie's a happy enough woman as it is." He looked over. "You do have me curious though. What's the news?"

"Your wife's dream may soon come true. There's talk of transferring you to Ottawa for a bit, and then shipping you and your family back over to London next year."

Kevin slammed on the brakes in surprise. "You're joking!"

"Now don't breathe a word of it to your lovely wife, Kevin. It's not set in stone. But... the conversation was that your presence in London would be an asset in England supporting them for giving Ireland its independence. There's a lot of squalling from the other side, and to have an Irish hero decorated by the King himself could calm frayed nerves. A gentle push to our cousins across the sea towards peace."

"I'd be part of the diplomatic staff?"

George nodded. "Their Parliament was open to the idea of Irish independence considering how awful it went for the Russians since the Great War. If they let the Irish make their own way, there'd be no risk of a civil war, you see." He gave a rueful smile. "But there's second thoughts a brewing and the thinking is someone like you can nip that in the bud." He sighed. "Everyone's tired of war."

Kevin shook his head. Melanie's dream was to leave Kingston for Ottawa, the nation's capitol. She missed terribly a large city since emigrating as his bride. But to be able to go home to London! She'd be in seventh heaven!

Kevin eyed his friend and mentor sideways. "Who introduced this possibility at the meeting?"

With a snort, George replied, "You even have to ask?"

His voice like a schoolboy's Kevin replied, "But Colonel Were I to go to London, who would be your protégé?" said it with a smile at the end, but was in fact more than a little curious.

"I'm going to be retiring, Kevin." George flicked his cigarette butt out the window. "I was informed that I won't be rising any further in rank." He gave his head a shake. "In fact, were I to stay on after my thirtieth year, I'd be transferred to the most remote command they can find for me." He gave a small smile. "I've gotten a little too long in the tooth for this young man's job." He held his hands apart. "Thusly and therefore 'Old Boy', I called in every favor, every connection and every smidge of good will to begin this next chapter in your life simmering." Turning to his side, he clapped Kevin's shoulder. "God could never give me a better son than you, 'Old Boy'."

Kevin gave a slight nod. In a low voice he said, "I'll ensure your trust isn't misplaced, George."

"When you're over there, just don't kill any more Germans, all right?"

Kevin's head twisted to look at his friend and he took his foot from the accelerator. George was staring at him silently. "For the love of God, George, it's been done with for years!"

"Ten years, Kevin." He held a hand up. "Let's not forget though, how much you *enjoyed* the killing. You were first over the trenches on our side so you could be first into their trench line." He leaned in, gently resting a hand on the man's upper arm. "I've never told a soul about those ears you took."

"I was young and full of blood lust, George. Those days are long past." The automobile had come to a stop on the roadway again as Kevin stared into George's eyes. He turned his head and the car started moving again. "Trust me, any Hun I meet in England will be safe."

"Good!" In spite of his satisfied tone, George still looked at Kevin as they continued on their way.

"Oh, and one more thing 'old boy'. You'd be kicked up a rank as well. Couldn't have a lowly Major hob-nobbing in embassies and so forth, wot?" George had a sly smile.

"George you should change your name to Nicholas! *Saint* Nicholas! This is like Christmas!"

The bridge traffic was quite light that afternoon and he pulled to a stop in front of the Prince George hotel.

Opening his door, George said, "Now mum's the word to the Missus, Kevin. You know how these things can get bollixed up at the drop of a hat, alright? Wait until the orders come through. It won't be until the end of the year at the earliest anyway." He raised a finger. "You best make sure to come to the May twenty-fourth Garden Party this year though, my friend. The Governor General is coming from Ottawa and would care to look you and your family over."

Kevin grimaced. "Oh? Sort of like an audition?"

George smiled. "I think he wants to ogle your beautiful wife if you want the truth. She's a smasher and you know it." He shrugged and held up his hands. "The court of St. James' *is* about as high class as you can get, you know. So for the love of God, don't be picking your nose or farting, all right?"

With a smile, Kevin shook his fist at his friend. "I'll just make sure I'm at your side through the entire affair. Next to you, a gorilla would look like a Lord!"

George stepped out of the car. Just before he closed the door, he said, "The party's not for another two months, and by that time we should have a good idea if this is still a live plan. If it is, you'll be able to give Melanie fair warning."

"Fair enough George. Thanks for the news!"

"Remember, mum's the word for now, Kevin." With a small wave, George turned and went in the side door to the Men's Tavern at the St. George Hotel.

***

The front door to his home opened when he reached for the door knob. Kevin's eyes widened in surprise to see Bridey Walsh holding the door for him. She was wearing a black dress, long white apron and maid's cap along with a bright smile.

"Welcome home, Major!" she said.

"Bridey... what...?"

"Mrs. Crawley would be seeing you right away in the parlor, Sir. Let me take your coat."

He slipped his uniform coat off, handed it to the girl and went to the parlor.

Melanie was on the settee waiting for him. Tea for two was laid out on the table before her. She was wearing a quite smart, orange dress trimmed in a blue that matched her eyes.

"Come in, darling and have a cup of tea. The girls are up for a nap." She gave a nod to Bridey, who pulled the sliding doors to close them.

"Melanie, you look lovely." He took a seat beside her as she poured. He shot a look toward the parlor door. "Bridey's in a maid's uniform?"

"Yes, dear. I've taken the liberty yesterday to hire her on, full time."

"Oh? Without consulting me?" He ducked his head and looked at her. "You must have a good reason for this I assume."

Melanie's lips formed a perfect Cupid's bow in a smile and she nodded. She turned to him. "I do, indeed. I'll need her help full time, you see."

He inhaled sharply. "Why is that? Are you ill, darling?" Oh God, please no!

"No... well, only in the morning. And that will pass in a short while." The bafflement on his face must have been too much for her to take. She burst out laughing. "I'm expecting another baby, Kevin!"

"What!"

She nodded. "The doctor confirmed it this week."

"Oh my love..." he scooted over, took her in his arm and kissed her gently. "That's wonderful news!"

"And yes, Kevin, you get to choose the name of this new baby as we agreed!" She rubbed his hair.

"Then it will be Eamon if it's a boy, and Sarah if it's a girl!"

"What? Sarah? Not Agatha or Annabelle?"She gave a small laugh.

"No. Sarah... for my baby sister back home who died of the consumption." He had a wistful look. I loved that child with all me heart."

"I know, Kevin, so you told me." She rubbed his arm. "And so you'll love Sarah as strongly then!"

He nodded, smiling. Then a shadow crossed his face. "Wait. You had a terrible time delivering the twins! What has the doctor said?"

"That's why I hired Bridget. I'm to rest in the afternoons; so she will look after the girls. I've given her the bedroom at the front of the house. She'll be here full time with Saturdays off and evenings free when the girls are down for the night."

"But I thought you were going to have an English girl, dear. I thought you wanted to have a proper Nanny."

She nodded. "This came up so quickly that I needed to secure someone right away." Her hand rose in a small, dismissive wave. "Besides, Bridget will probably be moving on in a year or so—*then* I can engage a proper Nanny."

"A proper *English* Nanny, you mean."

"Of course, dear." She arched an eyebrow at him and in an affected Brogue said, "*Or would ye be havin' ye're bairns soundin' like 'da washerwoman, laddie?*"

They both burst out laughing and Kevin raised his hands in mock surrender.

***

On the other side of the parlor door, Bridget's face flamed scarlet with embarrassment. She turned and walked softly to the kitchen where Mrs. Dowd was preparing the evening meal.

"Is there anything I can do to help, Mrs. Dowd?" she asked in the sweetest voice she could manage.

"Aye, Bridey. Keep stirring this soup for me while I get some more spuds from the pantry."

She watched the woman go to the closet. When Mrs. Dowd's back was turned, Bridget spat into the bubbling pot.

CHAPTER FOUR

Bridget settled into her position after that. Spitting into Melanie's soup and sauce became a daily ritual. She would start each morning by spitting into 'Her Majesty's' tea while filling the pot with water. 'Twas good practice. She was able to keep her resentment to herself while being sweet whenever she was in the presence of the English Crumpet.

But Lord, the workday was long! She had to be up in the morning to have Major Kevin's breakfast ready for him by six. As soon as he was out the door, she had to tidy up the home and every other day wash some clothing. The Crawley's felt that she had the spare time to continue to look after the wash if she did a load or two every day or so before Melanie and the twins woke.

Mrs. Dowd's housekeeping hours were cut back as well. "You're here night and day, Bridey," she told her. "Ye'll be busy enough!"

She had to prepare luncheon for Melanie and the twins, and then start supper to have it on the table when the Major arrived back home at five.

Melanie had asked her if she wouldn't mind too much, taking her own supper in the kitchen.

"It's the only opportunity for us all to be together as a family, Bridget. I hope you don't mind?" And what if she had? As if that would matter.

Busy enough? She was exhausted! Awake at five and not a minute's peace until the twins were down for the night at seven! Her belief that becoming the housekeeper for the family would be a step up, faded in the first week. While 'housekeeper' did sound more polished than 'washerwoman', her days never ended! Thank God she had Friday nights and Saturday mornings off!

When the Major's motorcar left the drive, she went to the mudroom and picked up a basket of clothes to get started on before making the morning tea for Melanie. Turning on the light for the cellar, she headed down.

At the bottom of the stairs, she jumped. She was so startled she dropped the basket of clothes.

On the opposite side of the landing was a rat!

She let out a squeal and flew back up the stairs. From the top, she saw the creature sit back on its hind legs, pawing and sniffing the air. Its long, pink tail curled around its body, the tip twitching while

it watched her with black, beady eyes.

"Shoo! Shoo, ya disgustin' beast!"

The brazen vermin tilted its head watching her until she grabbed a shoe and flung it down the stairs. It dodged the shoe easily and scampered away into the shadows.

Bridey leaned against the doorframe. Would she be held responsible for this infestation? WAS there an infestation?

Oh God! Were there more down there? Oh dear God in heaven, what was she to do?

She had no doubt that somehow she'd be held to account for this happening. She'd have to take care of this and quick!

That afternoon, she told Mrs. Crawley she needed to go to the market for some items while the twins napped.

"Very well, Bridey, although this is my quiet time as well." Melanie inhaled slowly. "Leave my bedroom door open so I can hear the girls if they wake up." She passed Bridey a small stack of papers she had on the bed that were covered with sketches of the girls.

"Yes, Ma'am." Bridget glanced down at the sketches. "These are quite good, Ma'am!"

"Thank you, Bridget. I had a flair for art as a girl, and Mr. Crawley felt this time of bed rest could be an opportunity for me to renew my endeavors. It's simply a hobby for me now."

Bridget leafed through the pages. With the faintest of lines and economy of strokes of the pencil, Melanie had captured the girls completely. She held up one sheet. "Agnes?" she asked.

Melanie clapped her hands. "Yes! How could you tell?"

"Of the two, she's the one with the habit of smiling with only half her mouth." Bridget thought it was an insolent smirk but kept that opinion to herself. She took the papers and placed them on the dresser. "I'll be back in a jiffy, Ma'am."

***

She didn't know the first thing about getting rid of rats and wasn't about to broadcast her problem to the local merchants. Luckily enough, there was someone in the town she could approach. Wicker basket in hand, she opened a gate that led into an overgrown front yard at the far end of Lowerton.

She wasn't halfway up the walk when the weathered front door opened, and a rail thin woman in a black dress stood in the doorframe.

"Bridey Walsh, as I live and breathe!" Deirdre O'Toole said with a smile, her gray eyes glittering like diamonds.

Bridey stopped in her tracks and stared at the woman. The last time they clapped eyes on each other, she was but a child of six. In fifteen years, she had never seen the woman once, and yet she knew her by sight? She tilted her head in wonder. And in fifteen years, not as much as a line on her face nor a grey hair on her head.

Despite the warmth of the April sunshine, Bridey felt a chill. When she stepped towards the house, a pressure without weight closed in on her. She stopped at the foot of the steps leading up to the front door.

"I'm... having troubles with rats," she said.

"Four or two footed rats, Bridey?" The woman's chin lifted and her eyes narrowed.

She inhaled sharply. "Vermin. With tails and whiskers." The words came out in a rush. She inhaled deeply. It was hard to take a breath, but there was no humidity.

"Very well. When you were last here your hands were covered by warts and I charmed them from you for a penny. Do you recall?"

She nodded silently. She had been too terrified to enter the house, and it was done right there on the steps.

"Now you're a young woman, and my help won't be charity to a child. My help and my silence will cost you a dollar."

"That's quite dear!" It came out like a gasp and she inhaled again, deeply. A low buzz began to hum in her ears.

Deirdre waved a hand at her. "Then off with you." She turned back to the doorway.

"No! Stop! I'll pay!" Bridey gasped, and the woman turned, a sly smile on her lips.

"Very well." Deirdre reached into her dress pocket and withdrew a small packet and held it out. "These are castor beans. The slightest peeling, like you would take from a carrot, mixed with a smidge of cheese or peanut butter will end your problems in a trice." She held out the packet. "Make sure you wash your hands three times with lye soap after handling these, Bridget. 'Tis a deadly poison. Half a bean will end the life of a two footed rat, no matter his size or build!" Her eyes glittered above a wide, toothy grin.

Bridey took the packet and dropped it in her basket. She kept her eyes on the woman as she pawed at her purse. Deirdre's teeth seemed to grow in her mouth when she smiled. She held out the dollar bill, and when Deirdre snatched it away, their hands brushed.

Deirdre's hand was like ice. It was so cold Bridey let out a yelp of surprise.

"I think you should leave, Bridey," the woman said. "Take care—that's a deadly poison!" Her grin expanded, filling up her entire face but for her eyes. Bridget could see no nose, nor hair; just a floating smile below two glittering eyes, shining like diamonds.

"Oh!" She turned and fled down the walk, hearing the door slam behind her.

***

Back down in the cellar, Bridget squatted down in front of the area she had seen the rat run off to. For some reason, having her poison ready gave her the courage. She had taken just a dusting of shavings and mixed them with a dollop of peanut butter that she spread onto the end of a fireplace match.

"Here ratty, ratty…" she said in a sing-song voice. "Come for your luncheon now."

When the rat peeked around from behind the furnace she was surprised at how calm she was. It looked up at her, whiskers twitching as it approached the peanut butter on the end of the stick. Slowly, she laid it on the floor and watched.

The rat kept an eye on her as it sniffed at the offering. Its ears perked, and it opened its mouth wide, showing two front rat-teeth and took a nibble from the dollop. It chewed and swallowed and returned to its meal.

Before it could take another taste, its entire body trembled. Its head lifted and it looked into Bridey's eyes.

"I poisoned, ye, ya vermin," she said quietly. "Now show me how long till ye die."

Its head shook from side to side, whipping back and forth. A quivering paw rose and then dropped, the rat rolling onto its side. Still staring at Bridey, it began to foam at the mouth while its dark eyes twitched and then closed shut. It kicked but once and deflated onto the floor as life left its body.

It was the first time Bridget had ever seen a creature die. She picked up the wooden stick and nudged the rat's paw. It flopped right down, no movement at all.

"Dear God in heaven," she breathed. Deirdre wasn't lying at all. A deadly poison indeed! She went to the dustbin and retrieved some old newspapers. Careful now, she wrapped the dead creature and the matchstick within a thick wad of paper and put the mass into the trash can.

At the laundry sink she scrubbed her hands with lye soap after retrieving the knife she had made the bean shavings with. She carefully rewrapped the other beans and tucked them in the back of one of the shelves in the cellar.

She didn't know how quickly she would be back for more.

CHAPTER FIVE

Melanie Crawley sat at the dinette maintaining an expression of perfect composure while 'The General's wife' mocked and scolded her. Since it was only the two of them seated there, at least it wasn't an out and out public thrashing, but it was a thrashing nevertheless. The rest of the officers' wives had left the garden tent to watch the magician perform some illusion, on the meadow leading down to the lakeshore.

Up until that moment, the May twenty-fourth, Victoria Day celebration had been wonderful. All along the meadow small tents had been set up. Long tables with linen tablecloths were manned by a cadre of cooks who passed out a scrumptious luncheon. The guests ate buffet style at the tables scattered both inside the tents and on the grass, while a string quartet provided background music.

After luncheon, they were preparing the two largest tents for a sit down supper to take place just before the evening fireworks that Kevin had said would be a *dandy* this year. The interim hours had been filled with games for the children and various entertainments. Several performers from the local theater sung the latest ragtime melodies, accompanied by a jazz band!

It had been such a jolly time until Mrs. Abbot, the wife of General Abbot— the Commandant of Kingston— tapped her on the shoulder and asked for a word. Melanie accompanied the woman to the back of the tent. Once seated, Mrs. Abbot placed her liver spotted hand on her wrinkled cheek, piercing the younger woman with her eyes.

The jazz music finished. Melodies from the string quartet once again drifted over them providing a stark contrast to the damage the old harridan was doing to Melanie's pride. The bitch was enjoying herself tremendously! Her diatribe had started with criticisms of the twin's posture, their clothing, and then she closed in for the kill.

"Honestly, Melanie, I cannot believe the language your daughters have used today! Is this how they speak at home?"

She managed a small smile, when she replied, "I'm sorry, but I have no idea what you're referring to."

"*Your daughters* called another child a '*bloody blaggard*'!" Mrs. Abbot sucked in her breath, expanding even further her considerable bosom. "Where, Mrs. Crawley, if not at home, did they learn such language?"

Melanie's jaw dropped in shock. "You're joking!"

"I *certainly* am not!" She leaned across the table. "In front of many of my guests, *including* members of the Royal Family!"

Melanie couldn't say anything. Her jaw muscle clenched and unclenched. Meeting Princess Mary, the King's daughter, and her two children had been such a treat. Princess Mary had greeted Melanie with a surprised squeal on the receiving line. They recalled their time spent together as children. Melanie's father had been a regular guest at Buckingham Palace and although Princess Mary was several years older, their friendship had been a bright part of her childhood.

No wonder the old woman sitting across from her wanted to take Melanie down a peg or two. Seeing Melanie's face flush brought such a triumphant smirk to the woman's face. She leaned across the table, her large eyes glinting. "*My husband* was passed over in favor of yours to take that post in London, young lady!" She waved her hand back at the garden party on the field. "*Why*, I haven't the slightest idea!" She paused, catching her breath.

'Probably because they didn't think either of you old windbags would survive the voyage!' she thought to herself. She kept silent. Kevin had been *unofficially* notified of his upcoming transfer to London, but it wasn't set in stone. They were to leave the following year; after she had given birth. The woman before her was a dangerous enemy. And, as the wife of The General, a formidable one.

Kevin would characterize her next action as a strategic retreat. She needed to regroup and plan her next moves, carefully. She stood, and a weak smile formed on her lips.

"Thank you so much for your guidance, Mrs. Abbot. I appreciate your concern for my daughters' well being and behavior." She put the back of her hand to her forehead. "Oh dear! The warmth of the day is having a terrible effect on me! I'm dreadfully sorry, but I believe I need to leave. My physician has warned me that I should take care, in my current condition!" She gave the old bat another smile and nod. "Good day to you and thank you for the *wonderful time,*

Mrs. Abbot. I'll be sure to inform *my dear friend* Princess Mary of your generous hospitality."

That last comment took the smugness right out of the bitch's face. Good.

She turned to collect Kevin and the girls.

***

Bridget was enjoying her free day. With 'The Major' and 'The Crumpet' and the girls away at the Victoria Day celebration, she indulged herself.

Because of the holiday, the Landmark Cinema had put on a matinee double feature. The latest Douglas Fairbanks film and the latest Charlie Chaplin comedy! Watching Mr. Fairbanks woo Mary Astor was thrilling, and she laughed herself to a coughing fit as Charlie Chaplin navigated a gold rush.

When she came out of the theater, she decided to visit the Ladies Room at the Royal Tavern. She'd have a cocktail and head back home, and return to the lakefront park for the fireworks display. It should be a magnificent one that year—the local paper had said they were going all out!

As she took her first sip of the vodka gimlet, feeling quite wicked for having a drink before six p.m., a man's voice behind her spoke. "May I buy you another?"

She carefully placed her glass on the bar and turned around slowly, forming a small smile on her lips that she hoped was worldly.

His pale, almost white, grey eyes peered at her underneath a shining head of bright, red hair. He had a small smile as well.

"I'll need to think about it, Sir, as we've never met before." She blinked slowly at him.

"Well, let's take care of that, shall we? My name is Devlin Griffin." His head dipped in a slight bow.

Returning his nod, she said, "I'm Bridget Walsh. How do you do?"

The Ladies Room was doing a bustling business, but when Devlin raised his hand, Danny Boyle appeared as if by magic.

"What may I get you, Mister Griffin?" he asked. Bridget had *never* heard Danny Boyle address any man using the term 'Mister'. She looked frankly from the bartender to her new companion.

"I'll be having what the lady's having," replied Devlin.

"Right, Sir! And that's a vodka gimlet, right Bri—" he shot a look at Devlin and back to Bridget—"Miss?"

"Yes, thank you, Danny," she purred. As he scuttled away she turned and looked at Devlin with newfound respect. "He's never called me 'Miss' before. It's always been either my first name or 'dear'. What an influence you have on the man!"

With a lazy smile, he replied, "He's smart enough to know what's good for him."

"Oh really?" She looked down the bar to watch Danny rummage with ice and mix to prepare Devlin's drink and turned back. "I've seen him bash drunken men twice your size, Sir." She appraised his perfectly tailored seersucker suit. "Why would a man such as you be a threat to his well being?"

Danny returned and placed the drink carefully centering it in front of Devlin. "Will there be anything else, Sir?"

"No. Thank you, Danny; I'll let you know."

"I'll keep an eye, Sir." He departed to look after other patrons, but kept glancing back every so often until Devlin took a sip and nodded in his direction.

"You didn't answer my question, Mister Griffin."

"Devlin, please."

"Very well, you may call me Bridget."

He gave a small smile. "Not Bridey? We both have a brogue, you know."

She closed her eyes. "I detest that name."

"Very well! Bridget it is!" She opened her eyes to see his smile. His lips smiled, yet his eyes watched her like a cobra sizing up a mouse. "I hail from Dublin itself. And you, Bridget?"

"My family's from the coast. County Kerry."

"You certainly don't look like a fisherman's wife..."

She replied with a shudder. "Not everyone in Kerry is a fisherman, nor a fisherman's wife, Devlin."

"Is it safe to assume you're no man's wife?"

"Tis. A simple housekeeper am I." She took another sip and looked at him. "I'm still curious as to the nature of your influence on our Mr. Boyle. His serving you so well, in such a crowded saloon... how is that 'what's good for him'?"

Keeping the same watchful expression, he answered, "You said our Danny was good at 'bashing' large men, yes?" When she nodded silently, he added, "There are things far worse than a bashing... and Danny knows enough about meself that he's cautious, is all."

Her eyes widened and her voice dropped to a whisper. "You've killed people!"

He gave a slight shrug. "Since the Great War, many men in this city can claim such a thing." He nodded in the direction of the military base, where at that moment Melanie

40

was directing her husband and children to their family automobile.

"Oh..So you've been in the war then?"

His face grew serious. "I've never worn a uniform." His lazy gaze took in the lounge where they stood. The noise level had grown with holiday makers enjoying themselves. "Let me put it this way... Danny works for the owner of this establishment, a man named Isaac Cohen. Mister Cohen and I have a business together. He has contacts that distill whiskey, and there's a great thirst for such a product in New York."

"You're a bootlegger!"

He gave his head a small shake. "No. I'm the man who solves the problems that bootleggers occasionally run into." He gave that smile again, with his cobra's eyes. "Do you understand now?"

She nodded, wide eyed. "But... what's it like...?"

His voice low, he said, "To kill a man? Killing's easier than people think, Bridget. Once done and done, 'tis nothing to do again. Aye, the first time's the hardest, but the others come easily... you'd be surprised."

As she watched his face, a thrill went down her spine. She believed every word he spoke because of how Danny Boyle acted in his presence. An actual hired killer! She was surprised at how she wasn't afraid of him.

***

A while later, she was walking up the drive to the Crawley home. She stopped short when she saw the car in the drive. The Major and Crumpet had said they were

41

planning to stay until after the firework display. What were they doing home so early?

She heard sharp words and loud voices coming through the open window of the parlor, and carefully crept forward.

"God damn it, Melanie! What do you expect of me!" It was Kevin, shouting at 'The Crumpet'. Bridget smiled and crouched beneath the window.

CHAPTER SIX

Bridget squatted down beside one of the rosebushes smiling gleefully as the storm raged above her head.

"What do I expect of you, Kevin? I expect you to side with your family!"

"What a terrible thing to say! Of course I side with my family!"

Melanie's voice took on a more reasonable tone. "Then why, darling is this even a question? Why, dearest, are we arguing? She can continue on elsewhere as a washerwoman. I absolutely refuse to have her in our home any longer!"

Bridget's ears perked up. They were arguing over her! Her position in the household! She eased closer to the window.

Kevin's voice took on a gentling tone. "Darling, don't you think you're being hasty? The twins love her."

"I wouldn't be so certain about how Agnes feels about Bridey, Kevin. And as far as Alice is concerned, the entire world is her friend—the child doesn't have a mean bone in her body!"

"Oh really?"

"Don't you 'Oh really' me, Kevin Crawley! You weren't the one having to sit there while that ogre of a woman chastised your children's language! *Thank God* I had been friends with Princess Mary when I was a girl! She said to me as I was leaving that she and her parents—*The King and Queen Mother* I might add—were looking forward to seeing me again when your transfer goes through! That took the wind out of the General's wife's sails for now, but Mary returns to England in a fortnight, and that ogre of a Mrs. Abbot will be spinning her webs until your transfer is official!"

"It sounds to me that our future is firm, Melanie."

"No it's not! When I give Bridey her notice, I'll be making a special visit to Mrs. Abbot and I'll act sooo grateful for her counsel over the girls' behavior. Only then will she be nullified!"

"I don't understand…"

"I'll be doing that at the Officer's Wives Luncheon. They have them monthly. I've not gone before, but by God, I'll be a regular attendee until we kick the dust of this town off our shoes. I'll butter up Mrs. Abbot in public. When word of that gets around, she won't be able to say another word against me to General Abbot nor anyone else in position to harm your career."

"Melanie, I'm terribly impressed by your skills at intrigue." Kevin's voice had taken a light tone. And in that light tone, Bridget felt her own future slipping away. She grasped a handful of branches of the rosebush, crushing them in her hand.

"My father, the Baron, had spoken to me many times of matters such as this, Kevin, that's all." Melanie's voice was

44

closer to the window; Bridget froze and kept her head down, facing the ground. Thank God she had worn her brown dress and black cape.

Kevin's voice had drawn closer too. They had to be standing together at the window. "So you're quite sure your mind's made up?" He sighed.

"Yes, Kevin. Absolutely." There was a rustle of her dress as she must have turned to face him. "What I fail to understand is your advocating so strongly for this... this *commonplace* girl. I understand that you share a heritage with her—you're both from Ireland—but really, is that enough?"

"I just think you're being harsh on her. You had already planned to hire a proper Governess after you have the baby."

"That was until I was so humiliated today, Kevin. I need to demonstrate to Mrs. Abbot a certain strength; terminating Bridey is just the ticket."

"So, a sacrificial lamb, eh?" Bridget wasn't sure if she heard a smile in his voice or not, until she heard Melanie's chuckle.

"I suppose so. But it's worth it." There was a pause. "But really, Kevin; you took that girl's side so strongly!" Another pause, and Melanie asked in a voice Bridget could tell was forced lightness. "Should I be threatened by this girl? Does she have you under some sort of spell?"

"Of course she does. She's a Druid, I suppose—wise in the ancient pagan ways of the Irish before St. Patrick!" It must have been a stunned look on Melanie's face that caused Kevin to let out a guffaw. "No darling! There's no hold she has on me! It's *you* I adore!"

"You're a terrible tease, Major Crawley!" Bridget heard the slap of Melanie's hand on Kevin's breast. They had to be right at the edge of the sill! One look to the side and she'd be caught out! She stopped breathing.

"All joking aside, Kevin—why did you defend her so strongly?" Melanie's voice was tender in its curiosity.

He let out a sigh. "I see a lot of me in her, I suppose."

Melanie's laughter tinkled into the evening air. "Really! Forgive me, but I fail to see a single common thread between you! A exalted war hero, handsome and dashing, on his way to pay court to the King of England and a common, horse faced, wall-eyed, washer woman!"

Horse faced? *Wall eyed?* Bridget's hand on the branches of the bush twisted in silent rage.

"Well, I'm not surprised, my dear. But there are aspects of Bridey I recognize. Like I did when I was young, I had a dream of becoming a soldier, and she has a dream of Hollywood and fame. Were you to traipse the back alleyways of Lowerton, you'd see clearly the obstacles in her upbringing she had to overcome to simply get a position here in our home; let alone fan the flame of such a dream as she has."

"Dream? Kevin, the girl's *delusional!* Do you really think she has the looks of a moving pictures star? Really! With that lantern jaw, broad cheeks and those eyes that go everywhere but straight?" Melanie ended her evisceration of Bridget's pride with a light laugh.

"Well, her chin's not nearly as pert and delicate as yours of course, and it's just a lazy eye. She's *not* wall eyed, Melanie. She's a sturdy young lass who will be a good wife for a man." He sighed. "And in America, who knows what she could become? After all, there are women who fly aero planes down there you know." His voice became more distant; they must have stepped back from the window. "When will you give her notice?"

"Not for a week at least; I want to put an advertisement in the newspaper and get some applicants before I let her go. So mum's the word, Kevin."

"Of course, darling."

They must have been leaving the parlor, because the last thing Bridget heard was Melanie's voice "Bridey Walsh, the washer woman movie star!" and her laughter.

Bridget twisted the branches until they snapped off in her hand. It wasn't until she flung them to the ground that she realized the thorns in the rose bush had left her palm bloody. She stared at the crimson stain in her opened hand, rage obscuring the pain.

CHAPTER SEVEN

Bridget woke with a start, drenched in sweat. Devlin Griffin's voice in her dream was still ringing in her ears. "God helps those who help themselves, Bridey," was echoing through her mind. She threw the covers off and sat up, planting her feet on the floor.

"Oh God, no! Sweet Mother of God, help me!" She panted, arms clutched around her stomach, she bent over at the waist. The very idea was too horrible to contemplate! Like a small mouse trying to fend off a cat, her mind fought against the other statement of Devlin Griffin's. "Killing's easier than people think, Bridget... you'd be surprised."

"No it 'tisn't! Tis a mortal sin!" she whispered hoarsely. "I'd burn in hell forever!"

She slipped from the mattress to her knees. Clasping her hands together, elbows on the mattress, she prayed with the fervency of Jesus in Gethsemane. "Oh God, don't let me do such a thing! Take this temptation from me! I beg of ye, Lord, help me ta' be good!"

She stopped breathing. She squeezed her eyes shut, so tight her lids hurt as she awaited an abatement of her black hatred, a sign from the Almighty.

With a whoosh, she sucked in a breath. Panting and gasping, she steadied herself and stood on shaking knees. She turned on the overhead light, and stepped to her dresser. She peered into the mirror. She couldn't see anything abnormal about her eyes at all, thank God. But wait...

She recalled earlier in the year when *Photoplay* Magazine ran a *Star Search* contest. She had gone to Mr. Hyfund the photographer to have a picture done to send in. He had insisted that a profile of her would be the best. She thought nothing of it; after all, he took photographs of people every day. So she had a profile photo done of the left side of her face and sent it in. It was a disappointment to read about the winners six months later, but at the time she resolved to enter every year.

But now the question was, why did the man cajole her into a profile photo? She gazed at her right eye, but saw nothing.

She opened the top drawer of her dresser and took out her hand mirror. Staring into it, she gazed at her image in the dresser mirror from an off angle.

"Oh my God!" she hissed. Her right eye was at an odd angle, floating almost to the top of her eyelid! Putting the mirror down, she clutched the edge of the dresser top, her knees watery.

She could get an operation! And what sort of surgery, Bridey? And pay with what money? There had to be exercises she could do! And if there were, don't ye think your Mum would have had it done then, girl? She had to do SOMETHING! She was going to be a Movie Star! Oh REALLY? Ye think so, lass?

A white hot pain skewered Bridget's head from behind her eye. She shut her eyes, tears of agony trailing down her face. Tilting her chin down, she could barely breathe, huffing for air like she was suffocating. The pain didn't let up; instead it wrapped itself around the back of her neck, a white hot brass rod. She pulled her lips back, her teeth clenched almost to the point of cracking. Huffing for air, she expelled snot and spit with each explosion of breath.

As quickly as it had come, the pain left—nothing but a memory of the agony she had just went through, not an ache nor a twinge remained.

She lifted her face again to gaze into the mirror. That flaming bitch! Damn her, damn her, DAMN THAT WOMAN!

"Killing's easier than people think, Bridget... you'd be surprised."

No, not really... she wouldn't be surprised at all. Of course.

She left her room, and quiet as a mouse, padded down to the cellar.

CHAPTER EIGHT

The poor Major looked as guilty as Judas. He couldn't look Bridget in the eye no matter how many times she tried to make conversation with him when he came down in the morning. She prattled on lightly about how enchanting the fireworks over the lake had been the evening before. When she learned that the Crawley's had missed them by coming home early, she cooed with sympathy.

"I'm doing all I can, Major Crawley, but I'm worried over the Missus," she said.

"Oh? What do you mean, Bridey?" Funny, when he called her by that name, it was as sweet as chocolate to her ears.

"I'm no doctor, Sir, but her color gets quite bad every day now. Just the other day she had a fainting spell, and it was the third one in the last week!" She knitted her hands together. "I know it's not my place, Sir, but I'm worried for her health. She gets these… 'spells' I suppose. They've been going on for the last two weeks and have been more and more frequent!"

"What!" He jumped to his feet. "What are you saying!"

She stepped back. "I'm sorry, Sir! She's gotten strange! She'd begin to tremble, and then she'd start shakin' or something so she'd have to sit down! Once..." she furrowed her eyebrows, "No, *twice* last week, she collapsed to the floor!"

"Why didn't you tell me!"

"I wanted to, Sir! But when I mentioned them to the Missus, she swore me to silence! She said it 'twasn't me place to discuss this!" She began to cry. "She said it'd be me job were I to tell ye!" She clutched her hands together and put them under her chin. "But Sir! She's carryin' a bairn and has two wee ones! If she's not taking care and I know but not be tellin', I'd be guilty of murder!"

"Murder! For the love of God, woman, you're looking out for her!" He collapsed back into his chair at the kitchen table. Staring at the table top, he muttered, "More than she you, I'm afraid..."

"Tisn't the Missus' place to look out for me, Major Crawley! Don't be cross with her over that. And if she decides to let me go for speaking out of turn, I wouldn't blame her in the slightest." She started to sob again. "I've betrayed me Missus' trust! I din't know what to doooo!"

"Bridey, Bridey..." the Major rose from his seat and crossed the kitchen to where she was standing. He took her by the shoulders. "You spoke on behalf of a greater good, Bridey."

"She'll hate me for it, Sir! But I don't care! I'm healthy and strong! I'll be able to find another position as long as she's well." She cast her eyes to the floor. "I will miss the twins... that'll be a hole in me heart a long time to fill back in..." another tear dropped from the corner of her eye. She looked back up to the Major. "What will you do? Isn't today that big meeting with the King's son?"

The Major shut his eyes. "Blast! It's his son-in-law, actually, but you're right!"

"Tis all ye've talked about all last week, Sir!"

The Major nodded. "Yes." He released her shoulders. "Come with me." Going into the parlor, he went to the secretary's desk that was beside the fireplace. He took a key from his pocket, unlocked the door and folded it down to become the writing table. Grabbing a pencil and paper from the work surface, he scratched out a note. Folding it, he handed it to Bridey.

"Give this to Mrs. Crawley when she wakes up, Bridey. I'll be home after luncheon and I'll have made an appointment with the doctor for her."

"Yes, Major Crawley," she held it in both her hands, eyes downcast and gave a slight curtsey.

"Don't do that, Bridey. Do not ever again curtsey to me. Let that remain an English tradition, alright?" She looked up and noticed the fleeting, harsh look in his eyes.

"Aye, Major." She smiled brightly behind her glistening eyes.

He took her chin in his hand. "My wife is fortunate to have someone such as you supporting her, Bridey. I'll make sure she knows that. You have a long future in this home if you want it."

She held his gaze. "As long as I'm wanted and needed, I'll be here, Major Crawley."

They held each other's gaze for three seconds too long and stepped apart. The Major headed for the foyer. Before leaving the house, he said, "Make sure she gets that note immediately."

"Yes, sir," she replied with a smile. When the door closed, she read,

I'll be home after luncheon. We
have to talk.

After luncheon. She'd have to move fast now.

CHAPTER NINE

Bridget opened the bedroom door and struggling with the tray, came through into the master bedroom. The English Crumpet was already awake and ensconced among her cushions.

"Good mornin', Missus," Bridget's voice was soft as she put the breakfast tray on the top of the dresser.

"It's morn*ing* Bridget. You really must work on finishing each word."

"Yes'm."

Melanie sighed, and gave her head a small shake. "Why is my tray on the dresser? Could you bring it to me, please?"

"Of course Ma'am. May I have a word first?" She stood eyes downcast and her hands clasped before her.

"Yes, of course. What's the matter?"

"I've learned I'm to be dismissed, Ma'am."

Melanie's eyes flew open wide. "What! How—" Then her eyes narrowed. "My husband has spoken out of turn, Bridget."

"Then 'tis true, Ma'am? Ye'll be lettin' me go?" Her hands knotted and tears sprang to her eyes. "What will I do, Ma'am? I've done the best here anyone could!"

Melanie held up a hand. "Now calm down, Bridget. It's not as bad as all that." Maintaining eye contact, she continued, "Your work is satisfactory, and that will be stated in the strongest of terms in your reference."

"*Then* what, Ma'am! What have I done that was so wrong, I'm to lose me job?" She clasped her hands to the sides of her face, eyes wide in panic.

"Bridget, it's not your work." She inhaled and blew out a strong breath. "It's your language and demeanor."

"I've never once swore nor cursed under this roof, Ma'am!"

"No, Bridget... it's... it's the *way* you speak. The girls are picking up your speaking habits and it's proving to be a terrible embarrassment to the family."

"But Ma'am! It's only how I was brought up! I didn't have the advantages the good Lord gave ye! I've been at work in one form or another since me twelfth year!"

"I understand, Bridget... but you see—"

"The twins love me, Ma'am! And I them!"

"I understand, Bridget. And were the Major earning a greater salary, we'd keep you on as housekeeper and have a governess to look after the children. But we aren't able to afford such luxuries." Her voice took a steely edge. "And for my daughters to speak and deport themselves in the manner you exemplify, their opportunities would be greatly lessened."

"I don't understand Ma'am! Ye need ta tell me in plain language!"

Melanie clapped her hands together sharply. "Bridget! I won't have my daughters talk and act in the common, shanty way that you do!"

The two women stared at each other.

Bridey sniffed. "May I stay on until ye find someone else? Or shall I leave today?"

"I'll be putting an advertisement in the newspapers shortly, and I'd appreciate you staying on until I can find your replacement. After that, you may go back to doing the laundry one day a week here if that is your wish."

"Yes Ma'am." She gave a short curtsey and turned to go.

"Bridget! My tea, please."

Bridey whirled in surprise. "Oh! Sorry Ma'am! Me head's a million miles away!" She placed the tray before Melanie and left the room.

Closing the door behind her, she folded her arms and leaned against the wall.

And smiled.

CHAPTER TEN

Melanie doctored her tea with the milk and sugar and took a sip. Her lips pursed. The milk must be on the verge of turning. Bollocks! Well, she'd have just the one cup now and get fresher milk from the kitchen for her next one. It wouldn't take long; with the caterwauling from Bridget, the pot had cooled off a great deal.

She sat back onto her pillows and took another deep sip. Poor girl. She felt somewhat badly for Bridget's plight, but the simple fact was she didn't belong in this household at all. Her influence on the girls would only lead to further embarrassments at best, and public humiliations at the least. The new girl would have impeccable manners, no matter the cost. Her daughters would be visiting Buckingham Palace and there was a mountain of work to be done, for them to be presentable to the Royal Family.

She drained the cup and as she placed it on the tray her arm took on a life of its own. It clutched the teacup's handle instead of releasing it and as she watched horror stricken, it lashed out in front of her going from left to right.

Oh dear God, what was happening! Her other arm began to tremble, but while she still had control she flipped the serving tray from her lap and tried to get out of the bed. Her legs moved like oaken trunks and she couldn't feel her feet! When she tried to cry out, all that came out of her mouth was a guttural croak.

Oh God! What was the matter!

Her body slid off the bed and flopped to the floor, her nightgown twisting around her legs. She rolled side to side, trying to get to the door when it opened. Oh thank you, Jesus!

Bridget stepped into the room, head tilted to the side, watching her intently.

Melanie tried to speak, but only grunts came out. She couldn't even open her mouth!

"My God, Dierdre was right!" Bridget said in whisper. Her eyes filled with wonder. She stepped up to Melanie and bent at the waist. Her eyes narrow and glittering like diamonds. "I'll be watching ye die, ye flamin' bitch! I begged you for me job, but nooo... 'Missus Oh So Special La-Ti-Da' needs a proper lady to look after her little wretches!" She spat each word like an accusation.

All Melanie could do was blink her eyes. She goggled them at Bridget and began to gasp. Her chest was getting tight. She's killed me! She's poisoned me! She felt her child in her womb begin to thrash as the poison worked its way to it. *Oh God in Heaven, my baby*!

"Aye, ye're bairn will be goin' to Limbo an' ye'll be goin' to Purgatory, 'English Crumpet'! Not so 'Mrs. Fancy That' now, are ye?" Her eyes were black crystals, but shining brightly like polished stone. She squatted down and ran a finger down Melanie's cheek. Lord, her finger was like ice!

"And that's not all, Melly. I'll be havin' The Major's heart as soon as he's over ye; and I'll be makin' it me business he forgets ye soon enough!"

No, no, no... Kevin!

Bridget gave a small laugh. "Yes, Kevin will be MY Kevin!" Her face took on a dark, loathsome cast. "But don't worry, I'll not be tryin' to replace ye in the heart of your twins! Oh no, 'dat wouldn't be proper now would it?" Her voice softened almost to a sing-song. "Nae, I'll not be replacing ye in their hearts, girl." She tapped the side of Melanie's face, then gave it a sharp, stinging slap. "I'll be sending them ta join ye as soon as I'm able!"

Alice! Agnes! No, no, noooo! Oh sweet Mother, not my girls! NO! Her chest froze and she felt her child within, go still. She stared at Bridget as a buzzing filled her ears. The edges around Bridget began to darken, first a thin grey, then a deeper charcoal until the edges became black and began to grow in towards the center. *I'll not leave the twins with you! I'll NOT leave!*

***

Bridget watched and waited until there was a long while since she saw a last breath. Deirdre wasn't the only one who was right. Devlin was right as well.

Killin was easy peasy. She smiled and whispered, "Of course."

CHAPTER ELEVEN

Good things come to those who wait. Bridey bided her time.

She became indispensible to Major Kevin since the day of Melanie's tragic seizure. She summoned him home right away, and when he came in the door she wailed and keened in grief and sorrow, blaming herself for not informing on the Missus earlier. Had she done so, she would be alive today!

She completely lost control and began to tear at her clothing in grief and guilt. The Major at first seized her by the shoulders in an effort to calm her, but she would have none of that. She shoved him away, and began to tear at her hair, crying over and over that she had killed the Missus!

She took care to not grab fistfuls, but enough wisps of her dark hair to highlight her own grief and guilt.

"I've killed her! She's dead because of me cowardice! Oh would the Lord take me instead!" She bent at the waist, pulling out the hairs.

"Bridey! Stop!" The Major again seized her by the shoulders and straightened her up.

She looked at him wild eyed, her grief and guilt slipping to madness. When she let a trickle of drool slip from her mouth as she keened again, he slapped her.

"COME TO YOUR SENSES WOMAN!" he roared. "We need you sensible!"

She wailed in response and he slapped her again. "BRIDEY!"

His fear for her mixed with his grief and shock. She went still and stood straight, feeling a trickle of blood escape down the corner of her mouth.

"Thank you Major Crawley. I needed to be brought to me senses." Her voice was shaky, but her tone steady. "What do we do now?"

**

From that moment on, every waking moment of Bridey's life was filled with the singular determination to be the helpmate Major Crawley needed. His daughters were heartbroken at the loss of their Mummy of course, but children were more resilient. Keep them fed, warm and entertained and their memory of Melanie would fade soon enough. No, it was Kevin who needed the help and support, and Bridey was determined he would have it.

Her first opportunity showed itself a month after the funeral. She had put the children to bed and came into the parlor where the Major was sitting by the front window. He had in his hand a sheaf of papers. From the look of the impressive letterhead, she knew it had to be official business.

"Excuse me, Major Crawley, the girls are in bed, and I'll be saying goodnight."

He glanced up at the clock in the room and back to her. "So early, Bridget? It's just seven now."

"Aye, sir. I have a novel I'm reading, but to tell the truth, I'm tired."

"Am I working you too hard?"

She gave her head a small shake. "No, Sir, 'tis just the burdens, Sir." She glanced down at her feet and lifted her head to him. "Ye and the children aren't the only ones missing Missus Crawley, Sir, that's all." She gave a sigh. "I know it will pass in time, aye; but the road to that is a hard one..."

"Aye Bridey, 'tis." His voice was soft and forlorn. He gave a small start. "Excuse me, I meant to say, Bridget."

"No, Major Crawley, 'tis music to me ears to hear it from your mouth. When you say it, your Irishness comes out a wee bit; soft and steady. Reminds me of home and a favorite teacher from back then."

"Then Bridey it shall be, henceforth." He gave a small nod that she returned.

The silence hung in the room and she turned to leave.

"Wait, Bridey, I would like your opinion on something."

She turned back and cupped her hands before her at the waist. "Of course, Major."

He held the sheaf of papers before him. "My orders have come through for my departure to London."

"I see... how may I help?"

He fingered a small note fastened to the top of the sheaf, held by a paperclip. "With them came a personal note from General Abbot. In it, he states that while he feels I'm most suitable for the task at hand, if I would instead prefer to withdraw my name, he would go in my stead." He sighed.

"Oh? I don't quite understand, Major. Is the General's offer genuine?"

Major Crawley gave a snort of laughter. "Oh, it's quite genuine indeed! He would be over the moon to take my place! His wife craves him to have that position quite strongly." He tapped the papers on the table. "And I must admit to you, that since Melanie's death my own enthusiasm has faded…"

"What can I do, Major?"

"Tell me, should I go or not."

"I think ye've already answered that question, Major. My opinion would be for different reasons, but supportive."

He blanched at her. "What is that supposed to mean?"

She kept her hands at her waist, but began knitting them. She again looked down to the floor. "I believe you don't wish to go, and I would support that decision because I think it's the correct one." She lifted her head and looked him in the eye from across the room. "I also don't *want* you and the girls to leave, Sir. That's what I meant." She turned to the open door.

"Bridey, wait." When she stopped, she kept her back to him. "Why do you say you don't want us to leave?"

She wouldn't turn to him. *Hoe this row gently, Bridey, 'tis only been a month!* "Because, Sir, I would miss the twins terribly!" she said in a hoarse whisper. "I know it's not me place and all that, but I've grown to—they've become quite dear to me, Sir."

"I see."

Now she turned back to him. "I don't know anything at all about your career and whether or not this move to England would help or harm it, Sir. England's not ye're home; 'tisn't the girls' home neither. An' with Missus

Melanie not by ye're side, how welcome would an Irishman be there?"

He cast his eyes downward. "Her family blames me for her death you know. Their letter arrived in the post this week."

"Major Crawley, you don't want to go then, do ye?"

He gave a small shake of his head.

"And the General is chomping at the bit for this?"

He nodded.

"So the power rests with ye?" A small smile curled her lips.

"Yes." He leaned forward in his chair. "Bridey, what is this leading up to?"

"The General wants something badly... perhaps you can make this work for ye. Missus Crawley had mentioned that ye would receive a promotion were ye to go. Is that so?"

He nodded. "A real jump in the ranks. I would bypass being a Lieutenant Colonel and go directly to the rank of Colonel, yes."

She brightened looking at him. "Then tell the General that you're willing to pass on this mission providing he promotes you anyway, and allows you to finish your career here!" Her hand rose to clap softly the side of her face, mouth open slightly. "I'm sorry, Sir if I'm being impertinent, but why not at least try?"

The Major grinned. "What a devilishly clever idea, Bridey!"

"Do you think he'd go for it, Sir?"

He gave his head a shake. "Absolutely! A Colonelcy! Here, in Kingston! Of course, he'd do it! High Command would jump *him* in rank before sending him—to demonstrate to our English cousins the high value we place on this mission. So he would be most open to the idea of sharing his good fortune with the man who opened the door for him! Yes! It could work!" He shifted to rest his arm on the arm of the chair. "It would take a bit of maneuvering, of course... dangle the bait out to him, get him all worked up in a lather, then strike when he's most excited!"

"You must be a fantastic fisherman, Major," she said.

"Why thank you, Bridey!" He was smiling as she took her leave.

So am I, Kevin. So am I...

***

For a full year, Bridey played the role of competent housekeeper and warmhearted nanny. The Christmas holidays were particularly difficult for the now *Colonel* Crawley. The happiness and joy of the season were dampened by his seeing how quickly his daughters adapted to the new state of their lives. While he cried on Christmas Eve after putting them to bed, they awoke greatly excited to see what was under the tree. Bridey had asked permission to give them each a gift from herself, as if she needed to! When they opened them they were greatly pleased at the small silver medals.

The girls held them in the palms of their hands.

"Who is the man?" asked Alice.

"He's St. Jude, dear," said Bridey. While the Colonel was sitting in a wing backed chair watching the children go through their presents, she stood by the door in her maid's uniform as proper as could be. "He looks out for people, like all the saints do." She wasn't going to tell them that he was

66

her favorite saint. "Now look on the edges and tell me if ye find anything else."

The twins bent their heads down to their medals, eyes focused.

"Yes!" said Alice. "A and C!" she looked over to her sister and pointed out the engraved initials.

"That's right," said Bridey. "For Alice and Agnes Crawley."

"St. Jude, eh, Bridey?" said the Major. "Patron saint of lost causes if I'm not mistaken."

She turned her head to him.

He leaned forward in his chair. "And what cause or hope might you be harboring that you would need such help?" His voice was soft and gentle.

The moment of silence between them drew out. As she felt his eyes on her she bit her lip and made herself blush as she had been practicing.

In almost a whisper she said, "I'll be starting breakfast now, Colonel," she said, and stepped from the room. In the hallway she paused and inhaled deeply.

'*Just a slight dangle of the hook in the water for now, Kevin. I've all the time in the world.*'

***

That Springtime, she cajoled The Colonel to put a swing up in the garden.

"It would be such a help to me, Colonel. They could frolic and play on it while I get the flowers in," she told him. He put up a sturdy one, with thick rope and an oak seat, making it wide enough that he could swing on it with each of his daughters beside him. She made sure to keep her back to him as she listened to the squeals of delight and his own laughter. He was beginning to come out of it now…

"Sing us a song, Papa," said Alice.

"Yes, please, Papa… it's been so long!"

She kept her back to him, yanking the weeds when he began.

> Oh Danny boy, the pipes, the pipes are calling
> From glen to glen, and down the mountain side
> The summer's gone, and all the flowers are dying
> 'Tis you, 'tis you must go and I must bide.

She turned slowly to him, and watched his eyes boring into hers. She put down her trowel and stood, listening. When he came to the final verse, she joined him in song:

> And I shall hear, tho' soft you tread above me
> And all my dreams will warm and sweeter be
> If you'll not fail to tell me that you love me
> I'll simply sleep in peace until you come to me.

> I'll simply sleep in peace until you come to me.

The twins' eyes flitted back and forth between the two of them as their voices faded, leaving the air thick.

"Bridey…" There was a catch to his voice.

She blinked three times at him then turned and fled into the house. She flew up the stairs to her room and slammed the door, her back to it, panting for air.

Moments later she heard his footfalls on the staircase and down the hallway. She could hear him on the other side of the door, his breath labored.

She could feel and hear the soft tap of his knuckles on the wooden door.

"Leave me be, Sir…" she said weakly. "Please!"

"Bridey…"

"Didja' leave the girls all alone in the yard below?"

Her question hung in the air.

"Aye, and I did."

"Please, Sir, go now to them. There's cold meat in the icebox ye can have for supper. I'll be down in 'da mornin'." She took a deep breath. "I've been foolish, and I'm too embarrassed to show me face tonight!"

"Bridey, you've been anything but foolish!"

"Please, Sir!"

She didn't respond again when he called her name. She bided her time until she heard him go back downstairs.

She smiled when she did.

The line's now cast, Kevin. Will ye be a good fish now and have a nibble at the bait?

***

She made sure that on the anniversary of 'The Crumpet's' death the bottle of sherry The Colonel would be drinking had been fortified a fair bit with some poiteen she had gotten the last time she was down to Lowerton. It was a powerful moonshine and she made sure not to add too much. She hummed a little ditty as she doctored the sherry:

'… and the juice of the barley for me…'

The Colonel didn't join them for supper. Instead, he slid the doors of the parlor shut while they ate. When it was time for their bedtime, Bridey lied and told the girls he had to go out in the evening for some special soldering duties but would be home in the morning. She watched them carefully for any sign that they knew what day it was; but there was nothing. The Colonel had decided that since they had no other family but their household, an anniversary Mass and commemoration would not be necessary, although he had gone to the seven o'clock daily Mass at St. Mary's that morning.

She crept back down the stairs and sat in the living room, across the hall from the parlor listening to the tink of the bottle against the glass as the night wore on. She sat primly, listening to him sob.

Not yet, Bridey. Patience, and just give him a nibble...

She waited until the caterwauling ceased and heard him refill his glass twice more. Lord Almighty, he could hold his liquor! Any other man would have been asleep by now.

Standing, she went to the door to the parlor and gently pulled it open.

He sat in a wing backed chair, his hair disheveled and looked up at her with owl's eyes.

"Time for ye to get some sleep, Colonel," she said in her softest voice.

His face crumpled. "I loved her with all me heart, Bridey! I miss her so!"

"As ye should," she stepped to him and put a hand beneath his arm, helping him to his feet. "A finer woman never lived, Sir. She was like a sister to me. The older and grander sister I never had!" The sharp intake of his breath was better than she expected.

"You're a kind and ignorant girl, ye know that, Bridey?" He sputtered as they began to climb the staircase.

"I'll take that as the backhanded compliment it was intended to be, Sir." He staggered on a stair and she righted him before things got worse. She gave a soft laugh. "Ye're drunk as a sailor!"

"A sister to ye, she was, eh Bridey?" He wheezed at the top step.

"Aye, Sir. Kind and good ta me every day."

When they got to the bedroom door, he weaved on his feet. He turned the knob and swung it open. "She was planning to sack you, Bridey." He put a hand on her shoulder. "Sack you for your Irishness!"

"Tis the drink in ye, talking, Sir. I'll be hearing none of it!" She turned him around and marched him to his bed.

He took her hand. "I'd like a son very much, Bridey. I'd like a son very, very much…" He kissed her hand sloppily.

A good nibble there, just tug it away now before he strikes.

"And ye'll be having many sons, Sir! You're a young man in ye're prime!"

"Oh? With who, Bridey? Who would bear my sons?" He grasped at her again.

She caught him by the wrists. "They'd be lined up outside the house if you gave them half a chance, Colonel!" She smiled sweetly to him. "And make sure ye pick the best of the lot!"

With a shove, she tumbled him onto the bed.

"Bridey, Bridey… don't be leavin' me in such a state…" he muffled into a pillow. She hoisted his legs up onto the bed and scurried to the door.

She stepped outside and spun around to peek through the opening. "I'll not be leavin' ye Colonel, don't you fret," Softly, she pulled the door shut.

Pulled it away, but dangled it back for a last lookie loo!

She went to bed smiling.

***

71

The next morning, she had his tea and breakfast prepared for him when he came down the stairs. She made sure to act as bright as a new penny in the face of his chagrined behavior. Each time he tried to 'discuss last night' with her, she shooed him away from the topic by mentioning the weather, new shoes for the twins and her plans for the upcoming weekend.

"More tea, Colonel?" she asked, holding the pot for him.

"Sit down, Bridey."

She replaced the teapot on the tabletop and sat down, perching on the edge of the kitchen chair. Keeping her face impassive, she asked, "Am I to be sacked *now,* Colonel?"

He dropped his eyes to the table. "I'm sorry I told you that."

"I don't believe 'tis true, Colonel. I don't understand why you would say such a thing about Mrs. Crawley."

He let out a deep breath. "It *is* true, Bridey."

"Was that your wish as well? Did *you* plan to sack me, Sir? Because if that's the case…" she willed her eyes to fill with tears.

"No! No Bridey, not at all!" He reached across the table and took her hand. "I was going to give her a chance to get over it, and then advocate keeping you on!"

She pulled her hand away from his. "Very well, Sir. I believe you." She gave a quick smile that was almost a grimace. "Tis water under the bridge anyway, Colonel Crawley. Is there anything else?"

"Yes. I would like you to stop addressing me as 'Colonel Crawley'. It's far too formal for my taste."

"Sir?"

"I call you Bridey. I would appreciate it if you were to address me by my given name."

She let the silence hang in the air and tilted her head at him. Speaking slowly, enunciating every word, she said, "You wish me to address you as *Kevin*?" When he nodded, she gave a small laugh and said, "No, no, no. I'm afraid not, Sir! Wouldn't be proper, you see."

His face fell to her satisfaction, but she became a wee bit concerned when it began to turn pink. Embarrassment? Or Anger? Not wanting to make the wrong choice, she stood quickly and smiled brightly, her eyes sparkling.

"How about a compromise, Sir?" She stepped around the table to be beside him, with just enough sway of her hip to cause her floor length skirt to whisper. "Could I call you 'Colonel Kevin'? I would like that very much."

His eyebrows furrowed with a look of disappointment. Men! When they try to look stern, more often than not, they take the face of a pouty boy! In spite of the urge to chuckle, she formed her face into an expression of anxious longing, biting her lower lip, eyes serious as he gazed into them.

With a cough, he regained his composure and said, "If that's what you feel is most appropriate, then I shall concede the field, Bridey."

She nodded. "Thank you, Colonel Kevin." When she turned away, he grasped her wrist gently.

"For now," he said, before releasing it.

Just one more dangle and tug and he's mine!

***

All week long she caught him from the corner of her eye, watching her, dewy eyed as a twelve year old. When she told him at breakfast on Friday that she would be going out with some friends that night to go dancing, he couldn't hide his unease—envy, actually—despite his effort to appear jovial about it.

"Now don't go falling in love with some lake boat captain, Bridey!" he said with a weak grin.

"Ah, Colonel Kevin, a dance card request is a long way away from a wedding!" She said with a giggle. "I won't be heading out until later in the evening after the girls are abed." She made a solicitous face. "Tis an important night for one of me girlfriends. May I have the use of the bath this evening?"

She had always taken her baths during the day when the twins were napping and he was at work. "Uh... of course!" She thought he was actually going to splutter at the idea, *knowing* she was going to be naked in a bathtub.

"Thank you, Colonel Kevin," she said with a smile.

Later, she came downstairs with her cape over her shoulders. She had a flapper's feather in her hair, held in place by a satin, burgundy headband. She went to the front door and looked to see the taxicab waiting for her. She opened the door to wave at the driver and went to the parlor where Colonel Kevin was seated, his sherry decanter open and a glass poured. The sherry was again doctored with poiteen for his 'nightcap'.

"I'll be leaving now, Colonel Kevin; I won't be home too late."

"Do I get the opportunity to admire your outfit, Bridey?"

He likes the bait and is taking his last nibble at it...

She pulled her cape about her. "Oh Colonel Kevin, it's quite daring! It's fine for dance hall wear, but for your living room...?"

He sat forward onto the edge of the chesterfield. "I'd like to very much, Bridey..."

She waited in silence.

"Please..." he said.

She rolled her eyes. "Now don't be getting any foolish ideas, Sir! 'Tis a party, after all, and it *is* 'The Roaring Twenties'!" She turned her back to him and undid the buttons holding her cape closed. Spreading it open, she turned around and dropped it at her feet, hearing his gasp suck all the air out of the room.

It was a rich, burgundy satin overlaid with jet black beads that ended in a series of pointed fringes above her knees. She gave a little spin, the hem of her dress floating out, right to the edge of wanton and dropping back down again. She knew Colonel Kevin caught the briefest glimpse of the black velvet garters holding her silk stockings up.

The kohl eye shadow and eyeliner, along with mascara made her eyes sparkle like jewels. When she smiled with her wet, red lips she thought he was going to have a stroke.

He's taken the bait! Let him run the line while she was away. He'd be ready for reeling in by the time she was back. She'd well and truly set the hook when she got home.

She bent down and picked up her cape. With a small wave she left the desperate man to stew in his own juices.

***

She came back home in the light of the full moon. As the taxi pulled into the drive, she noted the light was still on in the parlor. She only stayed for three hours—enough to dance up a nice sheen that released the perfume scent she had put on at the start of the evening. She hung her cape on the coat hook along with her clutch purse. She had checked herself in the ladies room mirror at the dance hall just before leaving and had freshened her makeup.

Entering the parlor, she noted that the bottle of sherry was not even half gone.

"Back so soon, Bridey?" he asked. His tie was off and two buttons undone. "Did you have a good time?"

"Yes, I did, actually! My girlfriend Daphne is always so much fun!"

He was watching her carefully now. "Did you have enough dances?"

She gave a small shrug. "I suppose… but I turned down more offers than I accepted…" She wandered into the room as coy as she could manage.

"Oh? Why is that?"

"Oh, I don't know…" She fingered her evening gloves, pulling them smooth and gazed at the floor. "The men there were rather childish, actually; not very sophisticated," Her eyes rose. "Not elegant at all."

"I see…" He stood and picked up two glasses of sherry. "Share a drink with me, Bridey?"

"Are you sure, Sir?" She smiled as she took it. He stepped behind her and flicked a switch. The Victrola that had been unused for over a year came alive with music.

"May I have this dance, Miss?" He bowed and held out his hand as '*Love Me Or Leave Me*' glided out of the speaker. The big band behind the woman's singing were strawberries and cream to the ear.

She took his hand and rested her head on his shoulder as they stepped and swayed in time to the music—not quite a waltz, but slower than a Charleston. His hand glided over her back, up and down, from her waist to the bare shoulders, sending a thrill right down through the soles of her feet into the floor.

"Ah... Bridey," he murmured, his breath hot in her ear, causing another thrill to jolt through her.

Play this one with care, Bridey! This trout could become Moby Dick in a flash and sink ye for good!

She wrapped her fingers through his as the song ended and another began in the same rhythm. She turned her head into his neck, breathing into the hollow of his throat. His own intensified response urged her other hand to caress his neck.

"Ohhhh..." With a groan, he took her chin in his hand and turned her face up. Their eyes sparked and he bent to kiss her. He kissed her long and deep, and her own knees began to knock. She clasped his head to hers as they clutched at one another.

Releasing her, he bent down and swept her up into his arms and deposited her on the couch as lightly as he would a child. He dropped to his knees beside her and began to kiss her again.

When his hands began to wander and fondle, she backed away. Still attached to her mouth, his hand began slipping and sliding on her legs, working up beneath the hem of her skirt.

She clutched at his face and nuzzled into his neck. "Oh Kevin! Please don't! I've never been with a man!" It took no effort for her eyes to tear up. "This is for a marriage bed! Please Kevin! I'm so tempted now!" As his hand delved higher she gasped. "Please Kevin! Stop! Tis for me husband! I'm to be a man's wife one day!" She wailed. "I'm to have me husband's sons!"

"Have my sons!" he growled. He whipped his head back to look into her eyes. His eyes were black and dangerous. "You're to be this man's wife, Bridget!" His voice was a rasp on concrete.

YANK THAT LINE GIRL! SET THAT HOOK, NOW!

She cupped her face in her hands. "Don't say things ta make me bend to your lust, Kevin Crawley! Be a better man than that!"

He took her wrists in his hands, enveloping them. "Marry me, Bridget! Be me wife, lass! I'll make ye as happy as an angel on Christmas morn!"

Her eyes flew open wide. "Is that your promise of honor, Colonel?"

"Bridget Walsh, will you marry me and be my wife to our dying day?" His face was smooth and open.

"YES! Oh yes Kevin! I've loved ye for ages!" She reached up and pulled him to her, making room on the couch as he climbed on.

Now reel him in quick as ye can!

***

It would be a year until her killing rage boiled again…

CHAPTER TWELVE

From that first night, Bridey took to Kevin's bed and didn't leave it until the day she died. They went to the priest that very week, and were married in a month. Good thing too, because Eamon came into the world eight months after.

When she told him she was expecting, he took the news rather matter of factly. Not the excited school boy way he had dealt with Melanie's last and final pregnancy.

"Very good," was all he said when given the news. He either didn't see or else didn't care about the hurt look in her eyes when he then kissed the top of her head. "And if it's a girl, we'll be naming her Sarah, and if it's a boy, his name will be Eamon," he said.

"Oh, Kevin? Do I have any say in the matter?"

"Certainly. You may choose the middle name."

She looked up at him levelly. "Eamon's a fine name. If it's a girl, we'll see."

As it was, that was a battle that never took place.

***

On the day Eamon was born, the delivery was simple-simon, no complications at all. Bridey felt rather smug as the midwife took her leave. Kevin wanted her to give birth in Kingston General Hospital and she would have no part of such an unnecessary expense. They had only one row over it, when she was in her eighth month. She vanquished him easily; it had to do with 'woman's things' and as far as he was concerned, the less he knew the better he felt.

"And no doctors either, Kevin! With their knives and their drugs! Women have been birthing bairns throughout history and Mary McGuire's the finest midwife in the city!"

Before she left, Mary McGuire had cleaned Bridey up with a sponge bath and brushed her hair. She put on a bit of lipstick before allowing him to enter. When she was ready, she called out to him. He had stationed himself just outside the door.

She almost burst with pride when she handed Eamon to his father for the first time. He cooed at the bairn and nuzzled into the boy's face and fingers like he were to eat the baby up, his love was so strong.

"You'll be having your hands full now with three of 'em, Bridey," he said to her, eyeing her over Eamon's swaddled body.

"I'll be up and about in no time, Kevin, don't ye be worryin' over me!" He was kind to be concerned though, and she appreciated it.

Handing the babe back, he said, "I'm not worried for you, Bridey. You're as strong as an ox," he held his hand up seeing the fire in her eyes. "And in as fine fettle as a minx! But darling, three children and this house! We have the money, let's spend it on some help for you!"

Eamon babbled for a moment and fell back asleep as she rocked him in her arms. "No!" she said, her voice a tight whisper. "We'll not be spending your hard earned money on a worker who wouldn't do as good a job as I, and work I should be doing in the first place!" She tilted her head at him. "A dollar's not an easy thing to come by as ye well know."

He smiled broadly and sat beside her on the bed. Reaching over, he stroked her hair, still damp with sweat from the birthing. "I'm astonished at how well you've come out of it already, Bridey," he said with wonder in his voice. Neither of them spoke of Melanie's frailty.

"Mrs. Dowd will feed and bed the girls down tonight, Kevin, and I'll be up and about tomorrow." She looked at him slyly. "Wouldn't mind getting another bun in the oven as soon as we can, I can tell ye!" She held up her hand. "Not right away, mind ye... but soon enough!"

He bent over and hugged her. "Let me bring in the girls. They're dancing a jig wanting to meet their brother."

She held the bairn to her face so her scowl remained hidden. *Tis only half brother!* "In a wee bit, darlin'... I'd like a nap if you don't mind?"

Sitting back, he said, "Of course, of course... before they go to bed, perhaps."

She leaned over and put Eamon into the bassinet beside the bed. It was one luxury she insisted on having custom made. It was at the exact same height as the bed, with a side that folded down so she could slide the babe in and out without any fuss.

"Thank you dear, just a nap and the girls can come in then…" she feigned a yawn. "Oh! I must not be quite the ox ye thought!"

He plumped her pillows and fussed with her comforter before quietly leaving the room.

When he left, Bridey lowered the side of the bassinet and whispered into Eamon's ear, "Those two curs will be keepin' their distance from ye Eamon, don't ye fear!" With a smile she glided her hand over the snoring form of her *first* son, then closed up the side and slipped into sleep herself.

***

A week later, she was back to being a wife and a mother to the twins. It was springtime and she had taken Eamon out for a walk. The twins were with her as well.

"May we push Eamon, Bridey?" asked Agnes, putting her hand on the bar beside hers.

She flew around and slapped the girl's mouth. Agnes let out a yelp and Alice gasped.

"Now, I'll be tellin' ye for the once and for the all, ye bloody blaggard! Call me Bridey one more time, ONE MORE TIME and I'll skin ye both alive!"

"But… that's what Papa calls you!" Alice spoke quietly. She had taken her sister's hand and they were both standing together.

"I've told ye time and again what to call me!" She was furious. What did these two expect, for her to get down on her hands and knees and beg? "Haven't I? And what has ye're father said about it?"

Agnes was rubbing her cheek where she had been hit. "He said we're to call you *Mother*." She dropped her hand

and stared defiantly. "But our mother's dead! You're *not* our mother!"

The defiant wretch! She resisted the urge to slap her again; Kevin would draw the line at bruising. "I'm the only mother the likes of ye will be havin'! And it's high time ye be giving me the respect!"

"Agnes," said Alice quietly, her voice quivering, "we won't call her 'Mummy', all right?" She tilted her head to her twin, their foreheads touching. "We've never called Mummy 'Mother', so it's all right." She looked back to Bridey. "Please don't hit her anymore..." her face shadowed, "*Mother*."

Bridey turned from one to the other. "And for ye?"

Agnes' face was tear streaked, but the anger in her eyes was unmistakable. "I'll address you properly... *Mother*."

Bridey watched them both. They had better. Now that Eamon was here, their father's son, their star in his eyes was fading. And would fade more as she brought more children into the world. Though they were but five years old, 'twas time they began to help with the housework. She'd have them scrub the kitchen floor when they got home.

"Very well," she said. "And no, missies, ye leave Eamon to me, is that clear?" She directed them to walk before her so she could keep an eye on them. She'd be giving Kevin a piece of her mind when he came home about his saucy daughters!

At the end of their outing, she noticed the rosebushes beginning to bloom along the walkway.

Melanie's rosebushes.

She had a head full of memories of Missus La-Ti-Da Crumpet tending the three bushes along the walkway back when she was but the *once a week washerwoman* for this house. Melanie had pointed to them with pride telling how she had planted them herself. As if being able to dig a hole and drop in a root ball was some sort of accomplishment!

The smell of these bushes would be wafting in the house before long. And when that happened, Kevin would become maudlin and tiresome in grief. He did so the first year after Melanie died, and the new blooms of spring told her that it would happen again.

Well, she'd be having none of that! She sent the girls to the back yard and went to the small shed at the side that held all of the gardening tools. Without too much effort, she found garden shears and a small bow saw. Still in her dress and hat, she set the brake on the perambulator and set to work.

It went quicker than she expected; the bushes were denuded down to the earth, their branches stacked alongside the house. Lord it was getting warm! The branches cut was only half the job. She'd root these bushes out for once and all. She returned to the shed for more tools, coming out with a pick axe.

Lord, she should have done this last fall! She took the pick axe and swung it down into the center roots of the first bush, impaling the point in the mass. She bent the handle back until she heard a soft crack under the earth. She repeated the action four more times.

"That'll do ye in good," she muttered as she wiped the sweat from her forehead with her sleeve.

She took off her hat, laying it upon the awning of Eamon's carriage. Grunting and chuffing she repeated the same destruction on the remaining bushes. One more memory of the *Crumpet* for the fire. She'd enjoy burning the woody debris in the fireplace.

She expected her husband to notice right away. When Kevin asked why she had done so, she'd tell him she found terrible leeches and vermin infesting them. She'd say that on her walk today, she had seen one of the neighbors taking their own bushes down and asked about it. She would say she learned this fungus was terribly poisonous—should the children so much as prick themselves on a thorn, it could kill them!

She was more than a little surprised when she shooed the girls into the house and put Eamon down that the scent of roses wafted through the entire downstairs. It was a warm afternoon, and all the windows were open. Her nose wrinkled at it. Certainly many people found the aroma of roses appealing, but to her it was the smell of weakness and snobbery.

Thank God it had faded by the time Kevin came home.

He didn't say a word about them all evening. She watched him carefully for the tell tale signs she had been able to pick up of him being annoyed, but there wasn't a one. He discussed the happenings at the base as usual, inquired about the children, as usual, and that was that. A normal evening at home.

The following morning she went to collect the mail and her heart stopped.

Each of the bushes she had torn out had been replaced.

And were in full bloom.

"How in the name of God had he done it?" Her eyes were wide as saucers. She strode down the walkway. Not a spot of dirt was on the paving stones. She bent down. And the earth was fully packed. She looked to each bush, finding the same thing. On one of the bushes she found a strange thing—while all the blooms were shell pink, one bloom had gone wayward and was pure white.

"Well, *Colonel* if it's a battle ye want, so be it!" She marched to the garden shed and got the clippers, bow saw and pick axe again. "I told ye I was not afraid of workin'!"

Being the second time doing, it went faster, and the scraps were piled up where she had put the original detritus. Why in the world Kevin had cleaned up so thoroughly, she had no idea. Except he hadn't been out of her sight all evening. He must have called some gardeners in to do the job while she was cooking supper. Sneaky, clever man. How much did he pay them to do the work overnight? And so quietly? She hadn't heard a sound.

Again, the house was filled with the bouquet of fresh cut roses when she returned to start supper. The twins were down for naps in their room, and Eamon was in a cradle in the living room. She went into the kitchen to prepare dinner, fuming at the man and his waste of money. For heaven's sake, they could plant other flowers!

When she heard the motor car pull into the drive she scampered outside. They'd have it out now!

"Meeting me at the car, Bridey? How romantic!" he said with a smile when she came through the side door. His second comment died on his lips. "Darling, what's the matter?"

She was bent over at the waist, her mouth gaping open, her face white. As white as the single wayward bloom on the rosebushes along the walkway.

CHAPTER THIRTEEN

A weaker woman would have thought she was going mad and Bridey did give into that temptation for a short bit. She took to her bed immediately, but didn't dare try to sleep until Kevin joined her later that night. She explained herself by saying she had some sort of cramps, but should be alright soon.

She had no confidence in that being the case when she finally fell asleep, hearing Kevin's deep breathing beside her.

She was surprised to wake the next morning fresh as a daisy. She was sitting in the kitchen with a pot of tea as she considered these strange events. Kevin was off to work and the children were still abed. He had been puzzled and concerned by her taking ill so suddenly and yet completely recovered in the morning. She calmed his worries by telling him she had tried too hard to be a good soldier yesterday and it was just a bit of overwork. He made her promise that she would at least consider hiring some help if only for a short while.

As if she'd let that happen!

She filled her teacup again, mulling over the strange occurrence of the day before.

Perhaps she was going mad; but she didn't *feel* insane! Shouldn't a madwoman be agitated? Shouldn't she be traipsing around the house singing lullabies or opera arias? Dressing in the oddest of clothes and eating raw food or something? She ought to be yammering to herself like a maniac were she mad, right?

Or else a quiet madness then—she should be sitting in a chair, huddled under blankets and coats maybe. Or hiding beneath her bed perhaps, drooling and pissing herself like some lump of flesh!

But no, she was having none of those experiences. She could recall the events of each of the last few days in order, from waking to sleeping. She could remember what she prepared for supper each and every night of the last week, what dress she wore to Church on Sunday, and what clothes she laundered three days ago!

No, her mind was clear as glass.

So if she was able to recall that she had washed and ironed Agnes' pink jumper and Alice's grey one two days ago, then her memory of destroying those rose bushes was accurate as well.

Her eyebrows drew tight and her lip curled. "Well, then Melanie *dear*, I think *three* will be the charm!" she said aloud.F

She rose from her chair and went out the side door into the drive. Hearing the noise of a motorcar's gears grinding, she looked down the street to watch a truck pull up to the Ashton home. *Rose Heating* was painted on the side. Two men got out, and as she watched, they opened the large rear doors of the truck and began to unload tools and equipment. Of course. Mrs. Ashton had told her just the other day that they were going to have a central heating installed. She hoped the racket wouldn't wake Eamon.

One of the men noticed her watching and stopped. He put his hand above his eyes shielding them from the bright morning sun and smiled.

"Bridey Walsh as I live and breathe! Is that really you?" he called out.

She sighed. Jackie Morrison was a regular patron of the Royal Tavern on Fridays after work. He had tried several times to chat her up when she had visited the Ladies' Room.

"It's *Mrs.* Bridget Crawley now, Jackie Morrison!" She called back. "I've married me a Colonel in the army almost a year ago!"

"And so you work there?" he spoke, gesturing at the home behind her.

Shaking her head she looked over with a rueful smile. Pointing at the brass plaque mounted beside the front door she said, "Now Jackie, I know ye weren't the brightest light when we were in school, but were ye to look beside the front door, ye'll see the name *Crawley*, will ye not?"

He tilted his head, his gaze following her finger. "Crawley," he said in a low voice. Turning back to Bridey, he added, "Aye and I do."

She folded her arms, thinking of the shanty where he had lived, in Lowerton. Probably living in a hovel not much better these days. "Me husband and I are the *owners* of this home."

The smile fell from Jackie's face. "You sound pretty proud of yerself, Bridey."

"Tis Missus Crawley to you, Sir!" She gave a wave like brushing away a mosquito and walked back up the drive. *Her* drive. She went around it to the side of the house, the noise of the two men resuming their labor fading as the structure came between them.

She didn't bother with the pickaxe this time. She planned to limit her efforts to the one bush that had the white bloom. She'd just cut its branches down and see what happened. She squatted down with the garden shears in hand.

"Well, Melanie dear, shall we try again?" she said aloud, and lopped off the branch.

With the crunch of the branch being cut, the world went still. The thuds and clangs of Jackie Morrison and his man down the street stopped cold. She glanced down the drive. They had just arrived and were now taking a break? She'd make sure not to hire *that* company if they were ever in need!

Looking down the driveway gave her a bit of a start. The world was *different* somehow. It was *still*. Not only had Jackie and his man grown quiet, but there wasn't a sound from the birds in the trees. Just a moment ago they had been peeping and squeaking to beat the band. Gazing into the branches, she didn't see a single one. Not only that, but she couldn't hear any more of the rustle of the leaves in the morning breeze.

There wasn't any breeze at all.

Nor a sound.

She looked down the drive towards the back yard. Everything *seemed* normal.

Or did it?

The day was as bright as ever; no sudden rising of storm clouds… but it was *different*. She looked about her. It was as if someone had turned up a gas light in a room too high. The light was stronger, almost washing out the color of her dress, and the green of the leaves on the branch she held in her hand.

"Oh sweet Jesus," she muttered in shock. The white rosebud positively *glowed* in her hand! She put her finger on it. It felt as cool as any flower that was freshly picked.

She walked down the drive to the street with the pace of a condemned man going to the gallows.

She rounded the side of the house and stopped.

Holy Mary, mother of God! The street was deserted. Jackie Morrison's truck was gone. She looked up and down the street. Not a soul. She peered into the park across the way to see it empty as well.

The air itself was dead. And was pressing in on her.

Just as it had when she visited Deirdre's a lifetime ago!

Her eyes flew open and a gasp emptied her chest. She spun and heaved in a lungful of that dead, dead air.

"Eamon!" she screamed. She flew up the drive to the side door. She flung the clippers and branch from her hand and yanked on the door. The instant it opened, she heard a loud clang from across the street and Jackie Morrison's bray of laughter telling his man to be careful or he'd lose a toe.

She froze in place, staring into the mudroom.

Stepping back out, she looked to the side. Laying on the ground to her right was the garden shears, but when she looked to the left, the branch she had tossed was gone. She closed her eyes and drew in a long breath and stepped back down to the drive.

Waving at her in the morning breeze was the white rose in full bloom, back on the bush.

Her knees became oatmeal and she collapsed onto the steps.

***

If Bridey Walsh was anything, it was pragmatic. All right, she was also a cold blooded murderess; she had to admit that to herself. Even so, it wasn't an angel of judgment sent by the Lord above. This was no Michael the Archangel sent to her home.

This was a haunting by the spirit of Melanie Crawley.

"Very well, Melanie," she said as she collected herself. "Ye may keep ye're bloody roses!" She collected herself as best she could and went about her day.

That night in bed, Kevin was feeling rather randy.

"Kevin, dearest, it's been only a short while since I birthed Eamon," she said. "I'll be needing a wee bit more time." Didn't the man realize how exhausted she was at the end of the day?

The look of disappointment on his face would break the heart of a marble statue. "Of course, darling," he said, "I'm sorry for trying to impose myself upon you so soon."

"Thank you, dear." She stroked his face, trying to wipe away his ardor. As she did so, the scent of roses washed over them both. She saw his nostrils flare in recognition... and a twinge of grief perhaps?

Damn you, Melanie. He's mine now!

She gave an impish smile. "You've been a gentleman to me, Colonel Crawley," her voice husky and smooth. "And it has been some time since ye've enjoyed the pleasures of the flesh, has it not?"

"Twelve weeks and three days, but who's counting?" he said.

She touched his shoulder and pulled him back when he went to roll over. "Well now, that's quite a long time, isn't it? Let's see what else we can do as a..." she wiggled her eyebrows at him, "consolation."

He gave a little gasp. "Oh! Mrs. Crawley! Console me indeed as best ye can!" He closed his eyes and crossed his arms beneath his head. "You're... giving me great... *great* comfort in my moment of need..."

As she tended her husband, the aroma of roses faded as quickly as they came.

Tis me bedroom now, Melanie.

***

"Ye'll come when I call ye, Agnes Crawley!" Bridey gave the child a swat on her behind. "Don't yell back to me 'What' ye heathen!" She gave the five year old another swat, eliciting an 'Oww!'.

It was two days later, and Bridey had been in the kitchen. Kevin and she were having the Ashton's over for supper and cards that evening and she was harried. When she had called out to Agnes from the kitchen to come and dry the dishes Alice had finished washing, the child's reply of 'What?' had been the last straw. That girl had been flip and nervy all day! She took the child by the ear, quick marching her to the kitchen.

As they went from the living room to the dining room, she heard the rattle of her favorite vase on the shelf. She looked over to see it dance on the shelf like a marionette. Her sisters had given it to her as a wedding present!

Oh REALLY Melanie? Ye don't like your precious daughter being punished? Let's see about that!

She scooped the child off the floor, and plopping into a chair at the dining room table, she put Agnes over her knee and gave her three quick cracks on her bum.

"Break that vase, and the child pays!" she said aloud, watching it.

The vase stilled. The only sound in the room was Agnes' soft sobs.

She hauled the child off her lap and stood her upright. "What will you say to me the next time I call ye, Agnes!"

"I'm coming?"

"Good. Now into the kitchen with ye and dry those dishes like a good girl." She gave the girl another tap on the bum and sent her packing.

Alone in the room, she said out loud, "We better be having a truce here, Melanie. Ye can't hurt me nearly as much as I can hurt the twins. If ye could, that vase would have conked me in the head! So leave me be, and all will be well, understand?"

When she smelled the roses, she knew she had won.

The truce held until she discovered Kevin's Last Will and Testament.

CHAPTER FOURTEEN

Bridget was able to put her battle with Melanie behind her in short order. As she regained her strength from childbirth, the entire episode began to fade in her mind as if it were a dream. She knew that it wasn't true, it was simply easier to not think about it. As long as Melanie didn't try to assert herself, Bridget saw no reason to do anything other than live her life.

Her situation changed in a single evening.

Kevin was at the secretary desk with his exchequer book open, paying the bills. Invoices from the food market, the dairy man, the coal company and others were arranged in a neat pile on his desk. He would write the cheque for each bill and leave Bridget the money for the postage to mail them the next day. For most of them, Bridget simply kept the few pennies and dropped the payments off when she was in the downtown area.

She was setting the table in the dining room when she noticed him reading through a sheaf of papers.

"And what's that ye have there, love?" she said.

"Nothing you need to worry about, my dear. Just some papers from the lawyers."

"The lawyers?" She straightened up from her task. She would set the plates and glasses, and would have the twins put out the cutlery. "What do they want?" To her, anything having to do with lawyers was never a good thing, and certainly was *something* to be concerned about. She stepped over to where Kevin was seated.

He folded the papers up and replaced them in an envelope. "Just paperwork settling the land and title to the house is all." He looked up at her. "Legal mumbo jumbo, that tells us we have a home to live in." He gave a small smile as he tucked the envelope into one of the pigeon holes that ran above the writing surface.

"Well, I could have told ye that!" She returned his smile and went back to the table.

He closed up the desk and put the month's bills and cheques on top of the desk. "You'll look after these, dear?"

"As I do every month, your lordship!"

He stepped to her and took her in his arms. "Lordship now? I'm now a grand lord, eh?"

"Ye are to me, Kevin Crawley!" She pecked his cheek and went back to the kitchen. She took the roast out of the oven and put it on top to cool and called the twins in from the back yard to finish setting the table.

She knew he was lying the second the words came out of his mouth, but she wasn't going to make a fuss yet until she found out what was in those papers.

***

The next morning, after she put Eamon down for a nap she went to the desk. She had never bothered with the bills and papers of the house. Taking care of three wee ones was work enough, and Kevin seemed to have all that well in hand anyway.

But why wouldn't he mention correspondence from lawyers? Anything that involved those shysters cost money, and more importantly, had to do with laws and judges in one form or another. Although Melanie was cold in the ground, she had nevertheless murdered her. So yes, she was quite interested in any communication from lawyers, thank you very much.

She ran her hand over the front oak panel. She would need to put a coat of furniture wax on it soon. It had been in the house from when she had started working there. It looked so small when Kevin sat at it, but he was a large man.

She pulled the knob on the panel, folding the cover down so it became the desk's surface. The thin squeak of the brass fittings told her that some oil was also going to be needed. Tucked among the pigeon holes across the top were a series of different papers—old bills, some letters Kevin had replied to from his brother who lived in Lanark, and some forms from the Army.

The envelope in question was at her fingertips. She looked aside for a moment feeling a twinge of guilt for spying on her husband. Ha! She smiled. It was her home too, was it not? She opened it and took out a sheaf of papers.

Oh! 'Last Will And Testament' was emblazoned across the top page. Under it, in calligraphic handwriting was 'Kevin Anthony Crawley'. His will! Now why hadn't he told her about this yesterday? These were very important papers! Back when she was a washerwoman, one of her clients had said that they kept important papers such as insurance policies and wills in boxes at the bank!

She opened it up to read the mumbo jumbo and soon discovered why he had been so evasive.

A discovery that led to a murderous rage.

CHAPTER FIFTEEN

Devlin Griffin was seated in a booth in the Royal Tavern when Danny Boyle approached him.

"Excuse me, Mister Griffin, but there's someone to see ya," he said quietly.

As usual, Devlin sat with his back to the wall. He scanned the room to see who was making eye contact and saw no one. Keeping his eye on the other men in the room, he said, "Well then, send him over, Danny." His right hand drifted to his vest where he kept a derringer pistol. He palmed it into his hand. It only held two bullets, but that would be enough to give him time to draw the larger pistol under his jacket.

"Well, that's the thing, Sir, it's a lady, and she's waiting for you in the Ladies Room. He leaned down. "It's Bridey Walsh, Mr. Griffin; you've met her before."

He lowered his head to think. The name did ring a bell, but... He smiled and his chin rose, to look at Danny. Ahhh... 'Bridget' Walsh! He hadn't laid eyes on her in a long, long time—well over a year. She was a different sort of girl, if he recalled correctly. And a real looker, too. With a glint in his eye, he stood. "Let's not keep the lady waiting then."

He gathered himself and walked towards the Ladies Room. His leg wasn't acting up at all today, so his limp was only slight. His step and pace was more like a man with a pebble in his shoe rather than a man who had been shot through the leg with a rifle three years earlier. That shooter had died screaming and begging for death.

Bridget was in the furthest corner of the room, away from everyone. She was sitting perched on the edge of a chair at a small table. Her skirt almost went to the floor, and matched her short jacket. Her cloche hat was pulled low, almost to her eyebrows. When he approached, she gave him the oddest smile; welcoming, yes, but was there a hint of fear as well?

"Miss Walsh... it's been some time," he said with his own smile.

"It's Mrs. Crawley now, Devlin. I've been married a year."

He sat back in his seat. There was a... a *different* sort of attractiveness about this woman. She didn't have the good time girl allure of a flapper of course. Her high cheeks became almost apples when she smiled, but it was the intensity of her eyes. Light brown, yes; but when they looked at you, you were the absolute center of her world. One of her eyes was just a tiny bit off center, but to him that made her face more... exotic or something. Just as a beauty mark did, this small flaw made her that more enticing.

"Well," he said, tapping his hat against his leg, "although I'm not the marrying kind, it is a disappointment."

She gave that smile again.

"What can I do for you, Mrs. Crawley?"

She tilted her head at him. "When we first met, you told me that men were afraid of you."

"Yes, I did, didn't I?"

"Do they still fear you?"

"I hope so, for their sakes."

She sat with her hands on her lap and never taking her eyes off him. "Have you ever done free-lance work?"

"You mean have I killed for hire."

She didn't so much as flinch. "Aye, that's exactly what I'm asking."

"Bridget…"

Before he could finish his sentence, she leaned into the table. "I have a frank question, Mister Griffin—do you enjoy your labors?" The smile she flashed was a flirty smirk.

"Why is that important?"

"Because when I committed murder, I felt an incredible exhilaration."

He knew as soon as she said it, she was telling the truth. The woman across from him *had* taken the life of another human being. And, just like him, was strong enough to admit the passion of it. More importantly, the look in her eyes, the satisfaction and zest in the words of her confession screamed in his mind a single message.

He was sitting with his soul mate. He nodded. "Yes; it is exhilarating."

"There's something about acting on our blackest and darkest natures, isn't there, Devlin?"

"I'm not sure what you mean."

She leaned across the table and took his hand in hers. "The purer the victim… the more innocent and good they are—taking such a life is a powerful drug, don't you agree?"

A lesser man would have found this conversation chilling. Except she was right. To be so utterly and completely evil was intoxicating. He nodded. "I completely agree." He covered her hand with his own. "And in the spirit of such honesty, I want to tell you that having this discussion is acting like an aphrodisiac upon me." He squeezed her hand, and she squeezed back.

"Me too, Mr. Griffin."

"I have rooms upstairs, Bridey."

She stood. "I thought you'd never ask." When she smiled, her lips glistened. And her eyes glittered like diamonds.

***

Two hours later Bridget entered the front door of her home.

"I'm back, Mrs. Dowd!" she called out as she hung up her coat. "I'm sorry I took so long, but there was quite a series of line ups!" She headed to the kitchen. Her timing was perfect, as Mrs. Dowd was alone.

"A series, Bridey?"

She nodded, her eyes downcast. "Yes. The Doctor said he 'found something' and I had to go for a few tests."

"Oh dear Lord!" Mrs. Dowd came from the stove where she had been working. "Bridey, whatever is the matter?"

She gave her head a small shake. "I'd rather not talk about it, Mrs. Dowd, but would you mind if I took a bath before the children get up?"

The woman looked at her with sad eyes. "No, not at all! Go on up with ye, girl. Everything's under control here."

"Thank you so much, Mrs. Dowd." She put a hand on the woman's shoulder." And not a word to my husband until I find out the results of my tests, alright?"

"Of course not."

In the bathtub she withdrew the thingamajig she had purchased at the pharmacy earlier in the day. There was no way she would bear Devlin Griffin's child! She rinsed it off under the faucet and after drying it replaced it in its holder and stretched back in the tub. She'd hide it someplace safe later. There was a shelf downstairs by the washing machine she had used before to hide secrets.

That betrayal was to repay yours, Kevin Crawley. To leave HALF of your estate to your two daughters and not the all of it to your wife? She smiled in satisfaction as she washed the dirt of the day off of her.

CHAPTER SIXTEEN

It was a beautiful summer's afternoon and Alice Crawley was on the swing in her backyard. Agnes was pushing her, trying to frighten her by pushing her higher and higher. Alice wasn't afraid at all—her sister wouldn't hurt her for all the world. She enjoyed the lurch in her stomach when the swing went as high as it could and then dropped back down.

The rush of the breeze in her hair kept mussing up the bow, but she didn't care. As long as Bridey didn't take notice, it was fine. Unlike Agnes, she was able to keep Bridey's name in her head, and 'Mother' for the out loud. Agnes let 'Bridey' slip out every so often though. But whenever she did, Papa was always present to rescue her.

She skidded her feet on the ground and brought the swing to a stop. "I think it should be your turn Agnes."

"No, that's all right! I like pushing you!" Her sister was wearing the identical outfit; the only difference was that the bow in her hair was on the opposite side. They did that on purpose, because then when they faced each other it was like looking in a mirror.

Alice giggled. "You *hate* pushing me! But you hate going up in the air more than pushing me, scaredey cat!"

"Don't call me that! You're the one who has to climb into bed with me when you have a bad dream!"

"Well, that's different. Those are dreams—this is only a swing!"

"Hmph. You can't fall off a dream and crack your head." She looked up at the ropes holding the swing. "I only get scared when you push me too high."

"Ohhh-kaayy… I'll only push you a little bit."

Agnes jumped onto the large oaken seat and grasped the ropes in her hands. She began to rock back and forth. "Okay then! Let's go!" Her sister began to push her gently. "You know, when you go slow like that, it's almost like floating."

Alice gave her a more solid push. "I like going up high in the sky!"

"Not too hard now."

The kitchen door at the back of the house opened and Mother Bridget stepped out onto the landing. She was wearing a light jacket and she had her hat on.

"All right, girls, let's go down to the lake now!" she called.

Alice brought Agnes' swing to a stop.

"I don't like that stupid lake," Agnes said quietly.

"Shh! She'll get upset if she hears you!" Alice whispered. "Mother! Will we be picking berries again?" she called out.

Mother Bridget tilted her head to the side and held up three wicker baskets. "Yes, we will. Now let's hurry along,

Mrs. Dowd can only stay for another hour, and your brother is still napping."

"He's *not* our brother, Alice, he's our *half* brother!" Agnes whispered as they crossed the yard to where Bridey was waiting.

"Shh! He's a good baby and I love him!" Alice hissed back.

"Hmph! You love *everyone*!"

Alice took her sister's hand. "And you most of all."

Mother Bridget handed them each their basket, and taking a hand from each of them, walked down through the park to the lakeshore.

"Do you think there will be any berries left?" she asked the girls.

"Well, they weren't ripe at all last week," said Agnes.

"Nor the week before," said Alice. "I hope they shall be ripe this week!"

"Well, said Mother Bridget, "three's the charm now, isn't it?"

Alice looked up at her step mother when she said that. She wasn't sure why, but there was something in her voice that was scary.

***

Mother Bridget had taken them deep into the berry bushes. She had been right, though; they were perfectly ripe! Alice's face was smeared with blackberry juice and her tummy was full. She was getting a little tired though.

"Mother, I'm rather tired, may we go home soon?" she asked.

Mother Bridget looked at her with a funny expression. "Oh, you're *raw-ther* tired, eh Missy? You sound quite like the proper Englishwoman, don't you?"

A chill went up Alice's spine. She wasn't being saucy or anything, but Mother Bridey was annoyed for some reason or another.

"I'm terribly tired too, Mother," Agnes spoke up. Mother Bridget shot her a nasty look and then smiled.

"*Ted-dib-lee* tired, little one?" she asked. Her eyes looked funny.

"Yes, Ma'am," Agnes said.

"Well, we can't be having you English princesses overtire yourselves, can we?" She gestured to the two girls. "Come here and we'll take the path down to the water's edge and sit for a moment. Then we'll head home, all right?"

The two girls picked their way out of the nest of blackberry bushes, holding their baskets high. When they got to the pathway where Mother Bridget was waiting, she folded her arms and looked at them sternly.

"Ye have mouths all purple and ye've stained ye'er dresses!"

Alice looked down the front of her dress in horror. Oh no! She looked over to see Agnes' frock to be even more stained.

"And I'll be having to work me fingers to the bone to try to get those stains out!" Mother Bridget clucked her tongue. Suddenly, she stopped with a jerk of her head. She gave her hand a wave, and her anger dissipated. "Oh well, 'tisn't the end of the world. Ye'll be too big for those dresses before long anyway, right?" She gave a strange smile to the girls.

Alice's blood ran cold. She should run away! Something was wrong! She looked over to Agnes to see fright across her sister's face too.

"Now come along down to the shore, then we'll go home. Mrs. Dowd has ice cream for ye today!

"No she doesn't," said Agnes.

"Agnes Crawley, are ye tellin' me I'm a liar?" Mother Bridget still had that terrible smile.

Agnes replied with a shrug.

"Well, never mind. Ye'll be learning the truth soon enough!" She took each of the girls by the hand and they went through a break in the hedges and were at the shore of the lake. Bridey tugged at their hands, pulling them along. Alice almost tripped as she was led to the shore.

"Quite soon enough," Bridey repeated in a low voice. She gazed down on each of them and said with a smile, "Of course."

There was a rowboat beached on the lake. A man almost as big as Papa was sitting on the gunwale. Mother Bridget walked right up to him.

"Hello, Bridget," he said quietly.

"Were you waiting long, Devlin?" She smiled.

"No, not at all."

"Did anyone see you?"

The man shook his head 'No'.

"Then we have a job to do." Alice watched Mother Bridget's face as she talked to the man. The skin had drawn tight to her teeth. She looked down at Agnes. Slowly, she turned her face to Alice's. Her eyes! Her eyes were all shiny, like pieces of broken glass were stuck in them! She was crushing Alice's hand in hers. Alice heard her sister squeal in pain as well.

The man gave a snorting grunt. "*We* have work to do? You mean me." Quick as a snake, he whipped out a black thing from his back pocket about the length of one of Papa's socks. He slapped it down on top of Agnes' head, the sound like a book being dropped. Agnes immediately fell to the ground and Mother Bridey released her hand.

The man spun to Alice and she looked up at him, her mouth open in astonishment. The last thing she saw as he raised that black thing again was his eyes. They were just like Bridey's! She started to let out a terrified scream.

He brought his truncheon down upon her head before a sound could escape her throat.

CHAPTER SEVENTEEN

THE KINGSTON WHIG STANDARD

MISSING CHILDREN RECOVERED FROM LAKE ONTARIO, ABDUCTOR BELIEVED DROWNED AS WELL

The twin girls abducted two days ago in the heinous attack along Lakeside park have been recovered in the most tragic way imaginable.

The bodies of Agnes and Alice Crawley, daughters of Colonel Kevin Crawley were found on Lake Ontario by searchers. They were tangled in ropes that were attached to a capsized rowboat halfway across the lake.

The police believe that the children must have attempted to escape their monstrous captor

and their activity resulted in the boat tipping over.

"We believe that we will recover the body of the perpetrator of this horrible kidnapping in the near future," said Chief Benjamin Hornsby of The Kingston Constabulary. The rowboat was discovered in the shipping lanes, a tremendous distance for someone to swim.

The children were reported missing two days ago by their mother, Bridget Crawley. They had been attacked by an unseen and unknown assailant as they picked the first ripened blackberries of the summer.

Mrs. Crawley was attacked from behind. The vile monster seized her, covered her eyes and bashed her head into a tree without warning, leaving her unconscious as he escaped with her children. She is still in hospital suffering the after effects of the brutal assault and the shock of the loss of her two daughters.

The police have notified towns all across the shore of Lake Ontario to be especially watchful for any suspicious persons lurking about.

Funeral arrangements have yet to be made, but a death notice will be published when they are finalized.

CHAPTER EIGHTEEN

For six months Kevin Crawley trudged through the endless trenches of his grief. He had only survived the deaths and funerals of Alice and Agnes because of shock. Had he been more in his right mind, he would have ended his own life, then and there.

What sort of animal would do such a thing as steal two babeens from their mother and let them die so? What sort of a world was it that such a monster could be allowed to exist by a loving God? Father O'Shea at St. Mary's vainly tried to give him some comfort; but the stupid, stupid man could not so much as venture to give any sort of reason.

You couldn't fault the man; he had made an attempt to bring comfort. But his weak and stupid clichés were lost on Kevin. All Kevin could do, during the entire two day wake was stare at the two coffins.

Sweet Jesus, they were so small! White boxes of enameled hardwood, with brass handles and—oh sweet Mother—hinges. The girls rested within on beds of pure, white satin. It had been a open casket wake, and he kept praying to God to wake his babeens up; call them from their slumber oh Lord, as you had called Lazarus! For two days and nights he was on his knees with his rosary, beseeching an uncaring God. For two days.

He screamed. He screamed himself hoarse when they closed the caskets. Forever and ever his tiny little girls would be in darkness below the earth! He tried to stop them, he fought and wailed and cried and begged them all to let him just take his little girls back home!

Oh please... oh please, oh please.... They would be so cold below the earth! Winter was coming and how, oh how would they ever, ever be warm again below the earth?

They were so afraid of the dark! You couldn't leave them in darkness forever!

Twas Bridey that called to him from the edge of madness.

"We'll have a lamp for them, Kevin," she said. "We'll have a lamp made for them, and they'll keep it filled with oil, and every night we'll light the lamp beside them and they'll have the light." He had fallen to the floor before the coffins, Father O'Shea and Mr. Thompson shushing the rest of the guests and letting her talk him back to reason.

"A lamp..." he sat on the floor between the two white coffins, a hand on each. He was wild eyed and his mouth hung slack for want of sleep. "A lamp..." he looked at Bridey, his eyes bleary.

"Aye, and they'll be resting with their beloved mother, Kevin. Right beside her so she will watch over them forever and ever..."

113

His eyes flew wide, a new pain skewering his shattered heart. "Oh sweet Lord... Melanie..." He whispered. He hid his face in his hands.

On her knees beside him, Bridey cradled his shoulders. "Aye, Melanie will be with them forever, Kevin. Forever and ever in the arms of their mother in Heaven."

His voice was a groan, "Beside them... forever...."

He keened himself to exhaustion and endured the funeral and grave service. Bridey was relentless with the men at the cemetery. Both coffins would stay above ground until everyone had gone; then and only then would they lower them into the earth.

***

He was inside a bell jar for six months. He could see the world, and hear it, but everything was muffled. When people spoke to him, their words barely made sense. His sleep was constantly broken; he would awaken in the middle of the night in tears, with no memory of what dream had come. Everything about his life was as if it were draped in a veil. He could make things out, but not the details. Not that he cared much anyway.

He could barely let himself look at his son Eamon. It broke his heart to do so because he could see Alice and Agnes in the baby's eyes and the timbre of his babbles when he'd try to speak. Each moment with the baby was a knife to his heart, twisting in the grievous wounds.

He dared not take a drink; not a drop. Were he to, he would kill himself and be done with it all.

All he could do was soldier on. He let one day bleed into the next, putting his head down on the bed at night to rise in the morning, go through some foggy motions of living to put his head back down again at night.

He never spoke unless spoken to; and when he was, his response was as short as humanly possible. If a grunt would suffice, so it did. Bridey had taken the message well, and looked after the bills and running of the household in its entirety. When a workman needed to be hired, she did so. When the automobile needed repairs, she made arrangements with the garage for it to be picked up and returned.

On Sundays she would take Eamon to Mass, alone.

Through fall and winter, he would be found either in his bed asleep or sitting on the couch in the parlor, staring out the front window at nothing.

He didn't think any thoughts, he merely waited to die.

It was the worst the following May, on the day of the anniversary of Melanie's death. He had decided in a muddled manner, that were he to throw himself from the bridge that connected the military base with the city proper, he'd drown. There would be enough money for Bridey and the boy to start a new life for themselves. She could sell this cursed house and perhaps move out west. Or further east, should that be what she wanted.

The decision made, he poured a glass of sherry and toasted Melanie's memory and went to bed.

And for the first time in months and months he dreamed.

It was a beautiful dream.

Melanie and he were walking by the lake. He had one of the girls' hands in each of his and they were chattering like magpies. He couldn't understand a word they said, but their happiness and joy of all of them finally being together was a warm shower to one who had spent the last months trudging through the roiling mud in the trenches of heartbreak.

He looked to Melanie and saw in her eyes eternal love. He looked down to his perfect, perfect daughters who returned his gaze with such love his heart would burst with happiness.

From behind him, Melanie placed a hand on his arm. "Now Kevin Crawley, you must put those foolish thoughts from your head." He turned to her again, to see a smile of such love and woe together. "You will not open that circle, Kevin Crawley. You must live in the world for the sake of your son."

"I want to be with you, Melanie... I'm sorry if I'm disloyal to Bridey, I truly am; but I want to be with you!" He felt her hand tighten on his arm.

"Bridey Walsh is the mother of your son, Kevin. You bedded and wedded her," she tilted her head. "I was unable to warn you from her." Her gaze dropped. "I should have though," she said softly.

His heart was so light until those words. "What do you mean, love?"

She gave her head a small shake. "We'll not speak of it, my dear... for Eamon's sake if for nothing else."

Agnes tugged on his hand. "We're so happy to be here with you, Papa! We can't come into the house though. We'd like to go back up to our room and play there, but we're only able to get to the swing in the back."

"Well then, my dears, I must spend more time in the back yard!" He began to spin in a circle, holding each of the girls' hand until they lifted off the ground shrieking and laughing. As he spun he watched Melanie. Again, joy and sorrow competed for expression on her face.

As he slowed down, setting the girls back onto the ground, she gave him a small wave.

"You'll know me by the roses, Kevin. By the roses…"

A pleasant golden glow, a warm late summer afternoon filled his senses…

The joy of his dream carried him awake. He opened his eyes to the new day.

CHAPTER NINETEEN

Those six months after the death of the twins passed quite differently for Bridget Crawley, thank you very much. Kevin had made an absolute fool of himself at the wake and funeral; she had lost all respect of the man for his weakness.

He was but their father after all! He hadn't carried them for nine months, and then endured the fear and pain of bringing them into the world. He certainly didn't bath them, or wipe their snotty noses. He didn't wash their underwear nor cook for them nor clean up after them. What in the world was he losing by their deaths?

He was being cowardly.

She remembered when the influenza had struck just as the Great War was ending. It took her youngest brother and sister with it, along with Granny. In a flash, they had gone from sniffles and coughs to corpses laid out in the parlor; one after another. Yes, of course Ma was beside herself— two bairns gone as well as her own mother. But Da was made of stone through it all, a rock to be leaned upon. Yes, he was sad for a few days, but had gotten over it. There was work to be done and other mouths to feed and that was that.

She and Da were cut from the same cloth. She had felt badly, but life goes on. Leave the wailing and keening for others, and let the dead take care of the dead.

She had been forced to take over all of the household's business affairs. Now it was she, not the great Colonel Crawley who sat at the desk in the parlor sorting bills and bank statements. Oh well, at least she had 'found' his will. He didn't express a single word of remorse nor offer an explanation to her, his wife! Nevertheless, she made him draw up a new one to bestow what rightfully should have been hers in the first place. She kept a copy of the previous one as a reminder of what his actions had driven her to.

She had to look after hiring workmen when the roof needed repair. While the carpenters were doing the work, she had them close up the stairway to the twins' bedroom. Kevin neither noticed nor cared.

Day in and out, week in and out, month after month the man was pitiful in his grief! He'd get up, go to work, come home and sit in the parlor on the couch, staring off into nothing for hours on end until she sent him to bed. Not a word of conversation, not a question after the health of his son. A bump on a log, day after day after bloody day!

In the mornings he would drag himself from bed, splash water from the sink and call that a bath. His face bore constant stubble from missed strokes of his razor. The only comb his hair would see was his wet fingers run through it. He would wear the same uniform day in and out, until it would be stained and stinking.

This was the great war hero? Bah. She was sick of him. Sick, sick, sick of him and his long face!

119

Was this to be her life now? Just two years ago she was going to go to Hollywood and become a famous actress. She was going to live in Hollywood Hills in a house with a pool and servants of her own. She was going to attend lavish parties, and give even grander ones. Handsome and powerful men would have vied for her attention. It was going to be such a magnificent life.

And now, here she was trapped with a man wallowing in self pity. He was a shadow of what he had once been; less a man and more a ghost…

A ghost.

By God, then why not put the truth to it? She had her whole life before her—why should she spend it in a mausoleum? Why should her house, her home, her very life be spent in this shell? If Kevin missed his twins so much, he could very well join them!

It would be a mercy.

***

She found herself at the gate of Deirdre O'Toole's home once again. Once again, the front door opened and the rail thin woman stepped onto the porch.

"Bridey Walsh, as I live and breathe!" she said, smiling as she had before, her eyes glittering.

"Tis Crawley, now, Deirdre, or haven't ye heard?"

"I'm aware of ye'er marriage, lass. And of ye'er son Eamon. Ye may wish to be known by the name some man has imposed on ye, like a slave bought in a market." She kept her eyes steady on Bridget. "But not meself. Ye'er name's ye'er name, for once and for all."

Bridget had come to the bottom of the steps leading up to the porch. She looked up to the woman unafraid. With a slow smile, almost a sneer, she said, "Ye sound like a suffragette, Deirdre. Did ye be marchin' for the vote back during the war?"

"Do ye want to be giving me cheek, darlin'? Do ye think that's wise?"

Deirdre's smile made her blood run cold. It was the same smile Devlin had when he bashed the heads of the twins. No— comparing Devlin's expression to the one before her was like saying a puff of wind was a hurricane.

She shook her head. "No. I'm sorry, Ma'am."

Deirdre returned to normal. "Now that's a bright lass." She tilted her head at Bridget. "More killin' to do?" Holding up her hand to silence Bridget's denial while it was still in her throat, she continued, "I warned ye about breaking open circles of life, girl."

"I need the beans, Ma'am." Her reply was a whisper.

Deirdre smiled again, and once more it blocked out the rest of the world, with only her glittering eyes above her lips. Blackness surrounded everything. Not darkness nor deep shadow; no, a pure and deep black. All that existed in Bridget's world were Deirdre's grinning maw and, sparkly shining eyes. "For raaaats," the words came out in a long rasp. The smile ended and the world collapsed back to normal. Bridget staggered under the stretch and snap of all about her.

The pain shot through her head. She had endured that stabbing agony for a month after the twins' death. Devlin had taken her by the hair and smacked her into the trunk of a tree after putting them into the rowboat. She had endured the agonizing headaches for a month; they would come from nowhere, crush her in a vise and vanish as quickly. She lurched to one of the posts of the porch to keep her balance.

The spear left her brain, and she gasped for air. Again it was gone, leaving her chilled to the bone. She looked up to Deirdre, wide eyed.

"Been some time since you had one of those spells, darlin'? And how concerned for ye has your Colonel Crawley been when ye've had them?"

She shook herself like a wet dog, shaking off her fear. Leaving only the disgust for Kevin. "As you probably know, Deirdre. He's never noticed." She reached into the pocket of her skirt and held out a dollar bill.

When they made the exchange and she took the packet of beans, touching Deirdre's icy hand didn't frighten her this time.

Deirdre stepped back to the door of the house. As she was closing it, she said, "Take care, Bridey; many circles have been broken in your home."

"Stop calling me Bridey!"

"There are other things I can call you... and I would, were I to ever see you again." She shut the door.

When Bridget got home, she left the packet in the kitchen, behind some canisters over the sink. She'd put it in his tea in the morning. That way she'd have a good night's sleep and energy to go through the day's tumult. Poor man would have died of a broken heart. Pity... he had once been a light in her life.

***

She woke even earlier the next day. She needed to shave the beans into his tea and have her hands washed before he awoke. She had the teapot steeping and was waiting for him to come downstairs. She made sure all else was in order; a normal day that would be visited by yet another tragedy to the Crawley household.

What needs to be done 'tis best done quickly. Of course.

Kevin bounced down the stairs fresh as a daisy. His hair was combed neatly, and not a spot of beard showed on his face. He was wearing a fresh uniform, his shoes gleaming with polish.

And for the first time since the twins died he kissed her good morning.

He held her by the shoulders, looking into her eyes brightly.

"Good morning, darling," he said with a smile that was almost shy.

She stood stiffly, teapot in hand. "And good morning to you, Kevin."

He still held her by the shoulders, but gently. "I feel as if I have come out of a dungeon, Bridey."

"Oh?" She held the teapot between them. It was quite warm in her hands.

"Yes… it was a terrible tragedy…" He looked down at the floor for a moment, then back up to her. "We'll never forget the girls, will we?"

She gave her head a slight shake, a lock of hair falling away.

He pushed it back into place, gently. "Ohhh Bridey," he said softly, almost in wonder. "You still bear the scar of that day on the crown of your head!" His finger stroked her scalp at the hairline where Devlin had left his mark.

She closed her eyes and nodded.

"Does it hurt still?" His eyes were filled with concern.

She dropped her head a bit. "Once in a while, but less often as time passes."

He kissed the scar tenderly. "Less often as time passes. It's been hard on ye too. You loved them so." His voice caught. "And I've been but another burden for ye to shoulder."

Her face tilted to look up at him and he kissed her. When the kiss broke, she bit her lower lip, staring into his eyes. "And now, Kevin?"

He sighed, but it was a soft one. "And now 'tis time for the dead to bury the dead, love. The girls are with their mother in Heaven, and I have a son to look after here on God's earth."

He gestured to take the teapot from her hands, and she backed away.

"No, Kevin, there's a smell from it I don't like. I was about to pour it down the sink." She gestured to the dining room. "Bring me the good teapot, the one we use for company, from the china closet. We'll have a fine cuppa this morning before ye go to work."

She dumped the pot of tea down the sink and made a fresh one, using the other teapot.

The sun's bright morning rays bathed them in the kitchen as they shared a pot of tea for the last time.

CHAPTER TWENTY

Alas, Kevin was somber again at dinner. When he came home, he dandled Eamon on his lap for half an hour, the first time he had done so in months. He did talk about the goings on at work somewhat as well. But when they sat down to supper and Eamon was abed for the night, a cloud came over his face.

She would have none of it.

"What's the matter?" she asked. If he slipped back into his ways…

"I had a telephone call from Sergeant Hornsby of the police today." He played with his food. "And I've been debating whether to inform you of it."

A tingle of fear skittered down the back of her neck. She forced her voice to remain calm. "Why should you debate informing me? Am I in trouble? Did I short change a clerk at the grocer's yesterday?" Her smile was weak as dishwater.

Still staring at his plate, he gave his head a small shake. "No, nothing of the sort." Raising his gaze to meet hers, he said, "They have a promising lead on what happened to the girls."

The tingle of fear became a block of ice. "Oh?"

He nodded vigorously. "Yes, and it's a strong one. It seems that Sergeant Hornsby, on his own time, had continued to go about the shore of the lake making inquiries."

"They did that when...when it happened?" She could barely take a breath, her body frozen to the chair.

"Yes and no. They asked at every home and business along the shore, yes, but not the people on the beaches with any consistency. They stopped visiting the beach and questioning people there, within two weeks. They had hoped that the reports in the newspapers would bring out anyone who had been on the beach and had seen something." He sighed.

"And to no avail."

"Until now." He still had his knife and fork in his hand, heavy silver cutlery given as a wedding present by Melanie's godmother. His fingers turned white clutching them. "Sergeant Hornsby reported that he spoke to a man who had been on the lake that afternoon and saw a man in distress on a boat. This witness was out bird watching and so had a pair of field glasses. He saw the man stand in the boat, toss his hat and coat into the water. He then stood and rocked the boat from side to side until it rolled over."

"Oh!" She couldn't think of anything else to say.

"The witness watched the man swim to shore, and as he did, the boat must have been in a current on the lake, because by the time the man reached the shore a mile down the beach, the boat had travelled quite far... too far for a man to swim back from."

"What will Sergeant Hornsby do now?"

"Bridey, the man swam back to Kingston. Sergeant Hornsby is going to move heaven and earth to find him." Bridey watched as the fork in Kevin's hand bent in two. "The hunt is on for a man my height, with bright red hair and who walks with a limp."

Devlin Griffin to a 'T'. Oh God.

"Tomorrow, Sergeant Hornsby will be mobilizing a house to house search for this man, and putting up roadblocks." He smiled. "We're going to find him, Bridey! And the bastard will hang!" He looked down at his fork in wonder and quietly laid it aside.

"I'm off to bed now, darling. I'll be up at dawn to meet with the Sergeant. I'll be bringing a company of volunteer soldiers to assist the police as they go house to house." He gave a snort. "The men will be lined up ten deep, fighting each other to be given the opportunity to help!"

If Devlin was anywhere in the city he'd be captured immediately! Her hands trembled as she stacked the dishes. She'd have to get word to him, but how? She looked into Kevin's eyes. "So with the help of God, this can be put behind us then," she said. "Sleep well, Kevin; I'll be up as soon as I have these done."

She stood at the kitchen sink filling it with water for the dishes. Oh dear God, what was she to do? She couldn't go down to the tavern to warn him—what if she was seen? But if he was captured, he'd spill the beans about her in a trice; she knew that because if the shoe were on the other foot, she'd do just the same.

She couldn't even pray for his escape. As if God were to heed her prayers!

The soft knock at the back door startled her.

She felt dizzy for a moment as she dried her hands, and went to open it, knowing who was there.

Dressed all in black, with a knitted watch cap pulled down covering his hair, Devlin gave her his most winsome smile.

"Time to go, Bridget."

She blinked at him in utter confusion. "What do you mean?"

"I have a car parked one street over. We'll make a run for the border and put all this behind us. I have friends in New York City who will help us get a fresh start."

She looked behind her to the steps leading up to the open kitchen door. "I'm not going anywhere!" She hissed in a whisper.

"We're two of a kind, woman, and you know that!"

"Keep your voice down, Devlin! The Colonel's only just now headed up to bed!"

"I don't give a fiddler's damn about the Colonel, Bridget! Get your coat and let's make a run for it!" He looked over his shoulder onto the darkness. "If the police don't have me identified already, they'll know me and all my business by morning. As terrified of me as people are, I'm sure Danny Boyle from the tavern will connect the dots for them." He gave an impish smile. "Danny remembers you going up to me room, *Bridey*."

Her stomach lurched in her mouth, her supper trying to come back up. She stepped back and Devlin entered the mudroom. "They'll be coming for you before lunchtime, you can count on that!"

Oh God! He was absolutely right.

"I'll get the baby and we'll be away," her voice was a whisper.

"No, leave the bairn with his Da. We must travel light, you fool!"

"I'll not leave me son!"

He slapped her suddenly, a taste of how her life would be forever with him.

He grabbed her by the arms. "Listen to me! We can't be saddled with a babe! We're not out of the woods, and if we're captured over the border, they'll put the baby in an orphanage!" He calmed down and smiled at her as he patted her flaming cheek where he struck her. "We'll go to New York first, then Chicago and then out to California."

California. Hollywood at last. Her heart broke at the irony. She dropped her head in surrender. "I'll get me coat."

Devlin stepped up into the kitchen, taking off his watch cap. "I'll pack some food to eat on the way. We'll have to drive all night if we want—"

"WHAT'S GOING ON HERE!" They both froze at Kevin's shout. He stood in the doorway of the kitchen half dressed.

"Damn it!" Devlin's teeth gritted.

"Bridey, what in the name of—" Kevin saw Devlin's bright red hair. "You!" He stepped into the room, hands outstretched to Devlin.

Like magic, a revolver appeared in Devlin's hand. "Uh, uh, Crawley! That's plenty close enough!"

Kevin froze in his tracks and turned to Bridget, his mouth hanging open.

"We'll just be on our way in a moment." Devlin nodded to Bridget. "Find some rope so we can tie him up and be done with it."

"There's a hank of it just in the cellar." Averting her eyes from her husband, Bridget scurried out of the kitchen.

"Ye killed me daughters, you animal!" Kevin's hands were clenching and opening.

Devlin tilted his head at Kevin. "I was hired to do a job, boyo." He smiled. "And she threw up her skirts and gave me a bonus for a job well done, I'll tell you."

"You *liar!*"

"Not this time, Crawley. A woman of dark and tasty passions is your wife. Something about a will, and you cutting her down by half to favor your girls or something." He shrugged. "Didn't matter to me what her reasons were. I was happy to bed her 'tis all."

Kevin's eyes narrowed and looked past Devlin. "Is that true, Bridey? You plotted the death of the girls?"

Bridget blew out a rush of air at the doorway to the kitchen. "Oh Devlin, you couldn't have kept your gob shut, could you? You've destroyed my life here now."

"Don't worry, *Bridey.*" Devlin kept his eyes on Kevin. He pulled something from his pocket and tossed it to Kevin. "Catch, boyo!" he said.

Kevin snagged the St. Jude medal out of the air and looked at it.

Devlin gave a chuckle. "I always keep a memento from my... err... 'projects'. That had been around the neck of one of the girls, you see." When Kevin took a step towards him, he raised the gun. "No, no, boyo. Not yet."

"Devlin!" hissed Bridey. "What are you doing?"

"Muddying the waters, my dear. I know that only one of the girls had a medal on them when they were pulled from the lake. The police believe that the beast who drowned the tykes would have that medal in his possession! So we leave it here with the famous Colonel, and the police will be so happy to deduce it was a case of a mad father murdering his children." His eyes slid over to Bridey. "We'll be home free!" Darting his gaze back to Kevin, he added, "We just won't leave him alive, is all."

With a sigh, she replied. "Of course. No, we can't, I suppose. I'm sorry Kevin." She stepped closer to Devlin. "Can you do it quietly?"

"Aye. I just put the muzzle to his chest and aim upward; you'll see." Devlin stepped to Kevin. "Now relax boyo; you won't feel a thing, I promise."

In the trench fighting, Kevin Crawley had confronted many an enemy holding pistols at him at point blank range. None of them survived. As soon as Devlin was with arm's length, he snapped a hand down and away from him in an arc, grasping the gun by the barrel. Devlin fired a shot, the report deafening everyone in the room.

Kevin did not let go. He heaved the barrel back up and over Devlin's wrist, a lever now that sprained the man's hand, breaking his grip. The gun was now his own. Without stopping his movements, he grasped at Devlin's throat with his free hand, and using the pistol as a hammer, pounded its handle into the man's face. The first blow broke Devlin's nose, the second crushed his brow above his eye. By the tenth blow Devlin was on the floor, his head a misshapen mess, the sound of each blow now a dull crunching noise.

Bridget stared in frozen horror.

From his position on the floor kneeling over Devlin's corpse, Kevin raised his eyes to her, black with fury. "You murderer." His voice low, he began to rise.

She ran from the room in blind panic. She had to get Eamon and run away! She flew up the stairs to his room at the back of the house. She could hear Kevin's feet pounding behind her as she threw the door open. When she got to the baby's crib, Kevin's fist seized her hair.

He spun her around, his hands clenching her throat.

"You murdered my babies!" he hissed.

She struggled for breath, gasping, "Don't hurt Eamon, Kevin! For the love of God, the boy's innocent!"

"As were the twins, ye whore!" He leaned into her, disregarding the scratches she was leaving on his face. "I'll kill him as soon as I'm done with ye!"

She knew by his eyes, she was done for. She knew Eamon's life would end soon too. She faded to the floor, feeling the world slip away. Something burst behind her eyes, leaving only red and black, and a red and black rage boiled over in her heart.

In her dying words, she croaked out, "Kill all of ye! I killed your English Melanie, and your half-breed daughters! I'll kill all of ye if given half the chance Crawleyyyy…" He wrenched her neck, silencing her with a crack of bone.

He knelt over the body of his wife, the murderer of his children. A sorrow and grief filled his heart. How could he be so blind? Panting, he got to his feet and looked to Bridget's son, stirring now in the crib.

"Kevin Crawley! *Leave the babe alone!*"

He jerked at the sound of Melanie's voice. She called to him again from the bedroom.

He crossed the hall and into the bedroom. There she was, lying on her cushions in the bed.

She was aglow; lit from within by an oil lamp it seemed. He could see through her. He ran to her, tears streaming, to take her in his arms.

But all he could grasp were the cushions and bedding.

"You're a ghost, Melanie." The only surprise he felt was at his lack of terror. God he loved her so; 'twas a blessing to see her face again, faded as it was.

"I cannot stay, Kevin... it takes all my strength to call out to you. Let the baby live... for the sake of your daughters, let him be..."

And like an oil lamp being turned down, she faded from him, leaving only the scent of roses.

He fell to the bed in tears, kneeling at it.

"Papa!" the twins' voices rang out from the back of the house. He ran back to Eamon's room but didn't see them. Oh God... were they trapped upstairs in their room? He went to where the wall had been closed up, and heard them call again. They were outside! He flew to Eamon's room again and looked out the window.

There in the yard, Alice was on the swing, Agnes behind her. They both glowed like their mother had. They blew kisses at him and smiled with such love his heart broke again. When he saw them also begin to wane, he threw open the window.

"No! Don't leave me like this! No my darlings, don't go!"

But they were gone. He collapsed at the windowsill, crying the most bitter of tears again. The pain in his heart was unbearable. *He* had brought Bridey into his home...

He had brought Bridey into his bed! He went back to the crib and looked down at the boy, his blue eyes gazing up at him. He still had the St. Jude medal in his hand. He set it around the neck of the babe and kissed the top of its head. He loved and loathed that child. He stood up and left the room.

Seeing the spirits of Melanie and the girls gave him the courage.

Without coat nor hat, with a note he scratched out at the desk in the parlor tucked in his pocket, he walked out of his home for the last time. He was as guilty for the deaths of his wife—no, his *wives* and children as the two corpses behind in his home. He walked alongside the park with Harvest Street at his back. He was heading towards the county courthouse. In his hand he held the hank of rope Bridey had retrieved from the cellar.

He walked up West Street to Court Street, his path taking him past the front of the massive limestone courthouse building. The darkened windows looked down on him as he passed the gilded fountain in front.. He wound his way along Court Street to Barrie. Off Barrie Street was a driveway that led into the city jail. The building had a light on over the entrance. He crept past quietly.

Off to the side was a structure that had been in disuse for years. Standing atop a group of posts more than six feet in height was a wooden platform. Nowadays, young boys would sneak in and climb the stairs to do a jig on the surface of the platform to impress their friends with their daring deed before being chased away by the jail's guards. One of these days they would have to tear down that hangman's gallows.

He crept up the stairs as silently as he could, pausing at each creak of the weather worn wood. He reached the top of the platform. Two more posts rose from the top of the platform, joined together by a lintel overhead. He uncoiled the rope in his hand.

He'd be doing a jig as well, but he wouldn't be running away.

Part II

Kingston, Ontario
The Present Day

MICHELLE DOREY

INTERLUDE...

The elderly man walked with tentative steps down the sidewalk of the residential street, leaning on his cane. His 'Arthur-i-tis' was bad today, despite the springtime warmth. In addition to the daily ache of ninety year old hips and knees, the soles of his feet were burning. He was almost there. Just this short sojourn and he could return to his room in the nursing home.

A liver spotted hand ran through the fine wisps of hair on his mottled scalp. What a doddering old fool he was. Day after day, for the last twenty five years, without fail, he would walk to this street and stand across from that house. Every day, for twenty five years he had been drawn to this tree lined street like a moth to a flame—or a gawker at a car crash.

And he didn't have the slightest idea why. He only knew that if he didn't make his daily visit, he would pay for it at night with horrible dreams, and upon waking feel a sense of such forlorn longing, that he would begin his day crying like a baby. So yes, he came day after day.

Stopping finally, thank God, he took his station across from the house. He knew from painful experience to remain on the opposite side of the street. Just like the moth and the flame, were he to draw closer he would suffer for it.

As it had been every day, his gaze was drawn to the dark, wooden door and he would wonder what was behind it. He lifted his head to stare at the bedroom windows on the second floor. Above them, like a jewel in a tiara, was the attic window, a half-moon shape, set just below the roof's peak. Every time his gaze was drawn to that top window his heart would ache; why, he did not know.

The house was old, older than himself he was sure. For another day, all the windows were dark. The vines of ivy at the top window spread outwards, clinging to the pitted brick, curling over the veranda and across the upper eaves. The house was being slowly swallowed up in it. The only other plants were the rose bushes out in front and up the side of the wide driveway.

His lips twitched in a sardonic smile. The last set of tenants was three male university kids swaggering in their yellow leather jackets, streaked with purple. They too were gone now. Engineering students, they lasted longer than most, a testimonial to their devotion at the altar of science. Still, that had proven to be no protection. No one who moved into that place ever stayed long.

He turned his head and his gaze swept up and down the street. The sunlight glared down, a steel brightness that faded the color of the grass and sky. And as always, the street was empty and silent. Not a whisper of a breeze in a tree. Not a single bird calling. Not even a barking dog. The street would remain still until the new tenants moved into the house. They would be the only people he'd see, until they too would leave. It had been so for twenty-five years.

"The circle must close." He muttered the mantra he'd murmured every day for years. He would wait. He would abide. Abide to who or what, he didn't know... and it didn't matter. He would abide.

His homage complete, he turned to leave knowing he would come again tomorrow. He would come as long as he was able. A sharp pain skewered his heart and he gasped. Staggering, he stabbed the ground with his walking stick to maintain his balance.

"No..." he croaked. Not yet. The pain was gone as quickly as it appeared, leaving him shaken from its memory. No... not yet... but...

The circle was groaning. It was stirring. It was preparing to close.

He sighed, and resumed his trudging gait. The tip of the cane clonked the ground next to him as he retraced his steps. Turning the corner and entering the park he saw the spring sunlight now filtering through the budding branches, patterning the sidewalk like lace under his footsteps. The burning in his feet ebbed away as he walked through the park back to the nursing home.

MICHELLE DOREY

CHAPTER TWENTY ONE

Sarah's eyes flew open and she jerked upright in bed. Gasping for air, her heart raced so fast it hurt.

"Owww!" A tear rolled down her cheek as she strained forward, her fingers spread over her chest. Where was Mommy, or even Nana?

The pain was gone in just a second, leaving her cold as a popsicle. She hugged herself but it wasn't enough. Throwing the top blankey aside, she popped onto the floor. She'd been coloring in her book, and never meant to fall asleep. At five, she was too big for naps, even Mommy said so.

Everything got fuzzy for a second, so she rubbed her eyeballs with the heels of her hands. Oh no!

"Grandpa?" Had that been Grandpa in her dream? Nana showed her pictures of him once, when Mommy was out. Nana had promised that one day, he was going to come to Mommy's place and they'd go for ice cream. He'd always been too busy to come, and Nana always told her that he sent his biggest love and hugs.

Nana was telling fibs when she said that. You weren't supposed to tell fibs.

Her forehead tightened when the dream once more, flashed in her mind. Grandpa... he was in a barn, laying down on the ground! And his heart was hurting! It was hurting bad! Real bad! She ran from her bedroom to the living room where Nana sat reading.

Mommy was there too! She was home from work? The question flitted and was gone because...

"Grandpa's sick! He's in the barn and his heart's hurting, Nana! His heart's hurting right here!" She slapped her hand over where her heart was. "He's sick and he's lying down on the ground! We have to help him!"

Mommy and Nana were still as statues looking at her. They were scared. She scared them, she could tell.

"Hurry! He's in the barn!"

Mommy scooped her up. "Good Lord! Sarah, you're cold as ice!" She turned her head, "Mom, Sarah's got one heck of a chill, and it's got to be eighty degrees in here!"

Nana stood up and walked over to them. She put her hand on Sarah's forehead. "Oh dear..."

Sarah batted Nana's hand. "Listen! Grandpa's sick!"

Nana's brown eyes became wide. "Sarah McDougall!"

"Easy, Moppet," Mommy was holding her tight. Mommy felt so warm. "Why don't you give him a call, Ma? He keeps his cell on him, right?"

Mommy and Nana look at each other for a long, long time.

"Call him, Nana!"

They both whipped their heads around to look at her.

"Call him now! He's sick!" She squeezed her Mommy's arm and turned to her grandmother. "He's dying, Nana!"

Nana didn't move. She was like a statue again!

"Okay, that's it, Missy." Mommy plunked her down onto the floor and grabbed her phone off the table. She looked at Nana. "First time I've called him in more than five years." Her voice was low as she tapped her fingers on the small screen. She took a deep breath and held it to her ear. "It's ringing."

A cloud of sadness shrouded Sarah. She sniffed. "He won't answer, Mommy. Grandpa died." She looked at Mommy, then at Nana and started to cry. "He'll never take me for ice cream now."

***

Nana drove really, really fast. Mommy had barely finished buckling her into the car seat, when Nana wheeled the car out of the driveway. The tires squealed.

"Slow down, Ma! You'll get us killed!" Mommy was scared, yelling from the back seat.

Nana didn't pay her any mind. They car sounded like a lion on TV as it roared down the street and out of town. Nana was hunched over the steering wheel like she was trying to push it with her hands to go faster.

"Ma, you're scaring me," Mommy gripped the seat ahead of her. Sarah's lip quivered.

"Call 911, Gillian."

"Ma, we don't even know what's going on!"

"Call them, dammit!"

Nobody said anything about Nana using a bad word. This was really scary.

Mommy patted her pockets. "Oh shit, I left it at the house!"

Mommy said a really bad word, and nobody said nothing again. Tears welled in Sarah's eyes and she sniffled.

"Ma, you gotta slow down! You're scaring the baby!" Mommy put her arm around Sarah and held her tight.

She looked up at Mommy. "Are we gonna have a axe-ci-dent, Mommy?"

"Shush baby. Just hang on. It's only a few more minutes."

Nobody said anything else as the car raced forward. After a few minutes, it slowed coming to a dirt road with big green fields on each side.

"He's got the cows in, Gillian! He *is* in the barn!" Nana turned hard on the steering wheel and the car squeaked really loud and jiggled as it turned onto the road. Sarah peered out the front window. There was a big house—bigger than their house back in town. There were a bunch of other buildings near it.

" Maybe he's in the house, Ma! Would you *slow down*!"

Sarah saw the big, brown cow barn. It had to be the cow barn because there were cows around Grandpa when she saw him in her head. And even though Grandpa was dead, she felt him there too.

She pointed her finger. "He's in the cow barn, Nana!" She and Mommy strained forward when the car came to a skiddery, bumpy, stop by the big doors.

"Stay in the car!" Nana jumped out and ran to the barn. She hauled open a door at the side and disappeared inside.

"Like hell," Mommy's face was tight. She leaned over the front seat and turned the key and the engine stopped. Her fingers shook undoing the buckles of the car seat. "Let's go, Sarah."

Sarah held Mommy's hand until they got inside the big barn.

The cows were mooing *really* loud. There was a long row of heads sticking out of some sort of thing that looked kinda' like monkey bars at the park. There was hay and stuff in front of them, but they were looking at her, the whites of their eyes showing.

Sarah took one look at Nana, kneeling down on the floor next to a man and thought the cows were crying like Nana was. She held the man's head in her hands, brushing back his hair.

Mommy had stopped running and walked slowly over to Nana. She had let go of Sarah's hand.

"Is he..."

Nana nodded a bunch of times. "He's so cold, Gillian." She looked up at her daughter. "Your Daddy's gone, sweetheart." Mommy was on her knees next to Nana and they both started crying.

Sarah stared at them. Why were they crying? Grandpa wasn't *just* lying on the floor of the barn, he was standing over all of them, right by Nana's side. His hands were tucked in the pockets of his blue overalls and his lined face was so sad looking down at Nana and Mommy. He took his hands out of his pockets and one hand lifted up the green ball cap on his head and his other hand pushed back his grey hair.

"Mommy—"

"Shhh Sarah! They won't understand!" Grandpa's finger crossed his lips.

Sarah gulped back her words and tilted her head. He kept his finger on his lips and walked around Mommy and Nana over to where she stood at the door. They didn't even look up at him.

He took her by the hand. "Stay quiet as a mouse, sweetie, and we'll talk outside."

She walked out of the barn with her hand in Grandpa's.

"We don't have much time, sweetie," he said. "I'm very sorry that this is the only time we're going to meet." He looked down at Sarah, with teary eyes.

"Why don't you like me, Grandpa?" She had always hid it from Mommy, but she knew that Grandpa didn't visit because he never wanted to.

He squatted down on his heels, eye level with her. "Because I was a stupid, stupid man, sweetie. I thought your mother was too young to be a Mommy, and I was too thick headed to admit I was wrong."

Sarah's lips curled in a small smile. "Nana tells Mommy that she's thick headed too."

"She gets that from me." He stood up. "Now come along, sweetie. I don't have much time and I have to make sure you do something." He held out his hand again and Sarah took it. His hand felt different from holding Mommy's or Nana's. It felt *thinner* sort of. Like if she squeezed it too hard it would smoosh through her fingers like Playdough.

At the front door he asked her to open it. It was only a screen door that was closed, and she was able to get it open standing on her tippy toes. She held it open for him and they went inside and up the stairs to a bedroom.

Grandpa stood by a bureau. "In the top drawer here, is a medal that I want you to have, sweetie." He bent over and picked her up. Holding her, he said, "Now you have to open the drawer."

She looked up at him. There wasn't any Grandpa smell. When Mommy would pick her up, she could smell Mommy's make up if she was wearing any, or the smell from her shampoo. When Nana would pick her up, she could smell something different, a smell that was just Nana. But Grandpa didn't have any smell at all. And his arms felt like they were smooshy too.

She shrugged and took hold of the two handles on the top drawer and pulled. One side came out a little, but the other side didn't move.

"It's stuck, Grandpa, help me," she said.

"I'm afraid not, darlin'. I can hold you and touch you because we're blood relatives and you have a gift. But I can't touch or hold anything else. You're going to have to jiggle it out, okay?"

That sounded silly, but she tugged at one handle and it pulled out a little, then the other and it came out some. Back and forth she tugged and pulled until the drawer was finally open.

"Good job, Sarah. Now you see that silver chain and the silver thing on the end?"

She nodded.

"That's called a medal. It's a St. Jude's medal."

"Like medals soldiers have?" she asked. "From being in wars?"

Grandpa shook his head no. "Soldiers get those as sort of prizes. This medal is to help remember."

"Remember what?"

"I'm not sure. Your Nana's mother gave it to me when we got married, and I want to make sure you have it." He nodded his head at the medal lying in the drawer. It had a thin silver chain and a delicate medallion. She picked it up and looked at it. There was a man with a beard and some writing on it.

"What's it say?" she asked.

"It says 'St. Jude, pray for us'. And on the back are the letters 'A and C'."

"Who's St. Jude?"

"He was a man from a long time ago who helped doctors and nurses." Grandpa sighed and made a funny kind of smile. "He's better known for being the Patron of Lost Causes..."

She brightened. "Mommy's going to be a nurse! She just found out that she got..." Her face screwed up.

"Accepted?"

"Yes! Ack-septed to a school for nurses!" Her face fell. "We're gonna' hafta' move away."

Grandpa nodded. "Yes. And that's why you have to put this medal on and wear it all the time for me, okay?" He put her down, and she looped the medallion over her neck. "That's a good girl." Now his face looked sad. "Darlin' I'm very sorry that I was so..."

"Thick head?"

He chuckled. "Yes, thick headed. Tell your Mommy how sorry I am when you get the chance, okay? And when you move away, make sure you always wear that medal."

"Okay."

"Promise me, Sarah. You know how to make a promise, right?"

She looked at him. He was starting to fade away. Her eyebrows knit together as she watched him trace his finger over his heart. She copied his gesture.

"Now say, 'Cross my heart'".

When she did, he nodded and kissed her forehead. She closed her eyes just for a second when he kissed her. His lips felt really smooshy.

When she opened them, he was gone.

CHAPTER TWENTY TWO

The smell of bacon drifted up the stairs and into Gillian's old bedroom. Her eyes creaked open, flitted past the bedside table to the pale roses etched in the wallpaper and then to the shafts of the August sunlight streaming through the window. How many mornings had she woken up, here in this room? It had been the room of her childhood she left behind years ago. It had been, since Dad's death, her 'old room' for the last few months. Of her twenty-three years on this planet, she had spent more nights in this room than any other. Well, last night was the final one.

She pushed the comforter away and sat up. Sarah's melodic voice and her mother's laughter sounded from the kitchen below. Gillian smiled. That was good, the two of them making breakfast but more importantly, her mother laughing.

She listened as the laughter continued. Mom's laugh was fuller bodied, rolling and throaty while Sarah's danced along the edges, sparkling and light. Gillian dropped her head with a smile of gratitude. She hadn't heard Mom laugh like that since before she got pregnant with Sarah. She didn't realize up until that moment how much she had missed her mother's belly laugh. She would take the laughter bounding up the stairs and filling her room as a good omen.

God only knew, they were overdue for a good omen after the last three months…

***

Mom had fallen apart when they found his body in the cow barn, and Gillian had to take over, hustling everyone back into the house so she could call the police.

She had to go back out to the barn to get the milking done; the poor cows were ready to burst. It was surreal for her, setting up the milkers with her father's body lying in the middle of the floor. But he would have been proud of her making sure the animals were looked after. She'd made herself do the milking; it was her penance for being thick headed.

When Terry Foiles arrived in his patrol car, he was gracious. He actually gave her a hand finishing up with the cows before starting his report. After that, it was just waiting for Hanson's Funeral Home to come and fetch Dad. It was then that she learned he had a heart ailment for the last three years. Terry had phoned Dad's doctor and they didn't need to do an autopsy.

She had an idea of everything else that needed to be done. She had been fourteen when Grandpop died and remembered what Dad and Mom had done then. Joe Hanson was a lot of help too. He ought to have been, for the money they paid for the funeral!

Grandpop had lived on the farm with them all her life. There was no extended family to call when he died. For the three generations of the farm's ownership, it had been passed down to the only child—always a girl, who had married a man from Far Away. Grandpop had been from Canada, Dad was from Maine. She didn't know much about the original founders or anything. Like Grandpop's, Dad's funeral was a small affair. Which was sort of a blessing as Mom was barely able to function.

Who could blame her? Forty seven and a widow? With no employment history for the last twenty-five years? She hadn't worked outside the home since she and Dad married. The farm had been profitable enough for them to live a snug life; Mom could milk a dollar for value as good as Dad could coax a cow's udder.

The farm community had rallied around. Mister Duffy from across the way had a herd of his own and did the morning milking for the first month after Dad's death. Manny Killaloe from the spread down the line had looked after the evening milking.

Manny had a crush on Gillian when they were in elementary school together, and Mom's hopes were high that things would click between them—until she learned that he was engaged to Lori Anders from Sparkill. Oh well.

Gillian and Sarah had moved in to be with Mom—the three of them against the world. She had taken over the milking and all the chores during the first month or so after Dad died. She had done them before when she was growing up, so she knew the ropes. Now, after being gone from the farm for five years, she'd get used to it again, she supposed.

But all that changed when Dad had been gone six weeks.

***

She had come into mud room and ripped off her Wellingtons, kicking them into the wall as usual. She took off her shirt and pants as she had done every night and stuffed them into the hamper. Putting on a robe, she went into the kitchen. Mom was there with her laptop and a bunch of papers.

"Take your shower and come right back down, dear," she said. "We need to talk."

"What's for dinner?"

"I don't know. Maybe we'll have a pizza or something."

"Where's Sarah?"

"I took her over to Mrs. Duffy's for the night. Now scoot and get that smell you hate off of you." Mom had a sad smile.

"What's wrong, Mom?"

She pointed to the ceiling. "It'll keep. Now go shower."

When she came down from her shower, having sluiced off cow stink as she had done every day, Mom had a frozen pizza in the oven. She was sitting at the table with papers and her computer.

"Mom, what's wrong?"

"Gillian, when does school start for you?"

She gave a short snort of a laugh. "Beats me. I asked for a deferral back when Dad died."

"Okay, we'll deal with that later. I've made a decision."

"What?"

"I'm selling out."

"WHAT!"

"And you're going to Nursing School in September."

"What!" Gillian looked around the kitchen. "You're getting rid of the place? But—"

"But I have to, Gillian. You *hate* dairy farming. And you're not letting any of the single farmers in three counties so much as take you on a date. You don't see yourself here; you're just going through the motions, biding time."

"It's only been six weeks, Mom. You're not supposed to make any major decisions for a whole year as a widow! This is a stupid idea!"

"Now Gillian…"

She slapped her hand onto the table. "Don't 'now' me! You're not asking my opinion or advice, you're telling me! What do I look like, a child?"

"Gillian…"

She leapt to her feet, fuming. "And furthermore, did you ever think of me? This is all I have of him! Ma! This is all I have! WE NEVER MADE UP!" She burst into tears, covering her face.

Maureen watched Gillian cry and her own eyes leaked tears, but a fire of anger flashed in her. "Don't you think I *know* that, Gilly? For the last five years of his life, and the years of Sarah's—both of you standing apart, arms folded, stubborn as a pair of jackasses. And for what?" She jabbed a finger at her daughter. *"You had to win!"* She held her hands up, encompassing the room. *"He* had to win!"

She sat back in her chair, spitting out the rest. "For four years each of you raked at my heart with your icicle silences about the other!" Shaking her head, she continued, "No, young lady, it's over. Your father's dead and you both can carry your guilt. Life has to move on. I contacted Queen's University and you simply need to phone them yourself and reactivate your acceptance."

"But this was my home!" Gillian's hands fell below her chin, clasped forlornly. "Mom, it's my home!"

"How *dare* you, Gillian McDougall!" Maureen ignored the wide-eyed shock on Gillian's face. "I have spent every *one* of my forty-seven years in this home! You moved away to the village five years ago and didn't set foot here until your father died! How *dare* you even imagine your loss can compare to mine!"

Gillian dropped her hands and hung her head. "You're right…"

Maureen rose from her chair and crossed to her daughter, taking her in her arms. "Daddy's gone, Gillian. And it's time we move on with our lives." Nestling her daughter's head to her shoulder, she stroked her back.

Gillian had been brave for the last six weeks. She had been strong for Mom's sake, and for Sarah's sake. She had misted and teared up, and a sob or two had escaped her throat during the service for her father, but the harrowing grief, the scraping, snarling beast that shreds one's heart with ragged talons of love lost and the finality of death rose from her feet to her throat.

"*Daaadeee!*" She clutched at her mother, holding on to keep from being pulled down and into the beast's hungry jaws. Crying out again and again she held on, the pain and sorrow never ending. It just went on and on and on…

***

The laughter from downstairs stopped and her chest grew heavy as she rose from the bed.

She grabbed the T-shirt she'd worn the day before and the jeans that were draped over the wooden chair. She would shower and get ready to take Mom to the lawyer later. This morning was a time for saying goodbyes. Her eyes began to sting and she blinked a few times to clear them as she thrust her feet into the legs of her pants. Clean pants that would stay that way—no more milkings.

She bounded down the stairs, showing a lightness that she was far from feeling. But Sarah needed to see her smile as much as Mom needed it. When she entered the kitchen, Sarah raced over, her arms high in the air, eager to be picked up. "Mommy! Nana made pancakes."

Gillian squeezed the tiny tyke's body close and kissed her cheek. "She did, huh?" She looked over at her mother, standing in front of the stove, a spatula in her hand. "Don't tell me. I bet she made it in the shape of a letter 'S'."

Sarah's eyes were like blue marbles, her lips wide, grinning. "Like my name. 'S' for Sarah!"

"That's right!" Gillian kissed her again. "My little Einstein." She walked over to the table and set Sarah on the chair. "Would you like some juice or milk?"

"Milk, please. Can we visit the cows one last time before we leave? I want to say goodbye to Bessie." She squirmed forward on the chair, barely able to contain the excitement.

Maureen's eyes met her daughter's and the smile on her face faded.

Gillian grabbed the carton of milk and a glass, filling it as she walked back to the table. "Sure. I want to say my goodbyes too." She set the glass in front of Sarah and turned around, walking back to the counter.

"Hey! The cows are just like us! They're going to a new home, too." Sarah's small hands closed around the glass and she took a long sip. She set the glass down and swiped the mustache of milk from her upper lip. "Tell me about the place we're moving to. I'm gonna have my own room, right? And you're getting me a kitten!"

Gillian glanced at her mother and continued pouring coffee. It was in the slump of her shoulders as she flipped the pancake over, her eyes misty as she stared down at the frying pan—the end of an era. It had to be killing Mom to be leaving this home, where she grew up. Where she'd loved and lived with Mike, raised their daughter, the surprise and joy of birthdays, Christmas days filled with wonder.

"Sure thing, Sarah." Gillian stepped to her mother's side and put her arm over her shoulders. "We're going to be all right, Mom. You made the right decision. You moving to Kingston with us...It will be healthier in the end. The memories here..." She sighed and squeezed her mother's arm.

Maureen sniffed and shook her head slightly, looking up at the ceiling for a moment. The wisps of silver hair framing her face fell back, and her lip trembled as she struggled to maintain control of her emotions. She inhaled slowly and her fingers plucked strips of bacon from the paper towel where they were drying. She placed a couple on a plate and slipped the pancake next to it.

"Doesn't mean it don't hurt." There was just a hint of a smile when she turned and handed the plate to Gillian.

Gillian grabbed the bottle of maple syrup from the fridge and poured it over the pancake before setting it down on the table. She took a seat across from Sarah, watching her bite into the crispy bacon strip. As she sipped the coffee, her eyes focused on her mother. Her chest filled with love and admiration watching the older woman's brave attempt to focus on the up-side.

"Do we have any family in Kingston, Mom? I wonder if there're many McDougall's or Crawley's there? McDougall's a pretty common Irish name." Gillian sat back in the chair, glancing from Sarah to her mother.

Sarah swallowed hard and her eyes were round when she looked at Gillian. "What's a Crawley? Is it a worm or a snake? I don't like snakes."

Maureen laughed while she ambled over to Sarah and mussed her pig-tailed hair. "It's our family name. It's *my* family name from long ago, Moppet. Not some wretched creature. Sort of like a maiden name."

Sarah brushed her hand away and looked up at her grandmother. "What's a maiden name?"

Gillian gulped her coffee and stood up. "I'll explain later. You better finish your breakfast now, if you want to see the cows and say goodbye to Bessie. The truck will be here soon to pick them up."

She turned to her mother. "Will you be okay while we're out in the barn? We won't be long."

Maureen tapped her daughter's shoulder. "Go on. Take as long as you need." Her eyebrows rose high. "Actually you've only got an hour. We need to get ready to go to the lawyer's office. I'd better clean up the breakfast things. I know you said the moving company will take care of everything, but I'm not leaving dirty dishes."

Sarah shoved the last bite of pancake in her mouth and scrambled from the table. "Wait for me, Mommy!" Darting to the door, she nudged past Gillian and opened it. She raced forward, tugging her mother behind her.

Outside, the temperature was already in the eighties, the sun warm on their faces as they stepped off the wide veranda and onto the flagstone walk. Sarah ran ahead, the gray soles of her sneakers flashing high, while her arms reached forward, the ends of the braids bouncing against her shoulders. She disappeared, rounding the tool shed and Gillian hurried to catch up.

Past the shed, Gillian's footsteps slowed and her mouth fell open watching her daughter at the barn door. She was tugging the thick, heavy slab by the handle to no avail. She stopped, tilting her head, and she smiled. She put both hands on the handle and pushed down on the catch. Now, holding the handle with both hands, she backed up, pulling the door open wide enough to enter. She tilted her head, again looking up and giggled before darting inside.

Uh oh, thought Gillian. If she walks behind the cows she might startle them and get kicked!

"Wait! Sarah!"

But Sarah had disappeared into the dim interior.

CHAPTER TWENTY THREE

Gillian's feet pounded on the dusty path and she lurched through the open doorway. She flipped the switch, flooding the barn with light, and peered ahead, craning her neck, looking for Sarah. Where was she?

She heard a rustle of hay from the far end and the soft murmur of her daughter's voice. Gillian trotted down the row and there Sarah was, standing in the low mound of hay, her hand extended offering the giant cow a handful of straw. In her other hand was a pancake from the kitchen.

Bessie was gently nibbling the pancake.

Sarah looked up at her mother. "She always likes pancakes, doesn't she, Mommy?" With a last slurp, Bessie polished off the pancake and turned to the silage Sarah held in her other hand.

Gillian remembered giving Bessie pancakes when she was a little girl and nodded her head. "Yes, she has, sweetie." It was probably the last pancake Bessie would ever eat though, and her heart pulled at the thought.

"Mr. Hawkins is going to give her one every morning whenever he has them for breakfast." Sarah looked into Bessie's eyes and stroked the animal's huge snout.

"You're sure about that?" Gillian couldn't remember which cows Hawkins had purchased. He was taking half of the thirty-head herd. He knew he was buying well cared for animals, and apologized that he didn't have room for them all.

"Yep!" When Bessie took the rest of the feed from Sarah's hand, she licked the palm and dropped her head to forage what was on the floor. Sarah let out a giggle and wiped her hand on her pants. Turning up to her mother's face, she said, "Bessie has eyes like Nana—big and brown. Mr. Hawkins will be as nice to her as Grandpa was." She giggled when Bessie lifted her head and her fleshy mouth nudged her fingers.

"How do you know that?"

Sarah rolled her eyes at her mother. "He told me!" She suddenly clamped her hand over her mouth, her eyes wide. "Oops! That was supposed to be secret!"

"Don't worry, I won't say anything, honey." Mr. Hawkins was nice, and to tell Sarah that was sweet of him. Gillian smiled and rubbed the hard patch of skull between Bessie's eyes. "This one was always Dad's favorite."

Sarah scooped up another handful of straw and held it out to the cow. "I know." She looked up at her mother and wrinkled her nose. "It sure stinks in here."

"You sure got *that* right."

She sighed and looked around at the other cows waiting, their feet shuffling from side to side while their tails swished. The stalls and waste troughs weren't as clean as when her father had done it. The hired hand that had been looking after the herd for the last week wasn't as thorough as she had been, but what could she do? Once the deal for the property had finalized, she and her mom had been a whirlwind packing and sorting three generations of possessions.

Well, that was all over now. The cows had been auctioned off and would be picked up this afternoon by the broker. At the lawyers, they would drop off the keys, sign some papers and that would be that. Soon enough, this would be another sub-division, jammed with houses. The surveyors had already been by, leaving their orange stakes all over the fields. She huffed a sigh. Dad would have hated seeing houses built on this land. He had loved the spread at first sight, just as he had fallen in love with Mom.

Well, that was all over now. "We'd better go. Finished here?" Gillian placed her hand on Sarah's shoulder.

There were tears in her daughter's eyes when she looked up. "Yeah." She turned back to the cow and stroked its nose. "Bye Bessie."

Gillian took her daughter's hand and they walked across the concrete floor to the door. Sarah turned her head and whispered, "Bye Grandpa." She reached into the neckline of her shirt and pulled out the St. Jude medal. Clutching it, she nodded silently, her eyes closed.

Gillian looked down at Sarah while she shut the barn door. That girl and that medal. She found it on the day Dad died, prowling and poking around in Dad and Mom's bedroom. Sarah hadn't taken it off ever since— not even when taking a bath.

Taking Sarah's hand, they headed back up to the farmhouse. Gillian would be happy to leave the farm again. These little strange things with Sarah were making her uneasy. She didn't realize at the time they were but thin, threatening clouds on the horizon, harbingers of a tempest.

CHAPTER TWENTY FOUR

The next morning, Gillian walked along the waterfront from the hotel, heading over towards the university. She had left Mom and Sarah back at the Radisson Hotel on Ontario Street where the three of them had spent the night. Mom and Sarah were going to hit the supermarket for some cleaning supplies while she picked up the keys from Jeremy Sloat, the rental agent.

The sky was overcast, with muddy gray clouds looming over the lake, threatening to downpour any second. She tugged the collar of the light, nylon jacket up in the face of a sudden gust of wind. It was only five more blocks to reach the house.

The house they had rented was incredible. Hard to believe that you could get a four bedroom house with a backyard, even a swing on a maple tree, for five hundred a month! The on-line, room to room tour had sold them both. It was the deal of a lifetime!

The street ended at the yacht club and she was forced to turn right walking away from the lake. As she passed the sailboats tied up there, the plaintiff whine of the breeze thrumming the ropes on the high masts filled her ears. A few sprinkles of rain trickled along her forehead and nose and she walked faster.

She crossed the street and entered a wide, walkway of a park. The age of the city was evident in the size of the trees, their thick limbs branching high, providing a canopy of leaves giving some shelter from the rain. She left the park's walkway, waiting for a break in traffic to dash across to Harvest Street and check the numbers on the houses. The campus was only a few blocks away, an easy walk for her, once she was settled in, and the playground and park nearby was perfect for Sarah. What a find.

There it was, number eight, looking more elegant than the pictures posted on-line could ever do justice to. Like the houses next to it, the exterior was brick and there were two floors. A half moon shaped window peeked out from the trails of ivy gathered at the peak.

As she mounted the steps to the veranda, the heavy, dark front door opened and a tall, gangly man stepped out. His fingers were threaded together, clasped in front of his chest and he leaned forward, peering at her.

"Ms. McDougall?" He seemed to glide across the floor and then perch on the edge.

"Yes." Stepping onto the porch, Gillian nodded, her hand extended. "Mr. Sloat? Pleased to meet you."

His hand was limp, barely gripping hers when they shook, and it was clammy. A dead fish handshake, her Dad would have said.

"Yes, yes. Please come in. You're right on time." He stepped back and pushed the door open wide.

Entering the house, her eyebrows rose high. Oh my. An enormous oak set of stairs dominated the centre of a wide hallway. The banister was thick and worn above intricately carved spindles and the steps were at least four feet across.

"Impressive, isn't it? They don't build staircases like that anymore." Mr. Sloat sidled past her, gesturing down the hallway. "Let's start down here, shall we? I'm sure you'll want to see the kitchen." He took a few steps down and looked over his shoulder at her.

Gillian stood stark still gazing at the staircase. She had known that this place was the deal of a lifetime, but seeing it for real amped it up like crazy. Who had built this house? What kind of family had lived there? But more puzzling was, why it was vacant? Who wouldn't *want* to live there, especially when the rent was so cheap?

"Mr. Sloat—"

He clucked his tongue while shaking his head. "Please, it's Jeremy." His gaze went past her, over her shoulders. The guy couldn't look her in the eye. She couldn't help but think if he was this shy, he shouldn't be in the people business, dealing with tenants and such. A thought tickled the back of her head—what if he wasn't shy, but instead had something to hide? She shook it off.

She shrugged. "Okay, Jeremy." He turned and she followed him into the kitchen. Dust motes flickered in the natural light streaming through the window at the back of the room. "I'll be honest with you. It seems like a lot of house for the low rent you're asking. What gives? I mean, not that I'm complaining but..."

He smiled and walked over to the counter, running his finger along the dark surface. "Take my word for it, the university is not in the business of fleecing tenants, especially when they're students. The house was bequeathed to Queen's and we rent it out, but actually it's listed for sale as well. Being a landlord is not a primary objective for us. The university's mandate is dedicated to higher learning."

The guy should have gone into politics with non-answers like that. Plus his answer was a crock; she knew the university owned a slew of houses they rented out. She stopped herself from saying anything though. The rent for that entire house was less than what she'd been paying for her one bedroom back in the village of Lanark!

Gillian walked to the cabinets pulling them open and peering inside.

Jeremy opened the fridge and turned on a couple of burners on the stove. "As you can see, the appliances all work. Actually, we replaced them all just a couple of years ago."

The coils on the stove were already turning orange and the fridge motor kicked in. Gillian nodded and he turned the stove off again. "There's a microwave, which is also new." He flitted around the kitchen, again never making eye contact.

Gillian wandered over to the window and looked out into the backyard. She smiled seeing the large maple tree; the swing suspended from a thick lower branch. Sarah would love that. The yard was bordered by a high, wooden fence, and a few clumps of white daisies struggled to keep aloft in the now steady rain. Mom could coax some life into the garden, maybe even plant a few tomato plants.

There was a fieldstone patio area next to the house and a hulking BBQ unit. "The BBQ was put in recently too, I guess." There. She beat him to the punch.

He smiled and nodded his head. There was a door next to him that he opened, dipping his head out before darting back quickly. "I'd take you out and demonstrate the BBQ, but it's raining cats and dogs."

She gave a small smile. "That's okay; I'll take your word for it." Mr. Sloat failed to hear the irony in her voice.

Sloat stepped back and opened another door in the kitchen leading to a set of three steps going to a landing. Holding his hands out from his side, he said, "The mudroom, of course." Turning, he opened a second door that led to the basement. Leaning in, he flipped a switch and his hand swept in front of him. Glancing over his shoulders, he said, "The electrical panel is down here. It was updated when the kitchen was redone." He stopped down onto the first step and turned to her. "Don't worry, there aren't many spiders down here... I hope."

She followed him, her eyes watching for anything creepy, crawly. Hah! She stifled a chuckle at the thought. Wouldn't Sarah think that was funny—Creepy Crawley. Probably her Mom wouldn't, but it was still funny.

The entire cellar was finished, after a fashion. The floor was cement, and the foundation stones she could see had been painted at one time. The furnace didn't look too old and had been set on a slab of concrete. The light hanging from the ceiling wasn't the brightest, leaving the corners of the room in dank shadow.

She walked past the furnace following Jeremy to the electrical panel. As he explained about tripped breakers or something, her gaze went around the room. Washing machine hook ups and an old wooden counter lined one wall.

She wandered over to them while Sloat returned to the bottom of the stairs. Without warning, a chill went up her spine and she shuddered. No freaking way was she going to have the washer and dryer set up down here. The kitchen had plenty of room for them, thank God. The cellar made her uneasy…there could be rats or something equally disgusting! There was no way she'd ever go down to the basement unless she absolutely had to. She turned and scampered up the stairs, suppressing another shudder.

Going now to the front of the house, Jeremy strode by her and his hand swept the air. "The dining room. The wall sconces are original, antiques actually." He stepped next to the archway leading out to the hall and flipped a switch.

The room seemed to glow golden from the amber glass in the wall lights. A light scent crossed her nostrils and she sniffed. Roses? She looked over to Jeremy, but he didn't seem to notice it as he continued playing tour guide.

"Across the hall is the living room or as it was probably referred to once, the parlor." He led the way past the large stairway and into the other half of the house. With a flourish, he waved his arm at the room and stepped back, so she entered first.

"Oh my." Gillian stared down the room that ran the whole length of the house. The floors once more were hardwood and there were windows at each end of the room casting a dull grayish light into the space. In the centre, set in the far wall was a fireplace. It was framed with a thick mantel at the top and two wide oak boards down the sides. An iron grate sat in the tiled cove flanked by a large metal poker.

How nice would it be to set a couple sofas near it, the fire blazing while the three of them sipped hot chocolate.

"Well?" said Sloat.

"We'll take it!" she replied. She jumped at the loud bang, like a gunshot. It had come from the back of the house. She looked at Jeremy; he was stock still looking towards the back of the house. "What the hell was that?"

Sloat sighed and closed his eyes for a moment. Opening them, he looked over at her. "Probably just the wind blowing a door open. I'll check." He was back in a minute or two. "Just like I said. It is a fairly old home, built in the early twenties, I think. The door didn't latch properly. That sort of thing happens." He reached into the pocket of his sports jacket and pulled out a set of papers and a pen. "Ready to sign your life away?"

She took the paperwork and pen, and walked over to the fireplace mantle. *'Sign my life away'? What an odd way of putting it.* But then again, Sloat was a little odd.

CHAPTER TWENTY FIVE

About ten minutes later, Maureen drove into the wide driveway that ran down the side of the house to the fenced-in, back yard. She and Sarah stepped onto the front porch and Gillian appeared in the open doorway, bounding across the veranda. "Isn't this place something else? I can't wait for you to see it!"

Sarah ran past her mother into the house. "I want to see my room!" She raced up the steps and into the house.

"My, oh my…" Maureen's mouth fell open, when she stepped into the foyer and saw the grand staircase.

"And that's just the start!" Gillian pointed to the parlor. "There's a working fireplace! Isn't that great?"

Maureen smirked. "Sure, as long as *you're* the one hauling the wood in February!"

Gillian returned the smirk. "At five hundred bucks a month rent, it's going to be Duraflame logs for this girl!"

Sarah called from the top of the stairs. "Nana! Come see, come see!"

The two women headed up the stairs. Sarah stood in the open doorway, her eyes bright above a wide grin. Maureen followed the child into the room, already sizing the space up for the bed, dresser and desk. It was plenty big enough to accommodate everything, with lots of room left over. She wandered over to the window and looked down into the backyard.

"I asked the guy about painting and wallpapering. They are totally fine with it, as long as we don't paint a really dark color." Gillian stepped into the room and swung Sarah up and onto her hip. "What do you think Moppet? What color would you like your room?"

"Pink! It has to be pink." She hugged her mother and then squirmed to be let down again.

"Look at those baseboards. They don't make trim the way they used to, back when this house was built." Maureen glanced at the walls and ceiling, looking for cracks or any sign of damage. "Pink would be an improvement to the bland off-white."

"Let's take a look at your room, Mom," Gillian said. "It's on the other side of the hall." They stepped out and down the hall to the room that overlooked the street.

"There's a ton of space in here." Gillian's head pulled back from peering into the closet and she wandered over to the window. "And the street is quiet. Plus the park across the way is pretty." She gave a cheese grin. "Just like country living, but in the city!"

Maureen forced a smile. Gillian was trying to sell her on the room, hoping she'd like it.

"I think the room's a good size and the view is great. But I agree with Sarah, it needs some color and life." She smiled and ruffled Sarah's hair as the young girl bounded by.

"Show her your room, Mommy!"

Gillian's lips spread into a wide grin. "I hope you don't mind, but I'd like the master bedroom. It will work out better for studying. You two can watch TV downstairs and I won't be distracted or nagging you about the volume."

Maureen patted her daughter's shoulder. "This move is for you, Gillian, finishing your education. Of course I don't mind." Gillian smiled and walked out of the room. "The bathroom is nice. It's got a big old claw-foot bathtub and shower." Maureen followed Gillian, poked her head in the bathroom, taking in the beautiful old tub and the newer fixtures of the toilet and sink. It was actually a lot more up to date than the one at the farm.

She walked down the hall and into the spacious bedroom that would be Gillian's. Wow! It was half again as big as the one she would have, tons of room for a desk, queen sized bed and dresser. The window overlooked the street and the park.

She paused for a moment, and looked around. "Gillian, what about the top floor? Where are the stairs going up there?"

Gillian put her hands on her hips and her head bobbed forward, a frown on her face. "Yeah. I asked the guy about that. He said it's been closed off for years and years. They never re-opened it for some reason. He wasn't sure why; I think it had something to do with insurance." She wandered into the hall and tapped a spot on the wall. "I think the stairway is behind this wall."

"That doesn't make much sense. You would think that using every room in the house would be important. After all the university had rented the house to students."

"Yeah, you'd think so, but Mr. Sloat just left it at that."
Gillian shook her head and shrugged. "Whatever. We've got
plenty of space without it and we're just renting it anyway.
Hopefully they won't sell it before I'm done school in four
years."

Maureen sighed. "I hope we won't have people traipsing
through, looking to buy it. That could be a nuisance." She
walked out of the room, following Sarah. "Let's see the rest
of it and then have lunch. I picked up some burgers and
fries."

Her hand trailed over the thick wooden banister as she
walked down the stairs. It was a period home, that was
obvious and the craftsmanship of the woodwork and stairs
was impressive. For sale, huh? Maybe she'd have to think
about that.

CHAPTER TWENTY SIX

Fine! Nana wouldn't let her help her wash the floor in her bedroom and now Mommy was mad.

'I'm not too little to help. I could help her sweep the floor. But she won't let me.'

Sarah watched her mother push the dirt onto the dustpan. Her eyes were narrow and her arms crossed over her chest. Couldn't Mommy see how mad she was?

"Hmph!"

Mommy looked over and rolled her eyes. Sarah hated it when she did that. She pushed her lower lip out and huffed a sigh.

"Look Sarah, I know you're bored. Nana and I need to get this done before the furniture arrives. Why don't you get your coloring book out?"

"I don't want to." She spun around and jerked her shoulders lower. Now she was facing the window. Outside, the swing was swaying slightly. The rain had ended and the sun was shining. "Can I go outside and play?"

Mommy set the broom down and came over to stand next to her. She leaned forward and looked out the window. "As long as you stay in the yard, I'm okay with that." She took her hand and led the way to the back door.

Sarah squirmed her hand free and raced to the swing. After giving the seat a good swipe with her arm to clear the water drops off, she turned and popped up onto the seat. "Can you push me?"

Mommy walked next to the house, tested the wooden gate and strode over to stand behind her. "I'll give you some pushes but you've got to learn how to pump your legs forward and back to keep yourself going. I'm sorry honey, but I've got too much to do to stay out here with you."

Her hand was on Sarah's back shoving her forward."Stretch your legs out when you go up!"

Sarah tried doing that, holding the rope tight.

"Bend your knees each time you come back and when you start to go forward again, stretch your legs out." Again, she gave Sarah a big push.

After four more big pushes, she walked around to face Sarah. "Keep practicing. Remember, don't leave the yard. I have to go back inside now." With that, she turned and went back into the house.

The next few times the swing went forward, weren't as high as when Mommy had pushed her. She swung my legs out but it didn't seem to be helping. After a few minutes, she was barely moving. "Hmph!" This was no fun.

She looked at the ground that her feet didn't quite reach. She kicked my legs back and forth, leaning over, staring at the ground. Darn it. It wasn't working.

There was a firm touch on the small of her back, pushing her forward. Her head spun around to see.

Two little girls stood behind her, their hands over their mouths hiding the giggles that shook their shoulders.

"Who are you? How'd you get in here?" Sarah kept watching them, as the swing fell back and one of them pushed her again. They looked alike, same short blonde hair, same bow at the side and the same dresses.

"I'm Alice." The one closest pushed her again and the swing went higher, sailing forward.

"I'm Agnes. We're sisters. Do you like the swing?" The other girl, her hand on the tree trunk, leaned forward, grinning at her.

"I'm trying to learn how to make myself go higher. Mommy said to pump my legs." They hadn't said how they got in the yard. They sure didn't come in the gate next to the house. She would have seen that. "Where do you live?"

Agnes spun around and cupped her hand next to her sister's ear, whispering. They both smiled and their gaze followed Sarah, swinging back and forth.

"We used to live here." Alice's smile faded and her blue eyes looked down for a moment. "Our Papa put up the swing for us."

"You lived in my house? Where was your room?" Sarah looked at the house and then back to where they stood.

Alice's hand rose and she pointed, her hand held high before her. "See the top window? That was our room."

Sarah looked up at the roof of the house and noticed the window tucked in, just below it. She hadn't seen it before. "Oh. My room is under that, I think. I didn't see that room when Mommy took Nana and me around. I wonder why she didn't show it to us. I might have wanted it."

Agnes's hands were behind her back, making the puffed sleeves at her shoulders look like small balloons. Her skirt ended at her knees, almost touching high, white socks. She had shiny, black shoes. It was like she was dressed up for church. Sarah had seen pictures of Nana when she was little and she'd had the same kind of dress and socks and shoes.

"Are you going to a party? Where are your sneakers? Does your Mommy let you play outside in dresses? Yours is pretty. I'd like a dress like yours." Sarah gripped the rope harder when Alice once more gave her a big push.

"We're going out in a boat later. Mommy died and Bridey—"

"You're not supposed to call her that! Remember? It's 'Mother' not Bridey." Agnes gripped her sister's arm and shook her. Immediately, Alice looked at the ground and she sniffed.

Sarah's stomach seemed to sink down into the flat board. Poor Alice. Their mommy died? She turned to look at the house, hoping Mommy would look out the window. She wasn't going to die, was she?

"Would you like to play Jacks?" Agnes reached for the rope and tugged it back, making the swing stop.

"What's that? I don't know what Jacks is." Sarah slid forward on the swing and her feet touched the ground.

Alice turned to her sister. "We can't play that. The Jacks are in the house. Let's play tag." She tapped her sister's arm and raced across the yard, calling "Hurry Sarah!"

There was a tap on Sarah's shoulder and Agnes laughed. "Tag! You're It, Sarah!" Her shiny shoes flew behind her as she raced towards her sister.

Sarah grinned watching them crouch next to each other, ready to run at any minute. They laughed and the bows at the side of their heads looked like they were ready to fall off.

This was way better than coloring! Friends! She'd made new friends!

As the children scampered around laughing and squealing, Sarah never noticed that in the bright sunshine, neither Alice nor Agnes cast a shadow.

CHAPTER TWENTY SEVEN

Maureen stood up and leaned back to stretch the cramp in her side. Time for a break.

She wandered out of the bedroom and into Sarah's room. Just a sweeping to get rid of any dust-bunnies was all that room needed. Sunlight streamed ribbons into the room and she sauntered over to the window. In the yard below, Sarah darted one way and then raced the opposite, a big grin on her face.

Sarah suddenly stopped, and there was a scowl on her face. She shook her head vigorously. Maureen could hear the child's raised voice through the glass of the window. "Did not!" she exclaimed. "You're still it!" Sarah folded her arms and stamped her foot. She flipped her head to the side and cocked it, as if she was listening, then smiled and nodded. In a flash, she spun and ran weaving and ducking to the back of the yard and back, laughing all the while.

Maureen smiled watching her granddaughter's antics. What the heck was she doing? Was this some sort of game? Whatever it was, she looked like she was enjoying herself.

At any rate, she was blowing off energy. The poor kid had been antsy since they started cleaning.

Gillian appeared in the doorway. "I'm done in my room. I want to give the kitchen cabinets a wipe down and then I'll take Sarah to get some groceries. She's probably bored as anything."

Maureen chuckled and beckoned her daughter over. "I think she's keeping herself busy."

Gillian bent closer to the glass and shook her head. "What the hell is she doing?"

Maureen chuckled. "Haven't you ever heard of imaginary friends?"

Gillian leaned into the glass. "Isn't she a little old for that?"

"Don't worry, hon. The girl's a little lonely, that's all. It'll all go away when she starts school."

"You sure?" Gillian's eyes were wide in concern.

"Yes, I'm sure." Maureen laughed. "You have the same expression on your face I must have had back on the farm when you were her age! You had your 'make believe buddy' until you started school, don't you remember?" She jerked her head back. "Scared the heck out of me, you being so alone on the farm and all back then." She put her arm over her daughter's shoulders and pointed at Sarah. "Don't worry– it runs in the family."

"For real?"

"Yes. For. Real."

"Alright, Ma, if you say so." Gillian grimaced. "Still looks weird." She glanced at her watch. "We've still got three hours until the truck arrives. I'd say we're doing pretty well for time."

Maureen nodded and took the broom from Gillian's hand. "I'll finish up on this floor. You go down and tackle the kitchen."

Gillian turned and bounded down the stairs while Maureen set the broom aside. There was just one thing left to do—get the bucket of soapy water from her bedroom at the front and pour it down the toilet.

She wandered over to the window and peered out, meeting the gaze of an elderly man standing in the park across the street. What was he doing staring at the house like that, just standing with his hands on a cane, not moving a muscle? She bent to the window to get a closer look. Elderly wasn't accurate. The guy was *ancient*!

Silently they stared at each other. The expression on his face didn't change; he just stood there impassively staring at a point above her head. All that was above her was the peak of the roof and the half moon window in the closed off upstairs.

She watched as he took in a deep breath and held it. Like he was waiting for something to happen. Her mouth twitched. What made her think of that? After what seemed like an hour but was really no more than a minute, his lips moved like he was saying something. Then, he turned and walked up the street, almost hobbling, he was moving so slowly.

Maureen bent and picked up the bucket of water. She had better things to do.

But boy, that old guy sure creeped her out.

CHAPTER TWENTY EIGHT

The old man was surprised to see the car parked in the driveway of the house. His bushy, grey eyebrows drew together and his jaw worked overtime, grinding his dentures as he stood quietly on the sidewalk. Movement in the second floor window caught his eyes and he blinked.

A woman stared back at him. She was too old to be a student. The hair that framed her jaw was silver. It was obvious that she was watching him, probably curious as to why an old fella' would be standing there gawking. If she asked him that question, he wasn't sure he could give her a reasonable answer. Not that it mattered. Like all the others, she'd be gone soon.

He returned his gaze to the sorrowful half moon window just below the peak of the roof.

He'd only missed a few days over the last twenty years, when there was an ice storm, or he'd picked up some flu bug. It always played on his mind to the degree that he was never able to sleep until he resumed the daily visit. There was something about the house that drew him back, every day.

He never understood why he moved to Kingston after he retired. He grew up on a farm, went to war, came home and spent his working life out west in the oil fields. But when it was time for him to retire, the only place he considered was Kingston. Not Victoria, and not even Florida. He never lived in Kingston until he became an old man. And with the universities and colleges in the city, it was more a city for youngsters, really.

And here he was now, living in a nursing home. The high point of his day was this daily sojourn; a walk through the park to gawk at that house. He couldn't explain it. He was drawn to the place, and yet at the same time repelled by it. Watching it from across the street was fine; but if he tried to cross the streeet, he'd get dizzy and feel very, very odd. He was a moth, and that place was a flame—he *had* to come near it, but *too close* and it would hurt him.

Still staring at the curved window, the sadness sharpened and took his breath away. He gasped and went still for a moment.

Finally, he said his daily mantra. "The circle must close." He turned away and ambled through the park, making his way home.

But make no mistake...he'd be back tomorrow.

CHAPTER TWENTY NINE

Gillian finished cleaning the kitchen and peeked out the window to check on Sarah. She felt guilty watching her daughter straddling the seat of the swing, rocking sideways. It had been a lonely afternoon for Sarah but she would make it up to her...Maybe buy her some art supplies, something a bit more challenging than just coloring.

She opened the back door and her eyes narrowed peering at the child. She was talking to herself. "Sarah?"

The young girl looked up and grinned. She swung her leg over the seat and ran towards Gillian. "Hi Mommy!"

"Were you talking to yourself?" She leaned over and kissed the top of her daughter's head.

Sarah drew back and her eyes were round staring at her mother. "I was talking to Alice and Agnes. They're my new friends. They're sisters." She turned to look at the swing, then turned back to Gillian, her face puzzled. "Where'd they go? They were right there!"

Gillian looked from the swing to the fence bordering the yard. "Well, I guess they just had to go home or something."

She sighed and reached for her daughter's hand. Mom was probably right; better to not make too much out of this. "Would you like to go shopping with me? I've got a surprise I want to get you."

Sarah's face lit up and she tugged at Gillian's hand. "A surprise? What is it? Tell me!" She started bouncing on her toes.

Gillian could only smile at the sudden about-face, the excitement in Sarah's eyes. "If I tell you, it wouldn't be a surprise, would it? You'll have to wait till we get there." She opened the back door and led her daughter into the house, ignoring the whining protests to tell her what it was.

Maureen's footsteps sounded on the stairway and a minute later she walked into the kitchen. "So you two are off now to get some groceries? Would you like my debit card? It's bound to be a big list of things to buy."

"No, that's okay, Mom. I'll get it this time. Anything special you'd like me to pick up?" Gillian grabbed her purse and smiled at her mother.

"Actually, why don't you pick up a bottle of that wine like we had last night at the hotel? Let's christen our first night here with a glass or two." Maureen walked to the front door with Gillian and Sarah. She peered out but the old guy who'd been in the park staring at her, was gone.

Gillian held her arm up and grinned. "Twist my arm."

***

It was ten o'clock that night when Maureen and Gillian trudged up the stairs. With a few glasses of wine coursing through their veins, easing the tension from over-worked muscles, they were more than ready to call it a day. The

184

moving truck had arrived on time, furniture placed, beds made and most of the boxes unpacked.

Maureen patted Gillian's shoulder and said 'good night' leaving Gillian standing in the doorway of Sarah's room. The night-light cast a soft glow in the room, revealing the small body curled into a ball under the comforter. Gillian stepped closer to the bed and checked her breathing like she did every night since Sarah had been born.

The easel that she'd bought that day was set up in the center of the room, displaying Sarah's drawing. Gillian bent over to see what her child had created. There was a big tree, a swing and three little girls playing next to it. The figures were crude, as any drawing a five year old would create but she'd put dresses on two of them. The third one was in shorts and her hair was braided. That had to be Sarah.

"Hello Agnes. How do you do, Alice?" she whispered with a soft smile. "School will be starting soon, so you'll be moving on I guess." She bent over Sarah's sleeping form and kissed the top of the child's head before heading to bed herself. She was beat to a snot.

***

A few hours later, the floorboards in Maureen's room creaked. She woke with a start and sat up. *Someone was watching her!* What was that? The room was pitch black. The window was covered with a dark towel. The shopping trip to get curtains would happen the next day. After that old guy ogling her, there was no way she was getting undressed in a room without some kind of covering on the window.

Creak. There it was again! It was those floorboards in the centre of the room. Her heart pounded in her chest and she held her breath, straining to see. "Gillian? Is that you?" Her voice was a fast whisper.

Silence was the only answer. But there was something there. The hair on the back of her neck rose, as the feeling grew. Someone was watching her! "Sarah?"

Again, silence.

She leaned to the side and reached for the chain on her bedside lamp. Immediately, light flooded the room. There was no one there. But she'd heard something. It had been loud enough to wake her from a deep sleep. She glanced at the clock. Twelve minutes past one. Oh my. She'd only been asleep a few hours.

She took a few deep breaths, willing her heartbeat to resume its normal pace. Old houses creaked sometimes. That was all it was. Maybe the temperature outside had dropped, or maybe the barometer, and the house was feeling that.

But what about that sense that someone was watching her? She shuddered. Actually, that feeling was still there.

The light gave some comfort. There wasn't anyone in the room. It was just her mind playing tricks on her. So much had happened over the past couple of months. Mike's death. Leaving a home where she'd always lived. The last three months had seen more changes in her life than ever before.

She settled down into the bed and pulled the covers tight. One thing was certain though...the bedroom light was staying on.

CHAPTER THIRTY

The next afternoon...

Another day and they were too busy to play or take her to the park. And they made it clear; she was too little to help put up curtains. They wouldn't let her hold the ladder, Nana scolded her when she picked up the pliers, and Mommy gave a big huff when she said she was bored and told her to go to her room and work on her drawing. Sara stomped out of Mommy's bedroom and down the hall to her own. Not fair!

Standing in front of the easel, she picked up the black pencil from the tray on the front. All of a sudden the room smelled really nice, like flowers. Closing her eyes, she inhaled deeply. She kept her eyes closed even when she felt a smooshy pressure all over. It was like she was all wrapped up in warm bread and soft fur at the same time. It felt so nice she shivered a little. Her hand moved around the easel for a few seconds and then everything went away.

She opened her eyes. The picture on the easel was... prettier or something. She saw that Agnes and Alice looked… *realer* somehow. And both girls were smiling, happier too.

Sarah's eyes sparked. "Maybe they'll come and visit again!" Putting the pencil down, she scooted back to where Mommy and Nana were working.

"Can I go out and play in the back yard?"

Mommy was at the top of the ladder fooling with the curtain. She glanced over and said "Sure, sweetie."

The day was hot and humid, making the strands of hair that escaped her braids stick to her neck. She raced over to the swing and hopped up onto the old wooden seat. Her legs strained out in front of her and collapsed quickly. This was the way Mommy had said to pump and go higher. It still wasn't working though.

"Hi Sarah!" The voices of the twins spoke in unison.

Sarah grinned and turned her head to see them, her eyebrows knotted. That was weird. They were wearing the same clothes as the day before and their hair ribbons were still slipping off at the side again. Mommy always made her change her clothes every day.

"Hi Alice. Hi Agnes. How come I didn't see you come in the gate?"

"No silly, we were already here! We were hiding! Want to play tag again?" Agnes reached for the rope, pulling Sarah closer.

"Okay. That was fun yesterday. But aren't you hot in those dresses and socks?" Sarah popped down off the swing and turned to look at her friends.

"No. We're fine." Alice tapped Sarah's arm. "Tag! You're It!" She grabbed her sister's hand and they raced around the thick tree trunk, with a flurry of lacy slip and black leather shoes flying high.

"Wait! Let's get a drink of water first. I'm thirsty." Sarah started towards the house and stopped midway there, turning to see if they were with her. "Hey! Come with me. I'll show you my drawing and my room."

The two girls stood on each side of the tree and their smiles faded.

"We can't." Agnes looked down at her feet, while Alice shook her head from side to side, her lower lip pushed out. For just a moment it looked like they were going to cry.

"What's wrong?"

"We have to go out on the boat later..." Alice's voice was low.

"Alice! Now you shush!" Agnes said sharply. "The circle's still open!"

Alice turned to her sister, holding out her hands like a plea. "But Sarah's little, like us!"

"What circle?" asked Sarah. The twins whipped their heads around to her. Their eyes looked a little funny. Sarah felt a little scared and took a step backwards.

Alice's face got funny, like she was gonna start to cry. "I don't know!" she said.

Agnes put her arm around her sister's waist. Still looking at Sarah, she said, "It just is." She gave a sad sigh and her eyes looked okay again.

"You're talking all mixed up," Sarah shook her head a little.

Alice stared at the door to Sarah's house. "It's Bridey, Sarah. She insists we go to the lake," her voice was just above a whisper.

"And she forbids us to go inside the house," added Agnes.

"Forbids? What's that mean?"

189

"It means we're not allowed," said Alice.

"How come? It's okay. I'm really thirsty. My Mommy won't mind." Sarah took a few steps towards them and crossed her arms over her chest. Bridey sounded mean. "Is Bridey your Mommy?"

"No!" they said together.

"We told you! Our Mummy died and Bridey married Papa," said Alice.

"She's your step-mother? Like in Cinderella?"

They nodded.

Agnes clasped her hands in front of her tummy. "We'll wait here for you, Sarah. Then we'll play on the swing and play tag and have such jolly fun!" She smiled, but it wasn't a for real smile, Sarah could tell when people didn't smile for real.

"Please, Sarah, let's not speak of this anymore," said Alice. "Fetch yourself a drink of water and we'll wait here for your return." She took Agnes' hand. "While you're inside, I'll cheer up my sister, don't you worry."

"Okay. I'll be right back." Sarah spun around and raced to the back door. When she got there, she turned before going in. Were they still there? Yesterday they ran away when Mommy came outside.

The sisters waved their hands and smiled at her, standing side by side holding hands. Agnes' face wasn't as sad anymore. Sarah turned and went into the kitchen. Thank goodness she had her real Mommy and not a mean step-mother like that Bridey lady.

CHAPTER THIRTY ONE

"Whew!" Maureen flopped down onto her bed and wiped her brow. What a day to be climbing up and down a step ladder; it was way too hot and muggy.

Gillian appeared in the doorway, taking in the newly hung rose-colored curtains and the matching bedspread. "This looks pretty nice. It's starting to feel like home." Handing a glass of ice water to her, she said, "Would you mind watching Sarah for a while this afternoon? The university emailed me that there's an orientation tour that I'd like to go to."

"Sure. I haven't really gone into the back yard to see what's what out there."

"Thanks Mom. I'll only be a couple hours." She stepped away and her footsteps sounded in the stillness, thudding quickly down the stairs.

***

An hour later, Maureen held Sarah's hand coming back from the playground in the park. Her back had felt a little stiff and they'd abandoned the gardening in favor of a trip to the nearby playground. As they approached the house, she looked at all the ivy clinging to the brick around the front door. She'd read once that the foliage could damage the brick and knew that spiders liked to hide there too. There was just too much of it; it needed to be cleaned up. You could hardly read the house number.

They crossed the street and Maureen looked down at Sarah walking beside her. "I'm going to snip some of those brambles off the front of the house. Why don't you get your drawing book and pencils and work on that while I'm working on the veranda?"

"Can I play on the swing instead?"

Maureen fished the front door key from her pocket and slid it into the lock. "Sure, go ahead." As she rummaged in the kitchen for garden shears, she heard the back door open, a giggle of laughter from Sarah before it closed behind her.

Clearing the ivy at the front wouldn't take that long. She tugged the branch of ivy that was threatening to cover the house number, and sliced through it cleanly. She tossed it aside and tackled another gangly twig, pulling it out and snipping it off.

She discovered a brass plaque above the house number, covered in thick brambles.

Suddenly, she stopped and looked over her shoulders. The air was filled with fragrance from the rose bushes that lined the front and side of the house. She inhaled deeply, feeling the fresh scent fill her head. What a special aroma.

Turning back to her work, she tugged at the stem and set of leaves that covered and clung to it. More 'feet' of the ivy had curled under the plate and resisted her first tugs. Her fingers coiled around it and she pulled harder against the gnarled vines and finally it gave.

A large embossed 'C' could be seen on the plate but the rest was still hidden. Once more, she attacked the growth, tugging and slicing until finally clearing the plaque of the overgrown coverage.

The brass plaque was almost black with age, the letters on it difficult to make out. She wiped the surface with her hand. Reading the word, her mouth fell open, gazing at the letters on the sign. She stopped breathing.

'CRAWLEY'.

In silent astonishment her eyes and her fingers glided over the letters. Slowly, she exhaled. This couldn't be. The coincidence was too unreal. Crawley? Her family name?

"What are you doing, Mom?" Gillian's voice interrupted, bringing her back to the heat and brightness of the day. "What's that you've found?"

Maureen turned to look at Gillian, still unable to speak. She pointed to the plaque.

Her daughter's brow furrowed and she strained forward to read it. Her eyes grew wide and her head jerked back. "Crawley? What the hell?"

Maureen felt her head get light and she caught herself from swooning. Her hand rose to grip Gillian's arm. "Don't you see? We were *meant* to live here!"

CHAPTER THIRTY TWO

The following evening as they were preparing supper, Gillian looked over at her mother. "The more I think about it, the idea of buying this house makes sense. Chances are, I'll stay in Kingston when I graduate. There're lots of employment options for nurses here." She brushed her hands together. "You're sure you're going through with this then?"

"Absolutely." Maureen opened the oven door and took the meatloaf out. She set it on the counter and then turned to face her daughter. "This house was built by a Crawley. It just seems right that a Crawley own it again. Our home in Lanark would never have worked out. You weren't interested in farming and I'm not getting any younger." She gave her daughter a smug look. "And when I gave the university a *really* low offer, they jumped at it. It's a once in a lifetime deal if you ask me!"

"Well, it's your money; and if you're happy, I'm happy."

A loud thud vibrated the ceiling above them.

Gillian and Maureen jerked back and their eyes were round staring up at the ceiling.

"What in God's name was—"

"Sarah!" Gillian raced out of the room and her feet flew on the stairs.

Maureen's voice called after her. "She's outside on the swing, Gillian."

Gillian's hand rested on her chest and she sighed with relief walking into her daughter's room. The bed hadn't broken and the desk and bookcase were still upright. Even the easel in the center of the room was the same...

Her eyebrows drew together. Except it wasn't. The drawing that Sarah had made of the three girls was different. The children were no longer stick figures. Sarah had fleshed them out so that they more closely resembled actual people—showing a talent for depth and proportion beyond her years.

"Gillian? Did something fall over? What made that racket up there?" Maureen's voice, calling up the stairwell, interrupted her daughter's thoughts.

Gillian peeked into the bathroom and her bedroom. Again, nothing was amiss. She strode down the hallway and opened the door of her mother's bedroom. The room was tidy, the comforter on the bed smooth and straight and the dresser and upholstered chair tucked neatly against the wall. She sighed and walked across the room to peer out the window. The noise had to have come from outside. Street repairs?

She turned and started to retrace her steps when the corner of a thick book caught her eye. It was half hidden behind the door and she'd missed it at first glance in the room. She picked it up. The family bible? She shook her head and propped it up on the shelf, next to the ancient photo album that her mother cherished.

She walked out of the room and peered at her mother's face as she stepped down the stairs. "One of your books fell off the shelf."

"Which one?"

"The family bible. No wonder it made such a thud, huh?" Gillian cocked an eyebrow at her mother. "The holy book scared the be-jezus out of me," she said with a half smile.

"Har-dee-har-har, such a punster." Maureen shook her head. "How about giving me a hand with supper?"

"Sure."

When dinner was just about ready, Gillian headed out to the back yard.

Sarah raced over and held her arms high, pressing her body against Gillian's thighs. "Are you coming outside to play with us?"

Gillian scooped her daughter up and balanced her on her hip. She gave her a kiss on the cheek. "Hungry Moppet? Dinner's just about ready." She walked to the doorway and stepped up into the house. Her head tilted to the side and she looked into her daughter's eyes. "Hey, I noticed your drawing. You're really getting good at it." She tickled her daughter's waist. "Did Nana help you with it?

Sarah laughed and pushed her mother's hand away. "Nope." She looked over her mother's shoulder back at the tree and smiled and waved. "See you tomorrow!"

"Who you talking to?"

Sarah looked at her like she was too stupid to live. "Agnes and Alice, silly!"

"Who?" Gillian turned around to the back yard. "Sarah, there's nobody there."

Sarah giggled. "I know. They go home *really* fast!" She shrugged her shoulders. "They were with me on the swing, but left when you came out." She gave a small pout. "They're shy I guess."

"Shy, huh?"

Sarah nodded.

"Shy like in make believe?"

Sarah looked off to the side and spoke slowly. "I don't think sooo..."

"But maybe…"

Sarah shrugged. "I like them! They're nice!"

Before it got any further out of hand, she gave Sarah a kiss on the nose. "Well, you're nice too!" She'd have to talk about this with Mom later on. "Let's head in."

When Gillian stepped into the kitchen she peeled Sarah away from her body and set her down. "Would you get the cutlery and set the table, Moppet?" She smiled when Sarah raced over to the cabinet and pulled the drawer out.

She finished tossing the salad and watched her mother mash the pot of potatoes. Once more she was reminded how much weight Maureen had lost and how the lines on her face seemed deeper. "Mom?"

"Hmm..." She glanced up and her eyes met Gillian's.

"In a few weeks Sarah and I will be in school. I was thinking... After you go to the lawyer's office and get the paperwork going, why don't the three of us take a vacation?"

"Go on a holiday while I'm buying a house?" Maureen's eyebrows lifted in puzzlement.

"Well, you're paying cash, and there's only been two other owners since it was built from what Jeremy Sloat said." She held up her fingers one at a time. "The guy who built it, the second owner who then gave it to the university. I don't think it should be very complicated."

Maureen shook her head. "Yeah, I'll be a real big shot, on the phone with my lawyers from poolside at a hotel."

Gillian nodded. "That's right, but nothing exotic and expensive. Maybe a week in Niagara Falls. We've never been there and Sarah would enjoy it. By the time we get back, the deal ought to be pretty much done!" Giving a cheese grin she added, "After all, we're already moved in, right?" She folded her arms. "What do you think?"

Maureen's hands stopped and a slow smile brightened her face. "It's been years since I've been there. That sounds wonderful. God knows, when you start school, there'll be no time for anything like that."

"Great! I'll pack while you visit the lawyer." Gillian picked up the salad and set it on the table. She ruffled Sarah's hair. "What do you say, Moppet? Would you like to go to Marineland and see the Falls?"

Sarah was carefully placing the cutlery on paper napkins. She looked up at her mother and then stared out the window at the swing for a few moments. "Can Agnes and Alice come? They play with me in the back yard all the time!" Sarah looked down at the floor and a dark look came over her face. "Bridey probably won't let them though..." she added in a soft voice.

"Your friends from the back yard?" The hair on the back of Gillian's neck stood up. What the heck was this now? Her imaginary friends had a mother named Bridey? "Who's Bridey, honey?" The expression on her daughter's face was disturbing for some reason. Gillian wiped a wisp of hair that fell forward behind Sarah's ear.

"Their step-mother. She's not very nice…"

"Oh?" Gillian tried to keep her voice light. "How do you know Bridey's not nice?" Who in the world *are* these people? She glanced over to Maureen asking the question with her eyes and got a shrug and a headshake reply from her mother.

"Alice and Agnes told me." Sarah was still looking intently at her toes. "They said it's a secret."

"Well, the next time you see your friends, let me know, and I'll ask their mommy, okay?"

Sarah's head whipped up. "SHE'S NOT THEIR MOMMY!" Her face was defiant; her lips pulled tight against her teeth and her hands had balled into fists.

"Sarah!" Maureen said, her own hand flying to her mouth, shocked at the little girl.

"Well, she isn't! She's mean and… and…" looking to her Nana and Mommy, Sarah burst into tears. Gillian scooped her up in her arms, and Sarah clung to her neck like a drowning man. She stared wide eyed at Maureen to see the same expression returned.

"It's okay, baby, it's okay," she said, rocking the child.

"I think Bridey's bad, Mommy. I think she's bad, bad!" Sarah had nuzzled into her neck at this point. Gillian held her, rocking her back and forth. In a few moments, Sarah's breath had evened out. Gillian kept gently rocking the child.

"Gillian," whispered Maureen. "She's asleep!"

"What's happening, Mom?"

"I think she's just overtired." The look in Maureen's eyes showed she was anything but certain of her diagnosis.

"Hey… hey Moppet…" Gillian rubbed Sarah's back as she cooed.

Sarah's head rolled in the crook of Gillian's neck. She leaned back, blinking her eyes open and smacked her lips. "Hi Mommy," she said. "Was I having a nap?" She smiled, thank God.

"Yes, Moppet, you dozed off for a bit. Feeling better now?"

Sarah looked puzzled. "Sure! I feel great! What's for dinner?"

Neither woman mentioned Bridey, nor Agnes or Alice that evening.

CHAPTER THIRTY THREE

Time flew, and before she knew it, Maureen had shook hands with the lawyer and stepped out of the office to join Gillian and Sarah in the reception area. She felt light, like she was floating on air walking over to them. In her hand was the folder containing the deed and survey of 8 Harvest Street.

Gillian looked up from the magazine she'd been perusing. "All done?"

Maureen smiled and nodded her head, not trusting her voice to answer. Her insides were quivering with excitement and she wanted nothing more than to race out of the building and get home as fast as humanly possible. The time spent in Niagara Falls had been fun with Gillian and Sarah. They had spent the days wandering around, seeing the sights and attractions with no timetables to meet.

When they returned home, they all decided not to do any more fixing up on the place until the deal had closed for once and for all. Now that the house was officially hers, she had plans.

"C'mon Sarah. Let's go *home*." Gillian tapped her daughter's knee and rose to her feet.

Sarah closed her coloring book and poked it and the box of crayons, into her knapsack. She scampered up to her grandmother and took her hand. "Nana? Now that you own the house, can I get a dog instead of a cat? I think I'd rather have a dog."

Sarah's big blue eyes, and hopeful smile tugged at Maureen's heart. She chuckled and turned to Gillian. "Did you put her up to this?"

Gillian's eyes widened. "No!" She glanced down to her daughter. "This is news to me, Mom."

Maureen gave a little snort. "Must run in the family then. I had my first dog when I was five, we got you Clifford when *you* were five, and now here's Moppet keeping up the family tradition." She turned her gaze down to her granddaughter, but continued addressing Gillian. "You're okay with it?"

"It's *your* house, Mom," Gillian said with a crafty smile. "But I think it's a good idea. Sarah's old enough, and the company would be good for her." She gave a little nod to Sarah who was watching the exchange between the two women. "Having a *real life* companion would be a good thing, don't you think?"

Maureen looked askance at her daughter. "It's *our* house, Gillian. Our house, okay?" She put her hand on top of Moppet's head. "If it's fine with your mother, I think it's a wonderful idea, Sarah."

"Now? Can we get it now?" The little tyke turned and pulled at her arm, her grin as wide as any jack-o'-lantern's. And just as toothy. She had lost her first baby tooth while they were away.

"Tell you what. Drop me off at the house and you two go to the pound together. Don't get something too big—"

"Gee and my heart was set on a Great Dane!"

Maureen shook her head. "It's your daughter, and her dog; you think I'll be cleaning up accidents?"

"Ick." Gillian's eyes almost crossed. "Maybe not so much a Great Dane."

Maureen laughed at the expression on her daughter's face.

Ten minutes later, Maureen got out of the car and walked up the steps to her house. Yes, *her* house. She gazed at the bronze plaque with the name 'Crawley' embossed on it. She was going to polish that plaque and gussy it up nice. She had put even *that* off until the deal was done, in fear of jinxing anything. Her mouth twitched for a second. Would she have bought the house if not for that plaque? Probably not. But there were no second thoughts that she'd done the right thing.

She slipped the key into the lock and turned it slowly. She dropped her head, a wound in her heart opened up with the realization that Mike wouldn't be carrying her over *this* threshold. With a small shake of her head she banished the pain to the back of her mind. She'd probably shed a few tears in bed tonight. Again.

"Sure you don't want to come with us to pick out a dog?" Gillian looked up at her mother.

Her hand rested on the door knob and she turned her head to answer her daughter. "Actually, I'd like some time alone in the house. I've never done anything like this before...I mean, buying my first home. It must sound silly but—"

"It's not silly, Mom. This is something you wanted to do and I agree with you. We'll be back in an hour or so. Enjoy the quiet while you can!" Gillian went back to the car and left.

Maureen pushed the door wide and gazed around at the foyer and entrance. Yes, it was good to be here, to own this home. When she turned to close the door, she stopped for a moment. That old man was back. He was across the street, on one of the park's footpaths. He was standing still, his hands resting his cane, watching her intently.

Who was he and why did he stare at the house like that? And he *was* watching the house, not her. The first time she saw him, she was behind the curtains at a window; even so, he had stood in that path, gazing at the building. Her eyebrows drew together and she exhaled slowly. Should she confront him, find out what the heck his problem was or just leave it be?

He looked ancient. He could just be senile or something. He wasn't any sort of threat... was he? Not at that age— he looked like he could barely stand, let alone hurt someone. Maybe he was just being neighbourly or something. When they made eye contact, she lifted her hand in a small wave. *Yes, I see you, mister.* She felt a sense of relief when he nodded back.

Closing the door behind her, she smiled and took a deep breath. Yes, it was *her house*. Gillian would probably inherit, but it was *her name on that bloody deed!* She could at least be honest about that to herself.

Standing in the hallway, she turned her head like a princess taking in her dominion, a kewpie doll smile forming on her lips. Her eye wandered up and down the oak stairs, and turned to first the dining room, then the living room. *No, ye eejet, it's called the parlour!*

She nodded with a small smile. Of course.

The only sound breaking the stillness was the click of the grandfather clock.

The heels of her sandals echoed when she walked into the living room. Dust motes, caught in the rays of the late afternoon sun, flecked the air beside the wide front window. She wandered over to the fireplace, and ran her fingertips over the mantel. It would be beautiful when a fire was burning in it..

She looked at the coved ceilings that curved into the plaster walls as she walked to the end of the room, pausing to glance out the window into the back yard. The flower beds lining the fence would need work but that was something she preferred to do herself rather than hire the job out.

The swing's gentle movement caught her attention, and her eyes hooded. *That should be cut down and burned in the fireplace!*

Of course.

The back of her neck tingled, and she blinked her eyes a few times. She was more tired from that vacation than she'd thought.

She walked through the rounded archway, past the back door and into the kitchen. She glanced at the swing again as she passed by the window, and exhaled softly seeing that it was now still. At the counter, she emptied the kettle to pour fresh water and make some tea—the first cup of tea to christen her new home.

While she waited for the kettle to boil she decided to make good use of the time. Upon entering the dining room, a faint floral scent drifted into her nostrils. She paused and sniffed again. Yes, not just floral but roses. The sweet scent was unmistakeable. She gazed around the room trying to find the source. Perhaps Gillian had left a potpourri or scented oil on the hutch or cabinet. *It was smashing how well the scent complimented the room.*

She trudged up the stairs, walked down the hall and opened the door to her bedroom. She'd have time and the peace now to catch up on any email or reading on her laptop. She hadn't had it with her while they were away.

Her head jerked back and she stopped short. The family bible was laying on the floor in the centre of the room. How did it get there? She always kept it in the bookcase by the door. Could Sarah have been in her room, looking at the book? She'd have to ask her. The book was old, a family heirloom that Sarah needed to be careful with.

The high pitched whistle of the kettle downstairs caught her attention. She picked up the book to put it back in its rightful spot.

At the kettle's insistent whistle, she hurried down the steps to go into the kitchen and unplug it. A few minutes later she settled at the dining room table with her mug of tea and opened her laptop. As the computer booted up she took a sip, her gaze above the rim of the cup flitting around the room. Aside from a fresh coat of paint, this room was fine. In fact it was her favourite room in the house. She sniffed. Pity, that sweet aroma had faded away.

The thump of a car door, followed by the squeals of her granddaughter could be heard outside. When she opened the front door, Sarah and Gillian were coming up the walk. A small, fawn colored dog was straining at the leash in Sarah's hand, scrabbling towards the house. Sarah was laughing and giggling as she was being tugged along.

It got to the top of the steps, looked up at Maureen and promptly sat down, cocking its head.

"Oh my God, what an ugly dog," she said under her breath. She looked up to Gillian. "You got a boxer?"

"No, silly!" squealed Sarah. "She's a Pug! This is Pearl the Pug! Isn't she cuuute?"

Cute? Maureen's mouth opened for a split second and she closed it again. Pearl was still sitting patiently at her feet, her large eyes watching her. Maureen squatted down to look at this creature more closely.

When she crouched, the dog perked its ears. Her large brown eyes were soulful as they peered at her from the folds of her coat. When Maureen held out her hand, the dog leaned forward, sniffing with its pushed-in, black snout. After a few quick sniffs, it gave her hand a lick and tilted its head up to her. Pleased to make your acquaintance.

Maureen's heart melted. Cute was an understatement. Pearl was adorable. "Yes… I think she is very cute."

"So ugly, she's pretty," said Gillian.

Maureen nodded in agreement.

"She's not ugly! She's cute!" Sarah said.

Gillian had a bag of dog food and another white plastic bag in her hand. She followed her mother into the house and shut the door.

"I'm going to show Pearl the house!" Sarah raced up the stairs, the dog two steps ahead.

Maureen turned to Gillian and smiled. "It *is* pretty cute and Sarah obviously adores it. I made a pot of tea. Would you like a cup?"

"Sure. I'll put the dog stuff away and join you."

Maureen led the way down the hall and into the kitchen and took a mug from the cabinet. "I've got a few plans for the house."

Gillian walked over to the counter and took the mug of tea from her mother's hand. "Oh yeah? What are you thinking?"

They walked into the dining room and took a seat.

"Well, the fireplace for one. I want to get it checked, make sure everything's in working order and that room in the attic. Maybe we'll—"

A loud thud was followed by barking and a low growl. The women jumped and Maureen looked past the archway to the stairs. Gillian was already on her way, bounding up the stairs, two at a time.

Maureen was right behind her, her heart thudding fast when the yapping became downright ferocious.

At the threshold of Maureen's bedroom, Pearl stood, snarling into the empty room, wild eyed. Sarah had her arms around the dog's neck trying to comfort it and pull it back to the hallway. She looked up to the two women.

"I was showing her the house and when we got to your room Nana, there was a thump when I opened the door and Pearl got scared!" She hugged the dog to her chest.

Pearl was having none of it. She was scrabbling at the floor and broke free of Sarah. She bounded into the room and let out a piercing yelp. With her tail tucked, she leapt out of the room into Sarah's arms, now whining, 'Aaarrroooo!'

Sarah was still on the floor and clutched at the dog. "It's okay, Pearl, it's okay." The dog began to lick Sarah's neck and ear. Sarah turned her face up to the women. "Close the door! Close the door!"

Maureen reached into the room grabbing the knob. As she pulled the door closed, she saw the Bible again on the floor.

"It's a Banshee, Mama! Pearl saw the Banshee!" Sarah's eyes were like diamonds, staring up at them. She stood, cradling Pearl who was still howling. *"She sees the Banshee!"* she cried out again as she stumbled to her room.

Maureen looked over to Gillian and the two women stared at each other goggle eyed.

"Mom, what's wrong with my child?" Gillian said in a whisper.

"I don't know…"

CHAPTER THIRTY FOUR

Maureen sat bolt upright in her bed. Her eyes peered about the room while her heart thudded fast in her chest. She glanced at the clock on the bedside table. Twelve past one. She sighed. That was the same time she'd woken up before, when the floor had creaked.

She pulled the cord on the lamp and tugged the comforter close around her neck. The only sound now was the ticking clock. She must be the only woman in the city that used a wind up clock in the bedroom. Since childhood, she had always had one, and wouldn't be able to sleep without its monotonous ticking.

She jumped at the sound of the loud creak from the center of her room, inhaling sharply through her nose. The stench in her nostrils made her start to cough. It smelled like something died under her bed!

She puffed her cheeks and blew out a blast. Great. As if Sarah's meltdown wasn't enough! She didn't know who was more frightened by the child's outburst. It was the *second* one now. And like the first time, after her outburst, Sarah cried, dozed off and woke up fresh as a daisy. What WAS wrong with that girl?

And now she had goblins in her own bedroom? Goblins that really could use a shot of air freshener? This was too damn much.

She sniffed the air again. The smell had gone. What the hell? And any presence she felt or rather *thought she had felt,* was gone too. She exhaled slowly and gave her head a small shake. This was crazy. It had to be all the stress. Leaving the farm, then buying this place, all in such a small space of time. Small wonder she was going crazy.

With a sharp toss of her hand, the comforter landed on the side of the bed and she stood up. A cup of tea or hot chocolate...She sighed. No. She'd have a glass of wine. *That* would do the trick.

She stood up, grabbed her housecoat and the family bible. She was going to leave this in the living room where she could keep an eye on it. She'd found it too many times in the center of her bedroom; she'd put it in a spot where Sarah couldn't get at it.

Making her way down the hall, she peeked in at Sarah, and her gaze softened watching the child's peaceful face, Pearl curled up at the foot of her bed.

The dog lifted its head and hopped off. She turned to go down the stairs, a small smile on her lips watching the dog step in line behind her. Even with only a dog for company, it was better than being alone in the night.

A nightlight lent a yellowish glow to the kitchen. She took a glass from the cabinet and when she'd filled it with wine, she wandered into the living room and sank down into the cushiony sofa. With the heavy book propped onto her bent knees, feet digging into the cushions, she sipped her wine. The dog hopped up on the sofa and nestled in at her feet. She plucked the crocheted afghan from the back of the sofa and settled in. She'd have her wine and hopefully get drowsy enough to go back to bed and fall asleep.

It was an enormous book, the size of a large old fashioned photo album, but much heavier. Each time it had slipped off the table in her bedroom, the thud it had landed with was as loud as if a concrete block had been thrown to the floor. No wonder; each page was a hardy vellum stock. Resting it on her lap, her fingers traced the embossed, gold edged title that read 'Holy Bible'.

She certainly didn't lug it all the way downstairs for night time reading. She hadn't given much thought or respect to the idea of God or Jesus since she was a young girl. She didn't even know what the illness was that took her Nan away. It must have been some sort of cancer though. When Nan took to her bed in the family home, Maureen had bloodied her knees beside her bed beseeching God with prayer to spare the woman.

As Nan worsened, she pled with God for at least a peaceful death. Her poor grandmother had wasted away so much, the last time she came home from the hospital, that she'd known there was no hope. But even a peaceful death wasn't meant to be; the shrieks and keens of agony from Nan when her morphine drip ran out was agonizing. That such a woman of indomitable will and spirit, reduced to a slobbering husk, was a condemnation of God. When Father Carson spoke to Maureen at the wake how her death was a blessing, she'd laughed in his face. It made more sense to realize that God didn't exist than to try to figure out how such a being could be 'the first mover' of such a chain of agony.

Ever since, she would describe her spiritual leanings as 'I'm an avowed agnostic'. One day, she would tell Sarah the stories of Nan she recalled from her own childhood. Life everlasting? Not at all; but she'd do all she could for Nan's memory to live on.

Leafing through the gilt edged pages, she had to admire the craftsmanship. On the inside of the front cover was inscribed the reason she had kept the foolish thing. Nan's own mother's name was at the top, Eileen Marie (O'Hanlon) Crawley. Below that was written 'Bestowed to Mary (Crawley) O'Neill, daughter. That was her dear Nan. A cascading chain down the cover showed the Bible being then 'bestowed' to Marie Aileen, her own mother. And below that was written 'Bestowed to Maureen Mary', which was herself. She would see Gillian's name below that before she died, and Gillian would inscribe Sarah's name when it was time.

In a way, it was the family tree. Going all the way back to Eileen Crawley at the top of the page, the family had survived though the birth of only children, all daughters. Not that she and Mike hadn't *tried* to have more kids; both of them were bawdy lovers with healthy appetites.

She grimaced a little at the ironic thought *'God didn't bless us with any more'*. Still, from the first time she thumbed this book open as a child, she could not understand why it also bore a name off to the side of the page in brackets 'Eamon Crawley'. Who was he? And why was a single line drawn through that name with a different pen? His name was inscribed in the timeline between the matriarch, Eileen's and her Nan's own name. Who was that guy?

Not for the first time had the mystery of Eamon intrigued her. She talked about this mystery entry with her own Mom a few times but had hit a brick wall. Even when she was alive, her Nan wouldn't discuss him. Neither woman knew anything about the mysterious Eamon.

She rubbed her finger over the name inscribed in the vellum and the hair on the back of her neck stood up. *'T'was a sweet name'* whispered in her head. *'He will guard the riches of this house forever! Eaaaamonnnn'*. Her eyes took on a diamond glitter.

"Of course", she whispered.

The pug at her feet stirred, then sat up suddenly with a soft whine, snapping her out of her reverie.

Maureen sighed and tossed the afghan aside. "Do you need to go out?" She set the book on the floor and tramped after the small pooch, down the hall to the back door. She flipped the deadbolt and opened it, clutching her robe tighter to her throat.

The dog darted by her leg, and scampered to the edge of the patio where it hunkered down to do its business. Mission accomplished, it darted back into the house and she closed the door and bolted it shut. When she turned to go back into the kitchen, the dog was at her feet, the hackles on its back standing high and stiff. She bent down and scratched behind its ear. "It's okay, girl. You're okay."

She went back into the kitchen and topped up the glass of wine. Instead of setting the bottle back in the fridge, she took it into the living room and set it on the coffee table. The first glass of wine had settled in and her muscles were beginning to feel heavier and much looser. She snuggled into the sofa, pulling the afghan over her, and reaching for the bible.

She finished the bottle of wine and climbed the stairs to go back up to bed. The wine and the reading had done the trick, making her drowsy enough that creaking floorboards and the wailing wind outside wouldn't keep her from passing out. She glanced at the clock. It was almost three in the morning. If she was lucky, Gillian and Sarah would let her sleep in.

CHAPTER THIRTY FIVE

The patter of Sarah's bare feet in time with the click, click of the dog's toenails on the hardwood floor intruded on Gillian's sleep. The door opened and Sarah rushed over and hopped up onto the bed, snuggling in next to her. Gillian's arm curled over her daughter and she kissed the top of her head. "Hi Moppet. How'd you sleep with Pearl on your bed? Did she keep you up?"

Sarah sat up and hugged it to her chest. "She was quiet as anything, Mommy!"

The dog hopped up beside them, wagging its tail and straining forward to lick Sarah's face. Gillian's hand drifted to its head and scratched behind its ear. The dog hadn't been there twenty-four hours yet, but already it was right at home.

"She probably needs to go outside for a pee. I'd better get up." She stretched her arms above her head and yawned loudly. The wood floor was cool on her feet when she swung her legs over the side of the bed.

When Gillian rounded the newel post of the stairway, she glanced across at her mother's room. The closed door told her Mom was still asleep. By the time Gillian was down the stairs, Sarah was on tiptoes, straining to reach the deadbolt latch on the back door. Gillian smiled and ambled down the hallway to help her.

When the door flung open, the dog rushed out but stopped at the edge of the patio. It turned and raced back into the house, hackles raised, letting out a low whine.

Gillian's eyebrows drew together as she bent down to pat the dog's head. The poor little thing's eyes were huge and its tail was between its legs.

"What's out there, girl?" She stepped down onto the patio and looked around. The yard was still. Pearl was at the door, hunkered down on her belly watching her. She walked down towards the end of the back yard, and when she got to the swing, from the door the puppy let out a yip. Scanning the rest of the yard from the maple tree, she didn't see anything out of place.

Maybe the dog hadn't settled in as fast as she'd first thought. Returning to the house, she scooped Pearl up and carried her into the kitchen, rubbing its head. Sarah had the bag of kibble under her arm, scooping some out to put into the dog's dish.

"Maybe after breakfast, we should take Pearl for a walk in the park. Dogs need exercise for them to do all their business." Gillian wandered to the counter and poured a cup of coffee from the gurgling machine.

Sarah sat crossed legged on the floor petting the dog as it snuffed and snaffled at its food. "You mean for them to poop, right?"

"You got it." Gillian opened the fridge door and reached inside for the carton of coffee cream. Her mouth gave a slight upward twitch when she saw the empty space where the bottle of wine had been. Sleeping in or sleeping it off, Mom?

***

An hour later Gillian and Sarah, led by the dog entered the front door of the house. Music drifted from the kitchen followed by the beeping sound of the microwave finishing its cycle.

Sarah grinned up at her mother. "Nana's up." She raced down the hall with the dog bounding after her.

When Gillian walked into the kitchen her mother was sitting at the table with a mug of coffee set in front of her. Gillian's eyebrows drew together. "Hi. Did you just get up? That's late for you, isn't it?" There were dark circles under her mother's eyes and her skin looked kind of pasty.

Maureen nodded and took a long swallow of coffee watching Sarah fill the dog's water bowl at the sink. "I didn't sleep well last night. I got up and had a couple glasses of wine."

Gillian laughed and took a seat across from her. "Yeah, from the look of you I didn't think you had a cup of warm milk."

Maureen set the mug down and sighed. "I feel like I've been hit by a Mack truck. Gosh, I'm tired."

"That's cuz you're hung over," Gillian said with a smug smile. "You're not a regular drinker, and there was a fair bit of wine in that bottle."

Maureen nodded. "Guilty as charged. I'll feel better after a shower and something to eat."

"Why don't you take it easy today? Sit and read a book or surf the web or something. I'm going out to pick up some paint for Sarah's room. She can come with me and we'll be out of your hair for a while."

Her mother exhaled slowly and her eyes were kind of hollow when she looked across the table. She turned her head when her granddaughter took a seat at the table. "Sarah, if you look at the old book that was on my night table, you have to be very careful. It's really old and you can't just leave it laying around on the floor."

"I didn't do that. I don't go in your room."

Maureen's eyes narrowed and she sat forward. "Oh? So it jumps onto the floor by itself?"

"I don't *like* your room, Nana! Even Pearl doesn't like your room!" The little tyke's lips were pursed together and she looked straight into her grandmother's eyes.

Maureen slapped the table top. "Enough of ye'er brass! Ye and that filthy cur stay out of me room ye bloody blaggard!"

Sarah's eyes widened and filled with tears and Pear let out a soft moan from her dog dish. "Nana…"

"Hey, Mom…" Gillian said softly. "Take it easy…" '*What the heck's a blaggard?*' she wondered.

Maureen shook her head and took Sarah's hand. "I'm sorry, Sarah… I'm not feeling too good this morning." She turned to Gillian. "If it wasn't her, then who was it? You? Me? C'mon, Gillian…"

"I won't ever, ever go in your room, Nana! I promise!" Sarah was on the verge of tears. Maureen reached over and gave her arm a squeeze.

Watching them, Gillian knew Sara was telling the truth. She was always able to tell when Sarah fibbed or didn't tell the whole story. This wasn't one of those times. Gillian sat up straighter in the chair. "Mom, remember that day we heard the loud bang upstairs? And we found your bible was laying open behind your door? Sarah was down here when that happened."

Still stroking Sarah, Maureen waved her hand. "It's okay. Don't worry about it. I've put it up on the top shelf in the living room bookcase anyway."

Gillian nodded. This wasn't worth making things worse right now. Mom's hangover was giving her temper an edge, so she decided to let it slide. "Is it okay if we leave the dog with you while we're out? We've taken her for a walk so she shouldn't be a bother." Gillian rose to her feet and walked to the counter to get her cell phone from the charger.

"It's fine." Her mother went back to sipping her coffee.

Sarah looked up at her mother, her eyes wide and solemn. Gillian ruffled her hair and winked at her before picking up her purse.

"Will you pop into the liquor store and pick up another bottle of wine? It helped me get to sleep last night." Maureen rose and refilled her mug with coffee.

"Sure." Gillian turned and took Sarah's hand, leading her down the hallway. "We'll see you later!" The words were more cheerful than the lump of worry in her gut.

When they were outside, Sarah tugged at her arm and looked up at her, the usual smile on her face no longer there. "Nana's wrong. I didn't touch her book, Mommy."

She leaned over and kissed the top of her daughter's head and pulled her in tight to her body in a swift hug. "I know, Moppet. Sometimes grown-ups make mistakes and forget things. I think that's what happened today. She made a mistake. But remember, she loves you."

"Very well, I suppose." Sarah looked up at her mother, her eyes like diamonds. "She was quite wroth with me. She was as frightful as Bridey."

Gillian stopped dead in her tracks.

"What did you say?"

Sarah blinked twice. "I said I didn't touch her book."

"No, after that, about being wroth."

Sarah tilted her head. "What's a wroth?"

Gillian huffed a sigh. "It's an old fashioned word." Taking Sarah by the hand, she said, "Let's go get the paint." Skip it. Imaginary friends, a hung over mother and she had a room to paint. It was going to be a long day.

CHAPTER THIRTY SIX

Later that day, Sarah sat on the swing in the back yard. She could see her mother through the window in her room, rolling pink paint onto the walls. Nana was in the dining room looking at her laptop. She'd been kind of quiet when they'd got home. It seemed like she was still a little mad about that book.

Pearl sat next to the back door, her head turned up watching it. No matter how hard she'd coaxed, the dog wouldn't leave the patio area. The dog shivered even though it was a warm day and once or twice she'd let out a soft whiney sound.

"Hi Sarah."

Sarah jumped and had to grab the swing's rope tighter to keep from falling off. Agnes's face appeared right next to her own, her eyes narrow and laughing. "Hi Agnes. Where's Alice?"

"Boo!" Alice popped out from behind the tree, her dark shoes landing next to Sarah's feet.

The dog let out a louder whine and scratched at the door, her tail curled between her legs.

"Is that your dog? I don't think it likes us." Agnes took a few steps closer to the patio, and giggled when the dog began to scratch and whine louder.

Sarah was about to run over to let the dog in when Alice spoke. "Agnes! Come back here! Hurry!"

Agnes spun around, and grabbed Alice's hand. Together they darted behind the tree.

The back door opened and Maureen appeared, casting a nasty look over at Sarah before the dog scampered inside.

Sarah slipped forward off the swing's seat and scampered round the tree. "Why'd you do that?"

"Do what?" Alice's fingers slipped inside the collar of her dress and she scooped out a silver chain. A ray of sunshine glinted off the metal she held between her fingers.

Sarah leaned forward and her mouth fell open. "I have one like that." She fished the St. Jude medallion from the front of her T shirt. "See?"

Agnes stepped closer and reached for it. "That's mine." Her eyes were narrow and her lips were a pouty line.

Sarah jerked back at the same time as Alice spoke. "No Agnes. It's Sarah's. Don't be mean. You scare me when you act like that." She turned and like flipping a switch, her face brightened into a wide grin. "Mine is engraved on the back." She twisted it in her fingers and leaned closer to Sarah.

"A. C." Sarah recognized the letters on the medallion. Her eyes grew wide and she smiled. "Mine too! That's what mine says!"

"Of course it does." Agnes's arms crossed over her chest and her shoulders jerked low. "The man stole it from me. Now you have it. That's not fair!"

Alice turned to her sister and cupped her hands over her twin's ear, whispering something. Whatever it was, made Agnes smile and nod her head.

She turned to Sarah and her hand reached out to grip Sarah's forearm. "Can you keep a secret?"

Sarah's eyes lit up. A secret! She loved secrets even though she knew she couldn't keep one if someone tickled her. "What is it?" There she hadn't lied.

Alice pointed to the top floor, to the half moon window tucked under the eaves. "If you were to make that your bedroom, we could visit you there."

Sarah's mouth closed and she thought. She had a Berenstain Bears book about Sister Bear having friends over for a sleep-over. Was that what Alice meant? In the book it had been lots of fun even though Brother played tricks on the girls.

"A sleepover? Your Mom would let you stay the night? I'm sure my Mommy wouldn't mind. She's really nice. So is my Nana usually, but not today. Today she's mad at me. She thought I was playing with her book when I wasn't. Honest."

"We know." Agnes reached for Sarah and put her arm over the tyke's shoulders.

Sarah's eyebrows drew together. "How did you know that?"

Alice looked down at the ground for a moment and her blue eyes were sad looking at Sarah. "She's in Bridey's room, silly!" She rolled her eyes when Agnes poked her in the ribs. "I mean Mother's room."

Agnes squeezed Sarah's shoulder. "You sleep in the nursery. It's a nice room."

Sarah took Alice's hand so that the three of them were joined. "I wish you'd come inside and meet my Mommy. I told her about you but I can tell she thinks I'm making it up."

The twins looked at each other, and their lower lips extended in a small pout. "We can't." Alice kicked at the ground with the toe of her shoe.

"If I move into that room at the top...you can then?" Sarah's voice was hopeful and her eyes were round as dinner plates.

Agnes nodded. "Let's play hopscotch."

CHAPTER THIRTY SEVEN

Maureen sighed and rose from her chair at the dining room table. The dog's scratching at the door was not only a distraction but it was probably ruining the door with its nails. The smell of fresh paint drifted into her nostrils as she walked down the hall. At the foot of the stairs, she called up to her daughter. "Gillian? Would you please open a window and close the bedroom door?"

There was no way anyone would be able to sleep up there with that reeking stench! She opened the back door and the dog scurried into the house. A ridge of raised hair darkened the centre of its back and its tail curled down between its legs. Across the yard her granddaughter's gaze met her own. What had the child done to the poor dog? Her lips were tight when she closed the door.

A throbbing ache began behind her eyes. She stopped in the kitchen and took a couple aspirin with a glass of water. Maybe the stink wasn't as bad in the living room. She picked up her laptop and settled on the sofa. She smiled and reached down to pet Pearl when the dog hopped up and plopped down at her feet.

Today she had decided, one way or another she was going to find out the history of this house. Considering that she'd never done genealogy before, perhaps a more useful tack would be going to sites specializing in that. After she typed 'researching my family tree' there were a number of sites offering help.

The next few hours flew by like they were minutes. When Gillian appeared in the living room later, Maureen was startled.

Her daughter smiled and flopped onto the chair across from her. "I thought you were going to take a nap." There was a smudge of pink paint on her jaw and the cuticles of her fingers were stained as well.

Maureen swung her feet off the sofa and sat up straight. She'd learned so much from her research! "I think I've found out, who built this house. If the records in my family bible are correct, and I'm pretty sure they are, then it was a great uncle, Kevin Crawley."

"What are you talking about?"

"This." Maureen got the family bible off the shelf and opened it to the back of the book. There, in swirly handwriting were the names of the parents and brothers and sisters of both Sean Crawley and his wife, Eileen. Sean had just one brother, and Eileen had come from a family of eight children.

"Look!" Maureen pointed to Sean's side of the family. "His brother was Kevin. Kevin Crawley!" She took a deep breath and went on in a rush. "Crawley was my great-grandfather. I came across an online entry that mentioned a Kevin Crawley living in Kingston. I have to go to the newspaper and check their archives to find out more, but I've got a good feeling about this."

"So?"

"That's right around when my great grandfather settled in Lanark. I think they may have come over from Ireland together, and settled down at around the same time in different regions."

"That's a real stretch, Mom. What you're saying is that there are two guys named Crawley who lived in Ontario at around the same time, and were some relatives of ours?"

"Yes!" Maureen's head nodded in excitement.

Gillian's eyebrows drew together and she leaned forward in the chair. "You're really interested in this family stuff, aren't you?"

"Well yes! It makes buying this house all the more meaningful, don't you think? It's history, right here at my fingertips." The clock in the dining room chimed five times and Maureen's eyes flew open wide. "Oh my! I've spent the whole afternoon doing this?"

Gillian nodded and rose to her feet. "Pretty much. It's time to start dinner." She headed out of the room. "Waste of time, if you ask me," she said in a low voice.

"Gillian MacDougall! How dare you!"

Gillian stopped and turned around facing her mother. "Excuse me?" She put her hands on her hips.

"How dare you be so flippant about this!"

"You're saying I'm flippant," she gave a small snort. "I think you're becoming *obsessed* to tell you the truth."

"What!"

Gillian folded her arms over her chest. "What's the big deal? So what if this house was built by some great-uncle, Whozis?"

Maureen's jaw dropped. "I can't believe this! I gave up my family home in Lanark to move here. I sunk my life's savings into this place! Now to find out that there could be a family connection? You don't think that's fantastic?" She shook her head. "What's the matter with you?"

"What's the matter with *me*?" Gillian's eyes flashed wide.

"Yes! You don't think it's great that this could be our new family home?"

"Ohhh! I get it! Our *family home*!" Gillian's eyes narrowed. "Just like the old farmstead back in Lanark, huh?"

"Yes!"

"The old farmstead back in Lanark I had to leave when I got pregnant? *That* old family home?"

Maureen waved a hand at Gillian. "Nobody asked you to leave! That was your decision!"

"Oh yeah! It sure was! The silent treatment was deafening! Dad didn't say two lousy words to me for four months! And you could barely look at me either!"

"It wasn't like that!"

"It certainly was!" Gillian stepped up to her mother, jabbing a finger at her. "Sure! I was eighteen years old, six months pregnant *and* on welfare in a one bedroom apartment in town! That was sooo much easier that living in my childhood home! You and *Dad* were ashamed of me and forced me out!"

"We did not! We loved you, Gillian!"

Gillian sighed and rested a hip on one of the arms of a nearby chair. "Not enough to ask me to come home, Mom. Not enough for Dad to *ever* come around." Her chin quivered. "Look— if this 'family connection' is important to you, fine. I got better things to do with my time." She stood up. "Like start supper." She stalked out of the room.

For a moment Maureen sat there in a daze. That had been harsh. Her daughter had snuffed out any excitement she'd felt a few minutes before. She snapped the laptop shut and set it on the coffee table. Gillian's and Sarah's voices drifted in from the kitchen, too far away to hear what they were talking about.

She got up and marched out of the room to join them. Sarah was sitting on the floor, tossing a rubber ball across the room that the dog raced to capture. Gillian was peeling potatoes at the counter.

For a moment it was like she was an outsider, intruding on their time and space. It didn't help when Sarah looked up and stayed silent—no joy in her eyes seeing her Nana. Even the dog was too engrossed with the ball to even notice that she'd entered the room. Well, like it or not she lived there too and it was time they showed a little gratitude.

Her back straightened and she strode over to the fridge and opened it. "I thought we'd have chicken. I defrosted some earlier today." She pulled the package of chicken breasts from the shelf and set it in the sink.

"That's fine. What about vegetables? Want me to make a salad?" Gillian's voice was cold and she didn't look up from her hands gripping the potato.

"No. We should use up the broccoli before it goes bad." She peeled the wrapping from the package and ran cool water to rinse the pieces of meat. "I'm going to call a contractor tomorrow to start work here. I want to open up that stairway so we can use the attic room."

Sarah scrambled to her feet. "Can I have that room for my bedroom?" She took a step closer and tugged at Maureen's shirt.

Maureen's eyes were narrow when she stared down at Sarah. She counted silently to ten before she spoke. "No." Sarah's face recoiled as if she had been struck. She took her hand away from Maureen's shirt.

Gillian wiped her hands and turned to her daughter. "Honey, I've just finished painting your room. You said you liked it. You picked out the color and you even picked that bedroom. If you're thinking of a bigger space, then when Nana moves upstairs, maybe we'll make her old room a playroom."

Maureen's heart had quickened and her mouth became dry at Gillian's words. "NO! Stay out of that room!"

Sarah's face twisted in defiance. "I wouldn't step foot in that room! I HATE that room, Nana!"

"Hey, hey... what's up with you two?" Gillian asked softly. Their heads pivoted to her, showing fire in their eyes. Gillian held her hands up. "Hey... we're all on edge today, aren't we? Let's all just take a breath, okay?"

Supper that night was eaten in total silence.

CHAPTER THIRTY EIGHT

Sarah's eyelids were heavy when Gillian rose from the bed. Before turning off the light, she once again looked at Sarah's drawing. It had been filled in with even more detail. She shook her head and turned the light off. There was just enough light in the room from the night-light to see Sarah tucking the bunny close and Pearl the Pug on the bottom of the bed. As she started to shut the door, Pearl raised her head. Goodnight pooch.

Her footsteps were soft on the stairs when she walked down to join Maureen. When she went into the kitchen, there was no sign of her and the bottle of red wine on the counter was only half full. She put her fingers to her mouth staring at it. Her mother had drank *that* much? Since supper? In all the time growing up, she'd only ever seen her mother drink at special occasions. Now, she was making up for lost time, it seemed.

She left the room and wandered down the hall to join Maureen in the living room. Once more, the laptop was open on her mother's lap and a glass of wine in her hand, as her eyes focused on the screen.

"Hey Mom." Gillian flopped down into the chair across from her mother.

Maureen glanced over at her. "Is Sarah settled for the night?" Her voice was a monotone.

Gillian ignored the slight slur in her mother's voice. "Yeah, I thought of letting her sleep with me but the paint fumes have pretty well faded." Gillian watched her mother empty the glass of wine and set it on the coffee table. It was probably too soon to have that conversation with her. She'd had a rough night, so see how it went when things settled into a routine.

She asked her mother, "Have you noticed Sarah's drawing?"

Maureen's eyebrows drew together and she glanced over at Gillian. "What about it? You used to like drawing at her age. You gave it up when you discovered boys."

"Really? I can't remember." She tucked her legs under her butt and leaned against the arm of the chair. "It's pretty good—Sarah's drawing. There's three little girls, one of which I'm sure is a self portrait with the braids and shorts. The other two girls are in dresses, old fashioned dresses. But it's the depth and realism in their faces that's kind of amazing--I mean that a five year old drew it."

"Your drawings were pretty good. At least your Dad and I thought so." Maureen lifted the glass and held it out in front of Gillian. "Would you mind getting me another glass?"

Gillian sighed. "Are you sure you want another glass? You've had a few already."

"Never mind. I'll get it myself." Maureen set the laptop on the table and rose to her feet. She took a step and stumbled.

"Mom!" Gillian jumped to her feet and grabbed her mother's arm. "You don't need any more wine, you've had enough."

Maureen's arm rose and sloughed Gillian's hand away. "Don't tell me what to do! If I want a glass of wine, I'll have a glass of wine. It's my life and it's my house!" Her eyes were narrow slits.

"Fine! Do whatever you want. I'm going to bed." Gillian stormed by her mother.

"Thanks, but I don't need your permission!"

Gillian's feet stomped fast on the stairs. Her mother was being a total jerk—had been all day. She was hung over all day today, and would be again tomorrow.

Great.

CHAPTER THIRTY NINE

Maureen's hand quivered pouring the last of the wine into her glass. She watched as a few drops splashed onto the floor. So what?

She took a gulp, feeling it burn the back of her throat when she swallowed. That bloody Gillian! The nerve of her telling her what she should do! She'd sacrificed so much to be with her daughter, help her out with her kid and *this wa*s the thanks she got?

How could Gillian understand what she'd gone through? She was too self-centered! As for Sarah, she was becoming a spoiled brat...and a little liar to boot. Maureen drained the glass of wine, feeling it warm her stomach.

She tossed the glass into the sink and smiled when it shattered. Let the *'English Crumpet'* Gillian, and her *precious babeen* Sarah clean that up! It was time for bed.

She tottered out of the room and clutched the banister as she walked slowly up the stairs. She'd sleep tonight, by hell! No creaking was going to wake her up, not tonight. Her hand skimmed the wall as she made her way down the hallway and into her room.

The bedside lamp cast a dim light, not daring to penetrate into the corners of the room. Maureen looked around the room, her body weaving, every piece of furniture blurring into duplicates. She flopped down onto the bed and kicked her slippers off. Her back fell onto the soft surface and she closed her eyes, not even bothering to get undressed. Her hand drifted in the air until it bumped on the lamp and she flipped the switch off.

A few hours later, she snorted and her eyes opened. *Oh God no.* That damned squeaking board. To hell with it. She closed her eyes, hoping to drift back into her dream. It had been nice; Mike was in it and they were driving into town in his truck. He was taking her to church, with Gillian as a child sitting between them.

But it wasn't a truck. It was a motorcar. And Gillian was wearing her lovely, summer dress with the large bow in her hair. Maureen felt somewhat uncomfortable in the fairing heat, with the layer upon layer of clothing she wore herself. Her chemise and pantaloons, under petticoats, and finally her dress itself. Thank goodness for the breeze in the air! She looked over at her husband, so proud of his new motorcar. She was baffled now. That wasn't Mike... it was someone else! He turned to look at her and smiled, his teeth white. But his teeth kept growing and growing...!

Her eyes opened, startled awake. She pulled the covers over her head shivering. It was cold, so cold in her bedroom.

That disgusting smell from the other night had returned. She hunched in the bed, breathing shallowly through her mouth. What the hell was wrong with her? The rancid stench took on a deeper layer of putrid. Rotting meat and now *death itself* flowed through her nostrils and into her brain.

She pulled the comforter from her eyes when she felt the pressure at the foot of her bed. *Someone was sitting on her bed!*

She blinked through her drunken haze at the shimmering face before her. It was a woman, her eyes piercing out from under a furrowed brow and her lips pulled back showing small white teeth.

"Oh!" Maureen shook her head and clenched her eyes shut. When she risked a peek it was gone. As was the stench in the room.

She jumped out of bed and raced down the hall to the stairs. The door to Sarah's room was open and the dog gave a soft whine from its place on the bed. Sarah was curled into a ball and sound asleep. Gillian's bedroom door was shut and no light shone from under it. She looked back at her bedroom, her heart pounding. Since she'd been in the house, she had hardly spent a single peaceful night in that room!

She crept down the stairs to the living room, her knees wobbly. She had never felt such dark and total hatred directed at her before. It was like a wave that crashed over her. She couldn't remember a single feature of that face... except those teeth!

She turned on one of the lamps in the living room and bundled the afghan around her. If it came again, drunk or no, she'd scream.

She clutched to the thread of that thought. She was drunk, thank God! Oh Lord, if that were to happen to her and she was sober!

Huddling onto the couch, the next thought came to her. Was she *that* drunk? She had to be. Otherwise she was losing her mind.

CHAPTER FORTY

Gillian finished in the bathroom and went downstairs to put the coffee on. The dog followed at her heels, wagging its tail and giving small yips. "Sorry Pearl. Let me finish this and I'll let you out." She got the coffee pot and turned to the sink to fill it.

Her head jerked back. Shards of glass and the stem of the wine glass sat in the sink. What the heck? Her Mom had busted the glass and just left it? She shook her head and sighed, setting the pot on the counter.

The dog continued prancing and yipping at her feet.

"Okay. Let's go." She walked to the back door and let the dog out. It would be okay outside on its own for a few minutes. She went back into the kitchen and picked the pieces of glass from the sink, muttering to herself. What if Sarah had reached in and cut herself?

She'd just begun to fill the pot with water when the dog began barking and scratching.

"Give me a minute," she said out loud. She still needed to get the can of coffee and fill the basket.

Pearl was having none of it. She began to 'Arrroooo' and was pounding on the back door.

"Sheeesh!" Gillian strode to the back door and flung the door open. Pearl was a fawn colored blur on the floor shooting past her, toenails scrabbling on the hardwood floor as she shot for the stairway. Gillian heard her head for Sarah's room.

What the hell spooked that dog so badly? She stuck her head out the doorway checking out the yard. Nothing. Go figure. Closing the door she glanced up at the ceiling hearing Sarah's laughter. Just as well, the girl should be getting up anyway.

She finished making the coffee and wandered into the hall while she waited for it to drip through. Entering the living room, her eyes closed for a moment and she took a deep breath. Maureen was passed out on the sofa, snoring softly. She didn't even bother to go to bed? Just stayed up drinking and passing out down there? Oh God.

She spun around and stomped back into the kitchen. She flipped the cupboard door open, grabbed a coffee mug and slammed it soundly. Taking the lid off the sugar bowl, she clattered it onto the top of the stove. After she added her sugar and cream, she clattered the spoon onto the stove as well. Mom better get her act together. School was starting soon for Sarah, and her own classes were about to begin. This was two nights in a row she'd gone to bed drunk!

Sarah entered the room holding Pearl in her arms. "Where's Nana?" She set the dog down next to its dish and turned to her mother.

Gillian's fingers gripped the box of cream tightly and her eyes narrowed, but she kept her voice light. "She's still asleep, but I think she's getting up soon. How about after breakfast we take the dog for a run in the park?" She took a sip of coffee and smiled at her daughter. "What do you think?"

Before Sarah could reply, Maureen appeared in the doorway, rubbing sleep from her eyes. Her hair was totally disheveled and the dark bags under her eyes seemed even worse. She glanced at the two of them before walking silently over to the coffee pot and pouring a cup.

Seeing the wide eyed puzzlement in Sarah's eyes, Gillian sighed and turned to her mother. "Would you like something to eat, Mom? I was thinking of making bacon and eggs. Sometimes grease is the perfect cure for a hangover."

Maureen looked down and muttered, "Sometimes you should mind your own business."

"Oh?" Gillian reached in the fridge and grabbed a juice box. She plucked a chocolate granola bar from the cabinet and handed both items to Sarah. "Can you play upstairs or outside for a little while, Moppet? Nana and I have to talk about some things."

When Sarah disappeared outside and she saw her heading for the swing, Gillian turned and faced her mother. The older woman leaned against the counter, the mug of coffee clasped in both hands. "Mind my own business, huh?"

Maureen took a sip of coffee. "I'm fine, Gillian."

"Fine? You're anything *but*, Mom!" Gillian ran her hand through her hair. Things between us were *fine* when we went to Niagara Falls, sure; but since we've come back, you've been…" she blew out a blast of air.

"I've been *what*?"

Gillian's eyes darted to the side, then back to her mother. "You've been... well, acting *odd*." She ticked off her fingers. "You're obsessed over this family history thing, you've been snappy at Sarah more than once, and good grief, you've passed out *DRUNK* twice in the last two days!"

"Oh, so now I can't have a drink *in my own house*? Is that it?"

"I'm trying to figure out what the hell's going on with you, Mom! Is this some kind of grief thing or something?"

"You leave your father out of it! As if you gave a damn about that man!"

The words struck Gillian like a blow. She staggered back and wiped her mouth. "How. Dare. You! What a rotten thing to say to me! He was my father!"

"He was my HUSBAND! *And ye shamed him so!*"

"Ashamed! Ashamed? Better I should have gotten an abortion? That would have made everything better?"

Maureen waved her hand in the air. "I didn't say that, Gillian." Dropping her hand, she took a sip of coffee. "But you have to admit, things would be a lot less complicated today..."

"Mom! What a crappy thing to say!"

Maureen's eyes were steely when she looked at her daughter. "It's true and you know it, Gillian." She took a deep breath. "I wish your father hadn't died. I wish I was never fool enough to buy this place."

Gillian shook her head, dumbfounded. "Just yesterday we had a fight over you being sooo in looove with this Crawley place. Now you wish you never bought it? Mom, what's the matter with you?" A sense of dread threaded across her heart. What the hell was with this woman? *This,* on top of Sarah acting weird was almost too much to take.

Maureen looked at her daughter silently for a few moments. Her eyebrows drew together and she opened her mouth to say something, but then shut it firmly. "I didn't sleep well last night. I tried sleeping upstairs but then I got up and came down here. I know I've been on edge, but I'm exhausted." She sidled past Gillian. "Now if you don't mind, I'm going upstairs to lie down in Sarah's room."

"In Sarah's room? Why not your own room?"

Maureen turned and faced her daughter. "They're *all* my rooms, Gillian. This is *my* house." She pushed past her daughter and went back up the stairs.

As she climbed them, she called back to her daughter, "Maybe I should have raised my voice to you years ago. I was too lenient with you. Maybe you wouldn't have had a baby when you were a child yourself and created this mess we're in."

Gillian stood in the kitchen stock still, her mouth hanging open in shocked silence.

CHAPTER FORTY ONE

The screaming match between Mommy and Nana rang through the air in the back yard. Sarah sat on the swing staring down, tears rolling off her cheeks onto the ground below her. It was all her fault. She shouldn't have asked for a dog. She shouldn't have asked for the room in the attic. Nana and Mommy were yelling at each other because she had done something wrong.

Her shoulders trembled as she clung to the ropes. At the light touch on her arm, she choked back a sob and lifted her head. Agnes and Alice stood at her sides, their eyes soft and welling with tears. They were still in the same dresses and the bows in their hair was still almost falling off. Sarah noticed, but was too upset to say anything about that.

"It's okay, Sarah." Alice rubbed Sarah's shoulder.

"No it isn't. It's all my fault that Nana and Mommy are yelling at each other." She twisted in the swing sloughing off Alice's hand.

Agnes stepped towards the house and stood staring in the window. Her hand rose and she pointed inside. "It's not your Nana, Sarah. It's *Bridey*. I hate her."

Sarah walked over to Agnes and shook her head watching the two women inside the house. "Where? I don't see her. There's just Nana and Mommy." She rose on her tiptoes to see more of the room, almost to the entrance of the dining room. It was definitely Nana and Mommy and they were still banging around in the kitchen, their voices loud.

A small hand closed over her fingers and squeezed. Alice was now next to her. "She's there, Sarah."

Agnes slipped her hand over Sarah's. "She wants you to leave."

CHAPTER FORTY TWO

Maureen was waiting at the kitchen table later that afternoon when Gillian and Sarah came in the front door. They both eyed her stiffly as they hung up their coats. She couldn't blame either of them; that morning blow-up between her and Gillian had been horrendous. As her daughter and granddaughter puttered around the kitchen and put some food down for the dog, she rolled her mug of tea in her hands.

Still looking down, she said, "I'm sorry."

Gillian paused and looked at her. "It's okay, Mom." Her voice was flat.

Shaking her head slowly, Maureen said, "No, honey, it's not okay. I said some terrible things to you this morning." She still couldn't look her daughter in the eye, she was so ashamed. "And about Sarah, too… I was horrid." Her voice hitched. "I don't know what came over me… I'm sorry, girls." She looked up, her eyes welling with tears. "I don't know what's wrong with me," she whispered.

Gillian crossed the kitchen and bent over hugging her. "You've been through a lot, Mom. And I was out of line too. I should have held my peace yesterday when you were talking about Crawley's and such." She gave a short laugh. "Maybe we're just trying to catch up with our lives or something? This has been one hell of a set of changes you know."

Maureen pressed into her daughter's arm. She'd raised a good woman. She glanced over to Sarah, who was on her knees petting Pearl as the pooch tried to eat. Sarah was watching the two of them. She gestured, and Sarah stood and flew into her other arm. The three of them stood gathered into each other.

"Let's order a pizza, what do you say?" she said when Sarah and Gillian smiled and stepped away.

"Sounds good to me."

After Gillian placed the order, Maureen said, "Someone's coming tomorrow to open up that third floor."

"Well, don't complain about the heat bill this winter, Mom. That's got to be a pretty big area up there." Gillian grinned.

"Do I get that room, Nana?" asked Sarah. "If you want it, it's okay though... I don't want you to get mad..."

Maureen tousled the child's hair. "Someone's got to sleep up there. We'll figure it out."

"What's the rush, Mom?" asked Gillian.

"Well, I slept in Sarah's room after I went back upstairs this morning, and I woke up feeling like a million bucks. I don't know what it is about me and my bedroom, but I don't..." she glanced away for a second. "You'd think it was haunted or something, maybe." She gave a snort. "Anyway, maybe the *feng shui* or something about that room is just bad for me—I don't know."

"More painting for me, huh?" Gillian said, smiling.

"Probably both of us. My old room will be a guest room—"

"For company we don't like!" said Gillian with a smirk. "If you hate the room, they won't stay too long, eh?"

Maureen gave a short nod. "Yeah, something like that. Anyway, we'll get the other room opened up tomorrow and figure out what needs to be done."

"Okay."

Maureen tilted her head at her daughter. "It was sort of funny when I was calling for a handyman. I was just going through the phone book, I spoke to two different guys—each time they seemed willing to come and do the job until I gave them the address."

"Oh?"

"Yeah. The first guy, when I told him where, said, 'Sorry, lady; something's come up. I won't be able to help you', and he hung right up."

"Pretty rude, huh?"

"Yes, but then it got strange. When I was speaking to the second fella' and told him the address, he tried to beg off too!"

"What?"

"Yeah! It was pretty weird. I told him that I was a widow and really needed help with this house... and if he wouldn't do the work, who should I call?" She gave a small smile. "I laid it on pretty thick, trying to get this guy to come over, you know?"

"So, he's coming?"

Maureen shook her head. "No… He gave me the name of a third guy—he's in the phone book too. He said that they used to work together as repairmen for the university looking after their rental houses, and that fellow would do the work."

"Mom, this is pretty damn odd, you know."

Maureen nodded. "Well, I phoned *the third guy* and left a voicemail. He called back just before you guys came home. He didn't sound too excited for the work either." She gave her head a small shake and her eyebrows rose high for a moment. "But he said he'd come by tomorrow when I told him it was a simple job of just popping open the plywood covering the stairway to the third floor." She shrugged. "He knew what I was talking about, and said that it wouldn't take him any more than fifteen minutes."

Gillian sat back, looking at her mother. "You're not having me on here, are you?"

Maureen shook her head. "No, I'm not. Scout's honor."

Gillian shivered. "That gives me the creeps." She looked around the kitchen. "What did we get ourselves into when we bought this place?"

CHAPTER FORTY THREE

Maureen was home alone when the handyman showed up. Gillian and Sarah had to be out for most of the day. Sarah needed to be registered for kindergarten, and Gillian wanted to get the jump on her orientation next week by going through the campus. They packed a lunch and were planning on having a picnic on the shore of Lake Ontario when Gillian was finished.

Maureen was waiting in the kitchen, finishing another cup of tea. She had moved some pillows and blankets to the living room last night and slept there. She woke up this morning the most relaxed and refreshed since they'd moved in. Her mouth twitched in a small smile—having nothing to drink for the last day and a half had nothing to do with that! Nooo... Pearl the Pug was curled up under the table softly snoring and performing foot warming duty at the same time.

She heard the truck pull into the driveway and the steps on the veranda before the doorbell rang, so she wasn't startled. When she moved her feet to get up, Pearl rose, stretched and yawned, and ticked after her as she went to answer the door. Maureen looked over her shoulder at the dog. Stranger at the door, doorbell buzzing and hardly a peep from her. But put her in her bedroom or out back and the dog would go bonkers.

"You got to work on your security skills, Pearl."

Pearl just looked up at her, eyes asking for a treat.

With a sigh, Maureen crossed the foyer and opened the front door.

"Mrs. McDougall?" the man asked. "I'm Jeff Comstock." He wore a red ball cap, and had a goatee flecked with grey. She felt the hard calluses in his hand when they shook, her fingers almost lost in his paw. She tilted her head and smiled. He was an overgrown teddy bear.

She took him right into the kitchen and bade him to take a seat.

"Would you share a cup of tea, Mr. Comstock?" she asked.

"It's Jeff, but sure."

"I'm Maureen," she said with a smile, pouring him a cup.

He looked at her from the corner of his eye as he added his milk and sugar. "Wait till you get my bill, then we'll see if I stay on a first name basis, huh?" He smiled as he said it.

She gave a small wave of her hand. "You're on the clock now, Jeff. I need a room upstairs that the previous owners closed off, opened up."

"Sure, I know what you're talking about. I've been in this house lots of times."

She put her elbows on the table and leaned across to him. "And that's another thing. It took me three phone calls to find a workman willing to come here!"

His chin jutted out. "Those guys are pu—" he stopped. "Pansies. There's a bunch of handymen, especially in this part of town, who won't come to this address." He arched an eyebrow at her. "Any chance you spoke with Allan Alder?"

"Yes! He was the first person I called! He hung up on me when I gave him the address!"

Jeff nodded. "Yeah, his listing's first in the phone book. I'm thinking of changing my listing to 'AAA' Home Improvements or something. We worked together doing jobs for the university on a lot of the houses on this street." His gaze went to the ceiling and walls of the kitchen. "He's scared to come here because of the stories his grandpa told him about the place when he was a boy."

"What stories?"

Jeff leaned over the table and lifted his teacup taking a long slurp. "Ahhh! You make a good cuppa, Maureen."

"What stories, Jeff?"

He sat back in his chair, interlacing his fingers on his rotund stomach. "I don't really know, to tell you the truth. That sort of stuff gives me the willies, so I stay away from it."

"What sort of stuff?"

"You know," he brought his hands up beside his ears waving his fingers. "Booga-Booga Boo kind of stories."

"Like ghost stories?"

"Yeah. Hauntings, spooks, things going bump in the night... stuff like that." He shook his head a little bit. "I never went for those kinds of movies or TV shows. Casper the Friendly Ghost was scary enough for me." He tilted his head at her and drummed his fingers on the table.

"What?"

He looked over his shoulder to the door leading to the back yard and peered through the window. He turned back to Maureen with a strange look. "It's still there…"

"What is?" Maureen leaned over the table to look out the window over his shoulder.

"The swing on the maple tree."

"What about it?"

"It's got a creepy story."

"Oh?"

He nodded and silently took a sip of his tea. Placing his cup back on the table top, he said, "I don't know if it's true or not, but I've heard you can't get rid of the swing, nor cut the tree down."

"You've got to be kidding."

He held his hands up, palms out. "Hey, it's just what I heard!" He looked away from her gaze, and said, "I was told that by a guy who tried *three* times to take the swing down. Each time he did, it was back up the next day. And when he tried to cut the maple tree down, the first two times, his chainsaw wouldn't work, and then his axe broke." He shook his head. "I always thought that Alan Alder was pulling my leg."

"The handyman who hung up on me."

"Yeah. He said it happened to him." Jeff tilted his head at Maureen. "He told me the other stories too."

"What other stories?"

Jeff pointed towards the side and front of the house. "The rosebushes. Same thing. You can pull them out all you want, chop them to pieces, whatever."

"And the next day…"

"Yeah. They'd be right back the way they were."

They both stared at each other in silence. What frightened Maureen the most wasn't the stories. What scared her more was how they somehow *made sense.*

"Well... Allan grew up in this part of the city; just a couple of blocks from here to tell you the truth. So he'd know all the old tales and whatnot. But it's the third story that's the creepiest."

"Oh, I can't wait to hear this one." Actually she could; but there was no way Maureen was going to stop now.

"Yeah... well... It seems the guy who built this house... *murdered his wife here.*"

"What!"

"Yeah, happened years and years ago—sometime between the First and Second World Wars. They had some kind of fight or something, and he chased her all around the house and killed her upstairs."

"In that room? Is that why the room is closed off?" If that was the case, she was going to bunk in the living room from now on.

"No... I don't think so."

"Why not?"

"Well, I've done work in this house, you know. That bedroom at the top, it's been closed off as long as I can remember. They wanted to open it up for more bedrooms, but weren't able to. Some kind of regulations about fire codes; it's on the third floor with no fire escape, so it stayed closed off." He shrugged. "It's too bad, because I'm pretty sure it's a huge room up there." He drummed his fingers again. "No... I think the murder occurred in a bedroom at the back of the house."

Maureen grew very still. "Why do you say that?"

"Nobody likes sleeping in it." His gaze went to the staircase. "Tenants that slept in it said it stank at night." He shook his head with a small laugh. "I never smelled anything in that room, and I checked it out a bunch of times." He made a gesture with his fingers pinched before his lips. "I think it's a case of college kids overdoing the wacky tabacky if you ask me."

"A bad smell."

"Yep."

"Any bad smells in the room that's closed off?"

He shook his head. "Nothing that I had heard about."

When Jeff headed out to his truck for his toolbox, Maureen sat there shaking her head smiling at the absurdity of it all. She bought a creepy house, no question about it. At that moment, it dawned on her that not one of their neighbors had knocked on their door since they moved in. Not. One. In fact, aside from that old codger who walked past the house every day and stopped to stare at it (which, as far as she was concerned was a little ominous in and of itself) she had never seen anyone on the block they lived on. Nobody coming or going to work, no mailmen or deliveries... nothing.

It was as if the neighborhood was holding its breath, waiting.

She jumped, startled when Jeff came through the front door carrying his toolbox. Pearl barely yapped at him, and he bent down and scratched her behind the ears.

"I'll have that open in no time flat, Maureen," he said. Will you want me back to install a door?"

His matter of fact tone, going about his business, anchored her to the present. "Yes, any chance you can do that today?"

"Sure; we'll head up to Home Depot after I get this done. You can pick one out as well as the hardware."

"Sounds like a plan, Jeff." She waggled her fingers beside her head. "Watch out for spooks!"

"That's the ticket," he said with a snort. Hitching up his toolbox, he left the sun bathed kitchen and Maureen refilled her teacup.

Minutes later his body was spread at the bottom of the stairs with blood seeping from his head.

CHAPTER FORTY FOUR

Maureen watched from the veranda as Jeff hauled himself into his truck, started it and backed into the street, driving one handed. His right arm was bent at the elbow and resting in his lap. Neither of them were sure if his wrist was sprained or broken; he was going to the ER at Kingston General Hospital and have it looked at.

Neither of them knew what had happened upstairs that caused Jeff to tumble down.

He was out cold when Maureen reached him. He was prone on the staircase, as if he had gone body surfing down the steps. There was a cut over his eye that was bleeding. She shook him, calling his name until his eyelids fluttered open.

"Ow-wow-wow-OW!" he said. He began to gather himself together, sliding his legs from the stairs down onto the landing.

"Jeff! What in the world happened?"

He looked at her, blinking his eyes slowly. His hand went to the cut and he rubbed the blood away and looked at it dumbly, before looking back up at Maureen.

"Wha— wha— happened where?" he said, squinting his eyes at her. He pushed his face up towards hers and squinted again. "Maureen, right?"

"Yes! Don't move!" She leapt to her feet and ran into the kitchen. She grabbed the roll of paper towels and a dish towel. She ran the dish towel under the faucet, soaking one end of it and flew back to where Jeff was. By this time he was sitting up on the stair landing. She bent forward and wiped the blood from his eyebrow gently. The bleeding was already slowing down, but he was going to have one heck of a bruise. He sat there quietly as she cleaned him up, then grabbing the newel post, he struggled to his feet.

Maureen stepped into him to help him up but he brushed her away.

"If I can't stand up on my own, I'm in really bad shape, Maureen." When he got to his feet, he let go of the post. He wobbled for a second. "Can we sit down in the kitchen for a minute?"

When they got to the kitchen table, he put his hands on the tabletop to support him as he sat down and let out a yelp of pain.

"Oh man, that hurts like a bitch!" he said. Tenderly, he rubbed his wrist with the opposite hand.

"Oh dear, Jeff... is it broken?"

He moved his fingers and sucked his breath in through his teeth. "I don't think so, but it's taken a hell of a shot," he said, his voice husky. He turned to Maureen. "What the hell happened?"

Her eyes flew open wide. "I don't know! You headed upstairs to start the job and the next thing I know I hear you tumbling down!" She took a seat at the table and looked into his eyes. There was something in books she read that the pupils of his eyes should look strange if he had brain damage, but she didn't have a clue what she ought to be doing right now. "Let me get you a glass of water," she said getting back up.

"What's that supposed to do?" he asked.

"I don't know! I got to do something, don't I?"

"Just give me a minute to catch my breath, okay?" He twisted his hurt hand in front of his face, his teeth drawing back in a hiss. "I think I need to get this looked at."

"What happened?" She was filling a glass at the sink.

His eyebrows furrowed. "I don't know... I went upstairs... and went to where the room was sealed off..." he lowered his head and closed one eye. "I remember tapping along the wall to make sure I was in the right spot. I put down my toolbox..." he looked up at Maureen. "And that's it. The next thing I know, you're shaking me." He shook his head from side to side slowly. "I was out cold." He picked up the glass of water and took a long sip. As he put the glass back down, he said, "I've never been out cold before in my life."

"My car's out front, let me run you to the ER."

He gave a short wave. "No, no. That's okay, Maureen. I'm okay. I'll take my truck up there and see a doctor or something." He finished the glass of water and stared at the glass in his hand. "I've never lost time like that though..." he said, his voice growing quiet.

No matter what Maureen said, he refused to let her accompany him to the hospital. Mike had been just as headstrong that time he broke two ribs falling off a ladder. But with Mike it didn't make any difference—she was his *wife* dammit, and so they had gone together. But she wasn't anything but a customer of Jeff's, and so had no rank to pull. She extracted a promise that he'd call her and let her know how he was later that evening, but that was all she could get from him.

After he started the truck, he rolled the window down and motioned to her.

When she stepped up to the truck, his face was pensive. She rested her hand on the edge of the doorframe.

"I'm not the kind of guy who buys into all that spooky crap, Maureen."

She nodded, silently.

"Two guys I've worked with think this house of yours is creepy. One of them thinks its haunted." He wouldn't meet her eyes, and she again kept her peace. "Something just happened in there." His gaze rose from the steering wheel and he turned his head from side to side. "I don't get it. It's a beautiful, sunny day, but it feels odd right now."

She felt it too. "Close. It feels close."

He shot a look at her. "Yeah, like it's really muggy or something... but it's not hot, right?" He rubbed the band aid above his eye. "I mean, I can breathe and everything... but it feels like I should be gasping for air or something."

She felt it too. The air was pressing in on her like a heavy winter coat. "I feel it too, Jeff."

When she said that, his eyes went wide and he gaped around again. "It looks so... so *normal*..." turning back to her, he said, the last words in a whisper, "but it's *not*."

She whispered back. "No. No, it isn't." Her gaze flitted up and down the street. It was completely empty. And completely still.

"What the hell is going on here?" For the first time since he walked in the door, he sounded frightened.

The hair on the back of her neck stood up when she replied. "Something *did* happen here, Jeff. And I'm going to find out what."

CHAPTER FORTY FIVE

"I get to go to school too, don't I, Mommy?"

Gillian and Sarah were walking home from the university. They had been there for a couple of hours while Gillian finalized her schedule and completed the registration process. There was an Orientation week that was going to begin right after Labor Day, but she didn't think she'd be a part of it. From what she read about Orientation Week at Queen's University, it looked more like some sort of glorified day care for eighteen year olds than anything a twenty-four year old single mother would be interested in.

"Sure, Moppet, you'll be starting Kindergarten right after Labor Day, and I'll start classes the following week."

Gillian was holding Sarah's hand, while they walked through the park, a shortcut to their house.

"Will Alice and Agnes be going to school too?"

A chill went down her back when her daughter mentioned their names. "Well… maybe if you ask them, they can tell you, okay?" She had to admit it to herself—this imaginary friend stuff was bothering her.

Since Sarah had started talking about her two companions, Gillian had kept an eye on her, looking for... well, more like *feeling for* any other signs of five year old psychosis or something. The 'drawing prodigy' was overshadowed by Sarah's two outbursts during the past week. She had been so normal before they moved here, but now her kid was getting... *strange*. She'd see how Sarah handled starting school before she'd get all worked up over it.

The path took them to the corner of the street their house was on. They paused before crossing and Gillian saw that old man standing across from the house. She shook her head. Mom had pointed him out to her just the other day saying the old fart came and watched the place from the opposite side of the street every day.

Get a life, Grandpa, you're weirding me and my mom out. And we've got plenty of weird already, okay?

He looked harmless enough from where she stood, so she decided to walk right past him and check him out up close. Then they would just cross the street and go inside. They crossed the street from the park onto the same sidewalk where the man was standing sentinel. Glancing at the driveway, she saw that the car was gone. Mom was probably doing some errands or something.

He turned slowly when they approached. The guy was older than dirt! He was a head taller than Gillian, and had wisps of baby fine white hair sticking out in tufts from his scalp. His eyes had that common cast all really old people had— watery, like they were facing a breeze and forgot to blink; and the edges of his eyelids were soft pink.

As they approached, his face broke into a beautiful smile. She felt Sarah's hand tighten in hers.

"Hello," he said. The guy might be as old as the hills, but his voice was strong and even.

"Hi!" Sarah looked up at him and smiled.

He nodded to Sarah, and looked straight at Gillian as he raised a hand to point at her house. "You live there, right?"

She bit her lip. Well, he'd know soon enough one way or another by watching them go inside. She nodded.

"We just moved in a couple of weeks ago and Nana bought it!" Sarah piped up. Gillian tightened her grip on Sarah's hand when she felt the child begin to squirm away.

"Stay with Mommy, Sarah," she said. Turning to the old guy, she said, "Is that important to you?"

The old guy scratched his earlobe and said, "Well, I guess it is."

"Why?"

"Beats me!" he said, and smiled again. "I've been living here in Kingston ever since I retired... been about twenty five years now. And ever since the first time I passed this place, I had to walk past it every day." He shook his head and glanced at the ground smiling. "I don't know why, but any day that I don't go past the place, I feel out of sorts or something." He lifted his gaze up to Gillian's. "Most of the time it's vacant. And when people did live there, it was always students."

"So?"

"You're the first *family* that's lived there for the last twenty five years." He gave a short nod. "That makes you special." He pressed his lips together and nodded again, like he just made some kind of important pronouncement.

Her inclination to laugh was overruled by curiosity. She cocked her head and arched an eyebrow. "What an unusual thing to say…"

He gave a short laugh. "You're telling me!" He ran his hand through his hair, fighting with his cowlicks and losing. "It sounded strange to me coming out of my mouth, but I just know I'm right."

"You feel the house, mister, don't you?" Sarah's voice chirped up. Gillian glanced down and a chill went through her. Sarah's eyes were like diamonds, glinting again. "And you can't cross the street to get closer to it, can you?"

"No…" he said, looking down at her. "No, I can't."

"The circle isn't closed yet, but it will be, don't worry!" She smiled up at him, her face shining.

"Okay… when, young lady?"

"Soon!"

Gillian watched the two of them as their gazes locked. Ancient old and a sprout. She gave a small tug on Sarah's hand. "What circle?"

Sarah turned to look at her mother. "I don't know, Mommy. I just know, that's all."

Gillian closed her eyes for a second. Now *that* makes all the sense in the world. She opened them and gave her head a small shake and looked back to the old man. "I guess you don't know what that circle thing means either, do you?"

"No… I only know that the young missy here is right," he said, studying Sarah. He flitted a glance to Gillian. "She's special, isn't she?"

"I think she is."

He looked back at Sarah. "So tell me, young miss; do you like your new house?"

"Oh yes! Nana sold her farm and she bought it!" Her face fell. "My grandfather died, so Nana decided to move away too."

"I'm sorry, young miss. That must have made you sad."

Sarah looked sideways at her mother. "Well... I never *really* met him when he was alive..."

"You never met him, Moppet..."

"Yes I did! He told me to make sure I got this!" She reached into the collar of her shirt and pulled out the St. Jude medal. It twinkled in the afternoon sun as it rocked at the end of the chain.

"Oh my God..." the old man whispered. He bent down and slowly extended his hand to Sarah, palm up. "That's a St. Jude medal, isn't it?"

"Yes it is! Alice has one just like it!" Sarah said. "They even have the same letters on the side!"

"A.C., right?" the old man said. His hand trembled as he touched the medal.

"That's right! How did you know that?" she asked.

"That medal used to be mine," he said. "I gave it to my baby sister when I left home ..." His eyes looked very far away.

"No, Agnes says it's hers!" She tucked it back inside her shirt. "She says it's okay that I have it now, but it *was* hers."

The man's voice was almost a whisper. "I don't know an Alice or Agnes. But I wore that medal my whole life growing up. My father made sure I always had it; but he wouldn't tell me anything about it." He straightened up slowly, his eyes wide with wonder. "Before I left for the war, I put it on my baby sister." His eyes filled with tears. "When I came back from the war, my Dad had passed away and my mother remarried." His voice hitched. "She turned me away at the door…" He covered his eyes with his hands and sobbed.

Gillian's heart ached for the poor man. She stepped to him and rested her hand on his shoulder. "What a terrible thing. Why would she do that?"

Through his hands, he whispered, "She said I wasn't her child, that my father adopted me and *made* her raise me." He took his hands away, reached into a pocket, drew out a handkerchief and wiped his face. "She said I was a demon seed and to leave Lanark and never show my face again!"

"Lanark?"

"Yes, it's a small town over—"

Gillian's hand began to shake. "I know where it is. I grew up there…"

"Really?" His face brightened. "I grew up on a dairy farm there, back during the depression and before the war. I left when I was sixteen; my parents signed papers so I could join up as soon as I was old enough."

"A dairy farm?"

He nodded. "It was a long, long time ago… and when I was turned away from home, I went out west to work on the oil rigs." He shrugged. "When I retired, I moved here to Kingston." He looked around, up and down the street. "It's a nice enough city, don't you think?"

"Yes, yes it is… Mister… what *is* your name?"

"I'm sorry. How rude of me. My name is Eamon. Eamon Crawley."

CHAPTER FORTY SIX

At that same moment, Maureen sat frozen in a seat at the Kingston Public Library's main branch. She had gone there as soon as Jeff's truck left her driveway and had been going through archived newspapers on microfilm for the last two hours. Her face was bathed in a green hue the microfiche reader emitted, tucked back in the corner of the main reading room. She sat with her hand to her mouth.

"Oh my God…" she whispered.

CHAPTER FORTY SEVEN

At the same time that Gillian and Eamon were chatting on the street, Maureen was sitting in the archives room of the local newspaper. She leaned closer to the screen of the microfiche and read the article.

THE KINGSTON WHIG STANDARD
MURDER-SUICIDE
MAJOR KEVIN CRAWLEY

In the early morning hours of Thursday November 1, the body of Colonel Kevin Crawley of 8 Harvest Street was found hanging from the old gallows behind the provincial courthouse. A staff member of the jail, John Bannister, arriving for his shift came upon the gruesome scene and contacted the police.

When Constables Gerald Waters and James Dunleavy visited the victim's home to notify the family, they came upon a horrific crime scene with two more corpses. The first body has been tentatively identified as Mr. Devlin Griffin; found in the home's kitchen bludgeoned to death. Continued search of the home turned up further mayhem. Major Crawley's wife, Bridget Mary (nee Walsh) was found in an upstairs bedroom, dead of a broken neck. Further searching turned up the Crawleys' son, a baby boy, unharmed.

The police recovered a note from the body of Colonel Crawley. It contained the name of his brother Sean Crawley of Lanark who was to be contacted regarding the baby, Eamon. It also contained a confession of guilt, 'I killed them all. It's my fault. God forgive me.'

Neighbors of the Crawley family, the Ashtons, were acquainted with the Crawley's for the past five years and commented on the family's tragic history. It was not the first time death had visited this home. The first wife of Major Crawley, Melanie Anne (nee Forsythe) born in London England died of complications in pregnancy, two years ago. Two twin daughters, Agnes and Alice, five years of age were kidnapped and drowned earlier this year. Until now, Crawley had not been under suspicion for their deaths.

Now, the police are no longer investigating circumstances surrounding the deaths of the other family members, given the admission of guilt in the letter.

An unidentified source at Headquarters has stated "It appears that the Major's thirst for blood was only whetted by his experiences in the Great War. His confession and suicide strongly support the theory of a man with a disturbed mind. What a monster to murder your wives and children! It's a miracle the baby survived at all."

Maureen clutched the edge of the desk to keep from falling sideways from the sudden dizzy spell. She exhaled slowly, unaware that she'd been holding her breath. Good Lord. All of that had happened in that house—*her* house.

And Eamon Crawley...the mystery name in the family bible. He was the baby, raised by an uncle in Lanark. Raised by *her grandfather.* She closed her eyes for a moment and shook her head. So much death!

What sort of man had Kevin Crawley been? What kind of monster? The 'unidentified source' in the article believed him to have been a child murderer. *His own children!* In all likelihood this animal murdered his first wife too! Then he killed his second wife! What a sick and disgusting man! There was death and sadness in that house, death at the hands of Kevin Crawley.

She was related to him. The realization made her head spin. Thoughts flitted through her head like fireflies. She and Gillian had been brought to the Crawley house for some reason. She knew in her bones their being at this house was no coincidence.

Her eyes widened and she gasped. Not just her and Gillian—Sarah! The two little girls, Agnes and Alice. Her hand flew to her mouth. Those were the names that Sarah called her imaginary friends. Oh no! *Not* imaginary at all!

A shiver scuttled up her back and her shoulders shuddered.

Not imaginary.

Ghosts.

The ghosts of the twin girls were still in the house! Sarah had no way of knowing about them, yet she'd seen them. To her, they were just regular kids! But they weren't. Not at all.

Her stomach knotted. Had she been sleeping in the same room where Bridget had been murdered? The memory of that frightful night when she felt she was being choked flashed in her mind, making her shiver again. Had that been Bridget? No, that *was* Bridget. And she was pissed!

What in the world was she supposed to do?

She pressed the buttons beside the monitor and the article hummed out of the attached printer. She shoved it into her purse. She had to get home and tell Gillian! She flew out of the library and raced home.

When she walked into the house, she did a double take at the sight of her daughter sitting at the dining room table with the family bible spread out before her. She rushed into the room. "Where's Sarah?"

Gillian glanced up briefly and went back to looking at the entries in the bible, the family tree section. "She's out in the back yard with the dog."

Maureen ran to the back door and looked out. Sarah and the dog were playing, wrestling with a stick on the grass. She went back to the dining room.

She pulled out a chair and sat across from her daughter. "Gillian, you'll never guess what I've found out at the newspaper archives." Instead of waiting for a reply, she continued. "The man who built this house was named Kevin Crawley. He murdered his wife—no, *two* wives, *and* his daughters, leaving their baby boy orphaned." Her eyebrows drew together and she leaned forward. "What are you doing with the bible out?"

Gillian's eyes were wide staring into her mother's. "The baby boy was named Eamon."

CHAPTER FORTY EIGHT

Maureen jerked back and her mouth fell open. "How did you know that?"

Gillian looked at her mother and smiled. "He and I had a chat right across the street."

"WHAT?" Maureen reached out and clutched at her daughter's arm.

"Yeah. You must have noticed the old guy standing in the park staring at the house? Well, he asked about us. We got to talking and he introduced himself. You could have knocked me over with a feather when he told me his last name was Crawley." She dropped her head slowly shaking it from side to side. "This is too weird, y'know?" She lifted her eyes back to her mother. "When he told me that he'd been raised in Lanark, I knew he had to be some distant relative of yours." She glanced off to the side. "Of *ours*."

"Oh my Lord, he has to be ninety years old! I've always wondered about his name in my Bible. How is it that he came back to Kingston?" Maureen's mouth opened and closed like she was totally gob smacked.

"He grew up on a dairy farm but he never liked it." Gillian gave a rueful smile and patted her mother's arm. "Kind of like me, I guess."

"More than you realize, Gillian. He didn't grow up on *a* dairy farm; he grew up on *our* dairy farm."

"You're kidding!"

Maureen shook her head. "He's my mother's cousin, Gillian. His father strangled his mother, and my grandfather took him in as a baby." She opened her purse and took out the copy of the newspaper article and handed it to Gillian.

She read it quickly, and nodded. "Now it all makes sense." She looked up at Maureen. "He said he loved his father but his mother always acted strange when she was around him. When the war broke out, he enlisted. While he was fighting in Europe, his father died. After the war ended, he went back to Lanark, but his mother turned him away. She had remarried and so he moved out west. He didn't come to Kingston until he retired." She tilted her head. "He had a St. Jude medal... the one Sarah's been wearing... it's *his* medal."

"My mother had that from when she was a baby. My grandma, *my Nan* never told her where it came from." Maureen chewed her lip. "My mom gave it to your father when we got married; she said that Granny never liked her to wear it."

"How did Sarah get hold of it?"

"From your father's dresser. She told me he wanted her to have it." Maureen's eyes widened. "I thought she meant that *she felt* your father would want her to have it..." Her voice faded and she looked over her shoulder to the back door. "But now... maybe he did tell her..."

"Now you're sounding crazy, Mom, Dad never laid eyes on Sarah from the day she was born!"

Maureen dismissed Gillian's rising ire with a wave of her hand. "I think Sarah has seen those two girls who drowned. She calls her imaginary friends Agnes and Alice, right?" She pointed to the line in the newspaper article wordlessly.

Gillian's eyes followed her mother's finger. "Agnes and Alice..." she looked up at her mother. "Holy shit..."

"Where is he, Gillian?" she asked quietly. When she started to tell her, Maureen shushed her. "Whisper it to me," she said softly. "The walls may have ears."

"Now you're sounding crazy."

"Just do it."

With a shrug, Gillian leaned across the table and whispered the name and address of the nursing home where Eamon lived. It was just two blocks away. Maureen rose, and picked up her purse. "I'll be back right away. We're going to have some company." She took her coat and left by the front door.

Listening to the car leaving the driveway, Gillian shook her head. Mom was getting pretty weird, that was for sure. And the whole whisper stuff was just too much. She leaned back in her chair and looked up at the ceiling.

"Is there anyone there?" She looked around the room. "Can you give me a sign? Anything?" The room was still. Almost *too* still. "If you can hear me, I got some news for you." She folded her hands behind her head and leaned her chair back on two legs. "We're going to have some company, what do you think about that?" She looked around the room, feeling like an idiot. "And the guest who is coming over is—"

The door to the back yard slammed shut and Sarah came running into the house screaming. "Mommy! We have to open the wall to the twinses room! WE HAVE TO OPEN IT NOW!" She flew through the house to the staircase and began to scramble up like a puppy.

CHAPTER FORTY NINE

While Maureen and Gillian were comparing notes in the dining room, Sarah was out in the back yard playing with Pearl. Suddenly, the puppy jumped up, and whimpering, ran to the back door with her tail between her legs. She stopped at the door and turned to look at Sarah, softly whining.

"I know you're right behind me," she said. "You *always* scare poor Pearl!" Hearing the twins' giggle, she turned around. Agnes and Alice stood there, dressed as always, covering their mouths with their hands.

Alice's hand dropped from her face. "I don't know why your puppy is scared of us, Sarah. We've never done anything to her."

Sarah looked from one Alice to Agnes. "I think it's 'cause you're not like regular kids," she said quietly.

"What is that supposed to mean?" said Agnes, her lips were thin and eyebrows furrowed.

"I'm not trying to be mean," Sarah replied. "It's just that... you know..." she held her hands out, palms up.

"Know what?" Agnes crossed her arms over her chest.

Sarah sighed. "I like you! I like playing with you! But… my Mommy and Nana have *never* seen you, even 'though you're here all the time! And…" she pointed the twins one at a time, "and you wear the same dresses *every day* and they never, ever get dirty, no matter what game we play!" She lowered her voice to a whisper. "And you're both afraid of Bridey, but won't tell me *why*. And I've never seen your mother!" She turned her head from side to side, taking in the fenced in yard. "I've never seen you come into the yard, and I've never seen you leave the yard, but you're here every day to play with me!"

"Because we like you, Sarah!" Alice's eyes filled with tears. "It's been ever so long since we've had a friend to play with!"

Agnes stepped to her sister and put her arm around her shoulders, trying to shush her. "You don't want to be our friend anymore? Is that it?" Her eyes were angry, but her chin was trembling a little.

Sarah blew out a puff of air. "No silly! We'll be friends forever and ever! It's just that…" she tilted her head at the twins. "It's just that… you're not *really* little girls."

"Oh? We're not?" Agnes picked at the skirt of her dress. "What's that supposed to mean?"

Sarah bit her lip and glanced to the house. "I mean… I think you're *ghosts*."

"Are not!" Agnes shoved Sarah, knocking her backward.

"Agnes Crawley!" said Alice. "Shame on you!" She went over to Sarah. "I'm sorry, Sarah, Agnes is just—" at that moment, Pearl The Pug ran down the steps barking and yapping at the twins. She was snarling as she raced across the yard. With open jaws, she leapt at Agnes.

And passed right through her, landing on the other side. She stopped and blinked. With another growl, she snapped at Agnes' ankle, but her snout passed right through. Like two images on a television screen, Pearl's snout and Agnes' foot passed through and over each other.

"Pearl! Be good!" cried Sarah, wagging a finger at the puppy.

Pearl sat down and cocked her head at each of the girls, her large eyes even wider in confusion. Sarah scooped the puppy up and held it in her arms.

"See?" she said.

The twins nodded, and Agnes burst into tears. Alice took her sister in her arms. Sarah set Pearl down and her arms rose to encircle both of her friends.

"I don't want to think about it, Alice! It was so scary! She shouldn't have said that!" hiccupped Agnes. She burrowed her face in her sister's shoulder.

"What was scary, Agnes? I'm not scared of you. I should be... I mean, you're *ghosts*! But you're my friends!"

Alice was patting her sister on the back. "No... it's not that, Sarah. Agnes is talking about..." her eyes filled up with tears. "About when Mister Griffin hurt us." She began to softly cry. "We don't like to think about it. We *never* talk about it, because it was so scary."

Sarah immediately understood. She put her hands on each of the girls' shoulders. "Did it hurt? To die? Does it hurt?" She was getting kind of scared talking about that, not a lot, but a little bit.

Alice shook her head. "No. Mister Griffin hit us on the head, and we floated up in the air over him when he took us out to the lake and put us in the water."

"Why did he do that?" asked Sarah.

279

Agnes yanked her head from Alice's shoulder. "Because he's mean! He's bad and he's mean and Bridey made him do it!" She pushed Alice's soothing hand away and marched to the back door of the house. "Nasty, mean Bridey Walsh! Mean as mean can be! Bad, bad Bridey!" She stood at the back door shaking her chubby fists at the house, consumed with rage.

Sarah and Alice ran up to her. "I'm telling my Mommy!" said Sarah. "She'll tell on Bridey!" She opened the door, just as Maureen was whispering in Gillian's ear at the dining room table.

"Sarah!" The twins spoke as one. "Sarah! Stop!" They each grabbed an arm and stopped her from crossing the threshold. They yanked her backwards onto the patio.

"Did you *feel* it, Agnes?" said Alice.

"Yes!"

"Feel what?" said Sarah. "What are you talking about?"

"Oh no!" They turned their heads, looking into the hallway and back to each other. The twins' eyes grew huge in horror. "Oh no! Oh no! NO!" they said at once. They whipped around to Sarah. "Sarah!" screamed Alice. "You HAVE TO OPEN THE DOOR! Eamon's coming! And if he comes here before we get back inside, BRIDEY WILL KILL YOU ALL! She wants the house for Eamon! Open the doorway, Sarah! We have to stop Bridey!"

"You can't stop her, Sarah! If we get inside, we'll be with our Mummy! She can stop Bridey!" Alice was screeching now, her hands to her face. "OPEN THE DOORWAY Sarah! NOW!"

Sarah threw open the back door, and like a bullet from a rifle, shot for the staircase, screaming at the top of her lungs.

CHAPTER FIFTY

Maureen parked her car right in front of the doors of Providence Care, ignoring the signs that promised all sorts of fines, penalties and doom from a wrathful bureaucracy. She wasn't going to be parked long, just long enough to fetch Eamon. Her footsteps crunched on freshly fallen leaves as she strode to the front door. The evening breeze was chilly. Fall was coming early this year.

She found him almost immediately, sitting in the common room watching the evening news. She recognized him as the man who had watched the house since they moved in. He was in one of those 'old people chairs' she had seen at nursing homes before. First Nan, then each of her parents had that type in their rooms. It was a large armchair, upholstered in a green vinyl. Eamon was sitting back on it, his cane between his knees, watching the TV screen intently.

She hesitated. What in the world would she say? *'Hi, I just learned your mother was murdered by your father while you slept in a room next door?'* She stood in the entranceway to the room; arms folded, chewing on a fingernail.

As if he woke up from a doze, Eamon's head gave a small jerk, then tilted. He adjusted himself on the chair and slowly turned around to face her. He smiled and waved her over.

They had never met, but he acted like he was expecting her. Maureen nodded to herself; just another oddity in a lengthening list.

"Hello Eamon," she said.

He looked up at her, smiling. God, he was *old*. It showed the most in his skin. It was paper thin, the surface crinkled and wrinkled with the passing years. His eyes had that watery, just finished crying look so common among the aged. But behind the film, he was watching her intently.

And with a kindness she had never experienced before. It emanated from him like an invisible wave, a gentle pastoral sonnet she couldn't hear, but felt. She squatted down to the floor, and knelt next to his chair and placed a hand on his arm. He covered it with his, and for a long, tender moment, they were just company.

"It's been a long, long time that I've waited for this, Maureen," he said, breaking the silence. "It *is* Maureen, right?"

She nodded.

"You're the vision of Katie," he said. "My dear, dear baby sister Katie. I can see so much of the woman she must have become in you, girl." He lifted a hand and cradled her face. His touch was dry and gentle. Tears leaked from her eyes when he raised her chin to him.

"I'm so sorry for what Nan did to you after the war," she said softly. "Did you ever see your sister again?"

He shook his head. "No, just that once, and she was but a sprout of five. The war had ended, and I stayed on during the occupation for a while. When I came home, Ma turned me away. She told me I wasn't her son, only my father's nephew."

He shook his head with a sadness and grief she prayed to never, ever feel. A loss of a lifetime that never healed. "Before I left, I went to Katie and gave her my medal." He raised his eyes staring off to his past. "I had worn it all my life, as a boy, and through the war. I loved that child with all my heart, Maureen. To me she was my sister, not my cousin..." He looked back to Maureen. "When I saw it on Sarah, I knew the circle will be closed."

She took his hand in hers and kissed it, gently. "I'm here to take you back home, Eamon."

"I know." He moved forward in his chair and stood up smoothly. Bending, he offered his hand to Maureen. "We must hurry, dear. The circles need to be closed, and this is our only chance." She took his hand and he lifted her to his feet. This fellow brought new meaning to the word 'spry'!

She looked into his eyes. She saw determination borne of certainty that gave her comfort. Truth be known, she didn't have the slightest idea what was going on. He broke their gaze and looked to the entranceway and sighed.

"Are you alright, Eamon?"

He began walking to the entrance. Keeping his voice low, he said, "Never better, but we must hurry. Sarah's in danger!"

***

The car stopped with a jerk at the curb in front of Crawley House. She and Eamon got out at the same time and stared at each other over the roof of the car. It was *so still*! Not a leaf stirred on the trees and the street was empty and silent. The only lights on were those in the house before them. She watched as Eamon craned his neck, looking up and down the avenue taking it all in. He closed his eyes for a moment, inhaled deeply and looked to Maureen.

"It's time."

When he placed his foot on the first step going up to the veranda, lights as bright as the sun in every color of the rainbow erupted from the windows of Crawley house.

And the screaming began.

"EAAAAAMON!"

CHAPTER FIFTY ONE

Gillian's chair thudded to the floor when she leapt up.

"Sarah!" From the bottom of the stairs she saw her daughter scamper down the second floor hallway.

"We have to open the room!" Sarah was still crying out.

"Come down here! Right now! You scared the *hell* out of me!"

"No!"

She heard the sounds of a hammer beating and flew up the stairs.

Sarah was at the wall that had been closed off. In both hands, she was holding the hammer the carpenter had left, beating at the barrier. The guy Mom had hired had gotten as far as peeling away the drywall, exposing the plywood underlayment. Sarah was pounding on it with all the might a five year old could muster.

"Sarah McDougall, you stop that right now!" She marched down the hallway.

Her daughter looked over to her wild eyed. "NO!"

Oh dear God, her eyes had that funny look about them again, glittering and sparking like diamonds. She turned back to the sheet of wood, dropped the hammer and began to pull at the seam where the wood had been nestled into the adjoining wall. "Help me Mommy! Eamon's coming and we have to close the circle!"

She had no sooner finished her sentence when the house... *pulsed.* The walls, floors, the air itself, suddenly expanded and contracted as if filled with a blast of air and emptied out. Light, coming from nowhere and everywhere burst and pulsed, almost blinding her.

A thick, hoarse grating whisper filled Gillian's ears. Like two plates of thick, rusty steel grinding on each other.

"EAAAMON!"

Gillian covered her ears as she stumbled down the hallway toward her daughter. Sarah shrieked in pain and covered her ears as well.

"Mommy! If we don't open the door, Bridey will kill us! Just like she killed the twins! Help me, Mommy! Open the door!" Sarah turned back to the edge of the plywood, yanking on it. Her fingers were already bloody.

A...a *pressure* fell upon Gillian, knocking her to the floor. It wasn't a wind; it was a shove. One that pushed every atom of her body and threw her down. She saw her daughter driven by the same force, flung down the hallway.

"LEAVE THAT BE YE WRETCH!" shrieked in her ears. It was followed by an animal panting, and at the same time the force vanished. Sarah jumped to her feet and ran back to the doorway, scrabbling at it with renewed fury.

"Sarah!" Gillian got to her feet. When she tried to pull her away, the child bit her forearm. Hard!

"Help me Mommy! I'm not strong enough! We have to close the circle!"

The panting sound picked up pace, like a wild dog about to leap. Gillian grabbed the hammer from the floor and jammed the claw into the crevice as deeply as she could. Once set, she heaved on the handle.

With a piercing squeal the board began to come away from the wall.

"*NNNOOOO!*" They were again buffeted by the force. Again the light burst all around them, and again they heard the shriek, "*EAAAMMMON!*" Gillian was driven to her knees and Sarah was swatted flat to the floor, screeching in anger and fright.

"Screw YOU!" yelled Gillian. She let go of the hammer, and with both hands, grasped the edge of the plywood. Splinters pierced her hand, but she didn't let go. She braced her feet onto the wall beside it and heaved again. Another squeal and the opening widened.

"*I'LL BE KILLIN' ALL YE BLASTED CRAWLEYS!*"

The shriek thundered in her ears, and she saw Sarah's figure rise from the floor. She began to spin around like a pig on a spit.

"Sarah!" Gillian reached one hand out and grabbed at her foot, clutching onto the ankle. She kept her other hand on the plywood, and yanked at it again. She only knew that she *had* to get this passage opened! The force began to pull Sarah away—to the top of the stairway!

"*DIE GOD BLAST YE! DIE!*"

The force began to spin and yank at Sarah, but Gillian held on with a might fuelled by desperate adrenalin. Her hand grasped at her daughter's ankle like a steel vise and she pulled it back towards her. The struggle and pressure, Gillian clutching the panel in one hand and her daughter's leg in the other stretched her like a piano wire.

The panel squealed open even more. She glanced back at it to see the gap just inches wide.

The evil force spun Sarah around again. Gillian felt, then heard her daughter's ankle snap.

"Sarah!" Her fingers opened letting go of Sarah's ankle. Even after the break, Sarah didn't make a sound.

"*NOWWW!*" Three feet off the ground, Sarah flew through the air down the hall. Gillian let go of the door and sprinted.

At the top of the stairs, the house rumbled, like a loud grunt. Sarah was launched headfirst down to the first floor. Gillian leapt at her and missed, crashing to the floor at the top of the stairs.

Time slowed to a crawl as she watched her daughter get hurled down the stairs like a javelin. The split second passed like five minutes; in her memory she saw Sarah take her first step, say her first words, and struggle with learning to zip up her winter coat all by herself for the first time. In the split second before her daughter's head cracked open on the landing, neck shattering, she began to grieve.

Please no...

The entire house pulsed again. This time a radiant, white light throbbed in the air.

In that eternal instant, Sarah stopped falling. She hovered in mid air a foot above the steps. And gently, like an infant put down for the night, she floated onto the bottom landing.

The scent of fresh roses bloomed around Gillian and she stared in wonder. Sarah's eyes opened and she began to cry.

From behind her, Gillian heard the voices of two children crying out.

"Mummy!"

She whipped her head around to the doorway. Two sets of tiny hands writhed at the edge of the plywood.

She struggled to her feet and staggered back down the hall. She pulled on the panel again. The gap widened and their faces peered out at her, wide eyed. With a final yank of outraged fury, she wrested the opening wider.

The children, mirror images of each other scuttled past her, their arms outstretched.

"Mummy! Mummy!" they cried, their voices as forlorn as a train whistle on the prairies at midnight.

They froze in their tracks when the house throbbed again. A purple blackness bloomed in the hallway. The smell of rotting meat filled the air, making Gillian's hand rise to her mouth blocking the retched gag that rose in her throat.

The twins screamed when the purple blackness roiled over them. As the children disappeared inside, blood red flashes flared within.

"I'LL SHATTER YE'ER BLOODY SOULS!" The banshee howl knocked Gillian to the floor. She clawed at the plywood, pulling herself to her feet and stumbled at the roiling image, her arms outstretched.

And passed through it, bouncing into the railing at the top of the stairs. She felt frozen to the bone, and her heart was black with despair from the encounter. She looked down to her sobbing child at the bottom of the stairwell.

Another vision bloomed in the stairwell. A rolling blossom of white, streaked with gold grew and rolled up the stairwell like a wave. It flowed over Gillian overwhelming the despair in her heart with hope and love, warming her chilled bones. It merged into the black roiling apparition like cream into coffee.

In the blink of an eye both clouds vanished, leaving four figures.

A slight young woman in a cotton nightdress knelt on the floor, clutching the two children to her. Across from her, hands outstretched like claws stood a more solidly built woman, dressed from bygone days. Hatred blazed from her eyes.

"I'll murder all ye Crawleys!" she hissed. But her voice was faded, as if she was calling from across a wide field.

The slight woman looked up at her. Each girl's arms were around her neck, their faces nuzzled into her. "It's over, Bridey. We can move on now." Her voice held a delicate English lilt.

"I'll not move on without me son! If ye are to have your bairns, where's me boy!"

"I'm here." Gillian had seen the old man enter the house with her mother. He had been leaning over Sarah. She handed him the medal she had been wearing since Dad's death. Holding it in his hands, he ascended the stairs. He was at the top, grasping the newel post and huffing from the climb. "I'm Eamon."

The four figures turned to him.

"Eamon, it *is* you!" one of the twins said.

Bridey flung herself at the old man, wrapping him in her arms. "Tis you! Oh Eamon, how I've pined for ye all these years!"

He pulled her arms from his body and looked at her with forlorn sadness. "Oh Ma… what you've done…"

"T'was all for you!" she said. She tried to caress his face, and he grasped her by the wrists. "You were me only dream! Me only love!" She looked at him with such fading joy, that Gillian felt pity.

"It wasn't just for me, Ma." Eamon looked over at Melanie and the twins. They returned his gaze in silence and he turned back to his mother. "I don't know *how* I know this, but Ma, you murdered them all! And drove my father to his death!" His eyes were wide in dismay. "How could you?"

"I..." Bridey's mouth opened and closed. He released her arms and they dropped to her sides.

He stepped over to where Melanie and the twins stood and got down on one knee. Reaching out with his hand, he glided a finger down a cheek of each of the girls' faces.

"I'm Alice..." she said quietly.

"And you were always kind," he said back. "I was but a babe and I was always your brother first," he said softly.

She nodded, and he turned to her sister.

"I'm Agnes," she said, eyes large.

"And you've always been strong," He took the St. Jude medal in his hand and looped the chain over her head. "And your strength got me through a war, and times of great sorrow." He took her by the shoulders. "I am now and have always been, your brother." He kissed her cheek.

He turned his head up to Melanie. "The circles once opened are closed," he said. "All my life, that phrase was in my head. I never knew what it meant until now."

She nodded softly as he stood. His eyes suddenly widened and his hand went to his chest. He looked over to Gillian, his face twisting in pain. "Thank you..." he gasped, and fell to the floor.

Except he didn't. His body lay in the hallway, but it was as if he was duplicated, because just as real, he continued to stand with Melanie and the girls. Numbly, he stared down at his own form on the ground and raised his eyes to his mother as he comprehended his own passing.

Bridey began to cry as she faded. "No, Eamon… don't leave me again…"

He gestured to the twins. "These are my sisters, Ma. You're free of Crawley House now. I'll be waiting for you on the other side when you're allowed to come the rest of the way." He sighed. "When you've repented for what you've done…"

"Eaaaaamonnn…" and like a light being dimmed, Bridey Walsh faded away.

The old man looked down at the twins.

"You look like Papa," Alice said. Agnes nodded.

"So I might," he said. His gaze lifted to Melanie.

She had a hand on his shoulder. "Let's leave here and say hello to him. He's been waiting." He smiled shyly at Melanie, and back down to the twins.

Whereas Bridey had faded, the four of them began to glow again; white and golden hues pulsed from within them. With each surge, the colors grew brighter as their images faded.

Until all that was left was the color, then that too was gone.

"Holy Toledo," whispered Gillian, awestruck.

CHAPTER FIFTY TWO

"Holy Toledo is right!" The whites of Maureen's eyes showed and her hand clutched her chest. "Did you see what I saw, Gillian?"

"Yeah."

Maureen and Sarah ascended the stair case slowly. Maureen's forehead furrowed. "Eamon... is he..."

"Yeah." Gillian looked at her daughter. "Are you okay, Moppet? Is your foot alright?"

Sarah nodded. "Alice and Agnes' Mommy kissed it and made it all better." She got to the top of the stair and saw the still form of Eamon lying on the floor. "Is he dead?"

Gillian turned to look down at Eamon. His face was peaceful and still, and she could see the pasty white of his skin. Just to be sure she laid her fingers under his neck searching for a pulse. Finding none, she nodded to Sarah. "Yes, I'm afraid he's passed away, Sarah."

"Well, he'll meet Grandpa then, and he is with the twinses," she said. Her face got sad. "He was nice. I hope his Mommy can come over to him soon."

"We're going to have to phone the police," said Maureen.

***

It didn't take long for everything to be settled. When the police arrived, they notified the nursing home, who took care of everything. Eamon had been quite old, and the surprise of learning that this had been the home he had been born in, must have been too much for the poor man.

When the funeral hearse arrived, Gillian went to the front door to let them in. She stepped out onto the porch and for the first time since they moved in, saw neighbors. A man her father's age wandered down the sidewalk towards her.

"Hi, I'm Dennis Doyle," he said. "I guess you're the new tenants?"

"No, we purchased the place."

"Really?" He adjusted his eyeglasses and rubbed his beard. "Welcome to the neighborhood." He gestured at the police car and funeral home vehicle. "Is everything all right?" He gave his head a shake. "Sorry. Of course it's not. Why else would the police be here?"

She came down the veranda steps to him. "That's okay. Thanks for asking. We had a visitor who was very old and got very sick suddenly. He passed away."

"Oh. I'm sorry. Some housewarming event for you." Dennis looked up at the house. "I didn't even notice when you moved in; was it today?"

Gillian tilted her head at the guy. There had been a truck, their car, and all that stuff weeks ago. "Uhh... no, we moved in a while ago."

"Really?" Dennis looked down the street to his house and back to Gillian. "I didn't notice anyone living here or anything until just now." He cracked a wan smile. "Guess I'm getting old."

Gillian gave a shrug. "No, I guess we just live quietly, that's all."

"I guess so." He stuck out his hand. "Like I said, welcome to the neighborhood. You'll probably have people from the block knocking on your door saying hi and all that. My wife Corliss will probably be over during the weekend to say hello. She's at work right now." He shook his head with a smile. "She's going to be pretty surprised to learn that you people have been living down the street and she hadn't noticed."

The front door opened again, and two men wheeled out a stretcher with Eamon's earthly remains. She and Dennis stood aside as they loaded him into the back of the vehicle and left.

Dennis kept his head bowed as the vehicle pulled away. "Did you know him well?"

"No, we had only met this afternoon. He had always walked past this house, and I said hello to him."

He lifted his head. "The old fella? I think his name's Eamon."

"Yes, that's right," said Gillian. "Turns out he was a distant relative."

"Oh. Then I'm sorry for your loss."

"Thank you, but it's okay." She turned her head watching the hearse drive down the now active street, slowing down for people crossing down at the corner. "He died a happy man."

Back in the house, Maureen and Sarah were in the kitchen heating up a frozen pizza. That was a good idea—she was hungry as anything. She plopped down at the kitchen table and Sarah hopped up onto her lap. The three of them sat quietly, eyes flitting from one to another.

"Is it just me," said Maureen, her eyebrows making a question mark. "Or does the house seem... I don't know... *peaceful* or something?"

Gillian turned to Sarah. "What do you think, kiddo?"

Sarah's eyes rose and scanned the ceiling. She craned her neck and looked all around her and turned back to the women. "It's not mad at us anymore." She tilted her head. "And it's not sad anymore... and it's not scared anymore," she said with a nod. She turned to Gillian and put her arms around her mother's neck. "It's *our* house now."

"You don't know how right you are, Sarah," said Maureen. When her daughter and granddaughter looked over to her, she continued. "I just remembered something I was told when I was about your age, Sarah."

"What, Nana?"

She drummed her fingers on the kitchen table. "It was my own Grandfather and Grandmother that bought the family farm in Lanark. Sean Crawley."

"Yeah, Eamon's uncle and Colonel Kevin's brother."

Maureen nodded. "Yes. But here's the thing—when I was a little girl, I remember being told that my Grandpa was able to buy the farm when his brother died. He came into some money and a house." She pointed a finger above her head. "This house. And from the money from Kevin's estate and the sale of this place, my Grandpa was able to buy the family homestead. Up until then, he was only a farm hand."

"Wait a minute," said Gillian. "You mean that *this* place made our home possible?" When Maureen nodded, she continued. "And selling the farm back in Lanark made buying this place possible?"

"Yes."

Gillian leaned across the table. "Ma, that's a circle."

"And now the circle is closed."

The End

A CLOSING WORD:

Kingston, Ontario teems with inspiration for tales of the paranormal. A short walk from City Hall can take you past a number of places where uncanny events have occurred. Within these nooks and crannies, the veil that separates planes of existence becomes quite thin. Stories of apparitions in church choir lofts, wandering spirits of executed criminals, and haunted residences abound. This tale of The Hauntings Of Kingston was inspired by a story I was told one crisp and chilly autumn night while I was near the campus of Queen's University. Listening to the story, my imagination took over, and the result was this, my debut novel.

Thank you for reading this book. Hopefully, you enjoyed it. If you did, please leave a review on Amazon. Reviews help struggling authors get their books in front of more readers. If for any reason, this book missed the mark for you, please accept my apologies. Hundreds of hours went into its creation and all I can say is "I did my best." If you want to let me know where it fell short, there will be no bad feelings on my part, I promise. I will take your feedback to heart, and try to improve—if not on this one, then certainly on the next.

If you would care to join my mailing list, I'm at michelledoreyauthor@gmail.com

UPCOMING RELEASES BY

MICHELLE DOREY

2016: The Lakeside Haunting (A Haunting In Kingston)

Made in the USA
Middletown, DE
17 March 2021